T UNWANTED DEAD

YORGOS PRATANOS

Black Rose Writing | Texas

ISBN: 978-1-68433-794-1
PUBLISHED BY BLACK ROSE WRITING
www.blackrosewriting.com

Printed in the United States of America
Suggested Retail Price (SRP) $19.95

The Unwanted Dead is printed in Sabon

*As a planet-friendly publisher, Black Rose Writing does its best to eliminate unnecessary waste to reduce paper usage and energy costs, while never compromising the reading experience. As a result, the final word count vs. page count may not meet common expectations.

THE UNWANTED DEAD

SATURDAY, OCTOBER 26 – SUNDAY, OCTOBER 27, 1957

Freiburg

"So? Have you finally found your God?" Helen asked her husband in the playful manner they loved to talk to one another, sparking a conversation that would surely help him forget the pain, even momentarily. But mostly, so that she might assess his clarity.

"No."

"So you won't find Him?" she insisted, even more playfully than before, as if his dry reply – a reply that hopefully could mean he felt he had ample time ahead to continue his quest – had not discouraged her.

"Others will," Nikos replied, exhausted, and went quiet. Helen fell quiet with him, hoping this silence was only temporary. Her wish came true, but not in the way she hoped.

"Water!" her husband suddenly cried out. "Water!"

She gave him some immediately, stroking his hair ever so gently, as if afraid the slightest human touch might hurt him. Silence led to stillness. The deathly calm that dominated the pallid room gave way to her outburst.

"Give me your blessing, my dearest, so that I will walk the path you forged," she cried out, sobbing.

Her left hand firmly on her tearful eyes, slowly and carefully, almost ceremoniously, she placed her right hand on his face and gently shut his eyes. Helen sat on the wooden chair next to the white iron bed, where the white sheets covered the lifeless body of her beloved husband. She hadn't realized how tightly she was holding his hand, her own hand dripping with sweat, so unlike his. She lost track of the time, leaning on him, her head laying on his chest, mirroring his body's rigidity in tender solidarity. Everything seemed to freeze in that glacial white, death laden room at the University Clinic in Freiburg – even Time. Her mind wandered across the seasons of their every shared moment, joyous or wretched, small or mundane, blissful or agonizing. In that modestly furnished ice-box of a room, she saw their life together flash before her eyes. Just ten days before, in that very room, her husband had smiled elatedly reading the telegram he had just received from Peking.

"The Peace Committee of China was apprised of my illness and sent funds to cover my medical care and hospital fees," he had announced to her exuberantly. A feeling of relief had washed over her then: the same relief she had experienced countless times throughout their life – as many as the moments they had been penniless and unable to cover the basic needs.

"We couldn't possible accept their kind offer," he had said to her, adding, "We will not take away one grain of rice that belongs to the Chinese people".

He had asked her, then, to send the money back immediately, to take extra care so that not even one penny should be lost in the banking process. She still remembered that peculiar feeling of pride she had felt then, walking to the bank to fulfill his wish; it was the same overwhelming emotion she had felt just nine days before, when they had found out that the Swedish Academy was going to give the Nobel Prize to the young French author, Albert Camus.

"Lenotchka!" he had bellowed, "come help me put together a decent telegram. Jimenez, Camus, now here's two people worthy of the Nobel Prize! Come; we'll send them a warm one!"

This was to be the last of the few thousand letters he had penned in his lifetime. For the ninth time, the Nobel Prize would end up in the hands of another, not because her husband was undeserving, but because his own countrymen stubbornly refused to accept that a "godless communist" could bestow upon his country a distinction of that caliber. With that congratulatory letter, Nikos had bade a selfless, noble and gracious farewell to the heartless world in which he had lived. Then again, was it coincidental that the last person to have visited him – only two days before – was his good friend and Nobel Prize Laureate, Albert Schweitzer?

That was to be the last time Nikos would open his arms wide to greet someone wholeheartedly, the final, and, joyful at least, surprise visit of his life. Struggling hard to sit up on his bed, he had suffered in silence through his pain and frailty, so he could take in all the stories his euphoric visitor had to share. Nikos had listened to his friend – the philosopher, doctor and humanist – and his eyes had glowed with interest at every critical instance, his spirit rallying against his own body's infirmity.

These images receded into the white of the surrounding walls when the nurses burst frantically into the room, upsetting the emotional continuum. Helen averted her eyes from the busy nurses, and transfixed them on the origami boat flimsily standing on the nightstand, a fragile gift from the political prisoners condemned to death at Corfu Prison. How many hours had he spent observing it, and how many seas had he traveled upon it! She wondered if he knew he would soon meet the ones who had created it?

She felt the urge to tell the nurses to lock the door, to leave them there forever in that room, together in the frost, but her dignity and the thought that her husband might have had different plans for her, gave her pause. She forced back a gut-wrenching wail as it tried to tear through her and turned to face the window. She saw three or four stars staring down at her; unashamedly, she allowed her tears to course their way down her cheeks.

Air! She needed air; but that would mean leaving him behind. She abruptly stormed out of the room, making her way towards the hospital exit in hurried, unsteady steps. This was the first time she had actually been physically apart from him in years, but she needed oxygen and that room had none. She tried to slow down, yet sensed somehow that the exit was farther still and quickened her step. She pushed open the main door with her entire body and was out. She breathed in deeply as she crumbled on to the front steps, letting out a long, repressed scream.

"She is not the first," a passerby might have thought at the sight of the woman weeping alone; "she won't be the last," another might have concluded as they crossed paths under the glow of the hospital lights. The last thing on Helen's mind at that moment was what random pedestrians might think of her; her mind was flooded by a torrent of words, images, and conversations, so recent and so intense that she had not yet had time to process them.

Just like that time in Denmark, when she had confided in her husband, not long after the doctors had mentioned the possibility they might have to amputate his right arm. A wide gushing wound caused by the vaccine they had forcibly injected him with so he could travel to China was not healing, and gangrene had begun to set in. Yet the gangrene had left as insidiously as it had crept in, and after, she had felt relieved enough to reveal to him her innermost thoughts.

"If they had proceeded with the amputation, I had decided to kill you and would then kill myself," she had said to him.

"You would... kill me?" he had responded in utter surprise.

"Yes!" she had insisted. "An author without a hand....you being unable to dictate.... now, if it were a foot..."

"A foot would have been terrible too..." he had replied.

A few moments later he had asked her for a pencil and a piece of paper, and had sat down, trying to teach himself to write with his left hand.

A warm hand on her shoulders startled her.

He's alive! The thought bolted through her mind, but it was instantly dispelled by the gentle eyes of Tapita Swetzer, the nun-nurse that had been caring for Nikos and who hardly ever left his side. Helen hung her head down and pressed her forehead to her knees. At his side she had experienced so many miracles; *why couldn't there be just one more*, she pleaded. *The sole certainty of life is death*, she thought. She had been preparing for this final parting for so long, even if she had never openly admitted it to him. They both had been preparing: in silence, protecting one another from the inevitability of his mortality.

The nurse led her back to speak to the doctor, and Helen felt herself transform, for by the time she had entered his office, her body stood erect, her head held up high. She was not just another woman who had lost her husband... no. She was the widow of a great man, and now, his earthly representative. Doctor Heilmayer welcomed her, crestfallen. He had become attached to this patient more than was allowed. At the sight of her he took her hands in his and held them tightly. What a role hands play in a moment like this! It is never quite appreciated, as if souls communicate through the entwined hands. He stood there, dejected, while she held strong – such a paradox. He was utterly distressed, speaking to her first, in English, then breaking into German, but she wasn't listening to him. Through his office window she watched the darkness descend to the ground and realized that after thirty-three years, this was The Dawn of the First Day without Him.

Was it the dawn of a new life? How could she start anything new when every time she closed her eyes, she saw him? No; nothing was starting because nothing was ending. This time the stairs leading up to the room seemed fewer than before, yet the muscles in her thighs burned; she tried to steady herself, to stand tall to the responsibilities galloping towards her. She had stood in the shadow of the willowy Cretan man for so long, and now she would have to emerge into the light, alone, and yet, it was to this very shadow he had cast upon her that she owed every second of her exhilarating life.

It had been late at night, the first time they had met on May 17, 1924. Helen had heard some awful rumors about him, courtesy of his ex-wife – a well-known author herself – who had been slandering him in the circles of the Athenian intelligentsia. How commonplace for an ex-wife, even for an accomplished author, yet Helen had trekked up Mount Penteli with her circle of friends nonetheless, to watch the sun rise from the beach in Rafina. The moon had almost reached mid-sky when she spotted him, tall and slender, standing among a crowd of people. As much as Helen tried, she was now unable to recall any of his ex-wife's vile words against him. Instead, she could recall ever so vividly the great impression those two deep lines in his face had left upon her. They had ridden on the same wagon, and he had stared at her the entire time. Then came his three questions: his approach had been almost methodical, easing toward her, inch by inch, until at last they were sitting side by side.

"Who is your favorite author? What is your favorite color? What has been your life's greatest joy?"

When they had arrived at the beach, Helen had sat on the sand, fully clothed, having forgotten to bring along a swimming suit. And he, as much as he loved the sea, had turned his back to the big wondrous blue and had stood before Helen, facing her. He had asked her about all that she loved, told her stories from the places he had visited, made her laugh, and all the while he had stood there, lest she be bothered by the sun and decide to leave him. That entire day he had only moved just so, following ever so slightly the sun's rotation, while she enjoyed the safety of his shadow.

"I am an African; I love the sun. But for you, my fragile Athenian lady, we need to take special care!" he had said to her, and so he had, for thirty-three years.

That longstanding care had ended tonight. She would now enter into the harsh light without a defender, without shade. Everything and everyone would zoom in on her now – eyes, cameras, and she would be alone in responding to each attack by his powerful enemies.

But would they continue to persecute a dead man? She glanced at the empty bed for a second, feeling the same wrenching sob tear through her once again. She ran to the window, opened it forcefully and expelled a bitter shriek into the damp chill, tears rolling down her eyes, crashing furiously on the white hospital floor. It was by this window that he had stood, waiting for her to bring him newspapers and books, and each time she returned from the library, she would see him standing there, seeking her out anxiously. She would now have to tend to the most tedious arrangements in her life; she would have to relay the news of his death to their friends in Crete and in Athens. She took a few more deep breaths and raised her gaze, but could not discern anything brighter than gray clouds.

She had never fathomed the possibility of such a somber return home. She had envisioned it quite differently: him, standing tall and smiling, with the Nobel Prize tucked proudly in his luggage, his gift to the Greek people. But that was not their reality; they had been persecuted relentlessly by the Church, the Palace, and the para-state organizations of Greece long after they had left, eleven years before. The attacks had been fierce, even from Nikos' "colleagues".

Would the news soften their hatred somehow? she wondered as she began to construct a convenient reasoning filled with rational arguments, as if hatred is mitigated or softened by logic. *He is now dead; he did not incite any form of violence, he never forced anyone to read his books; this warfare raging against him will surely begin to wane.* Helen's calming thoughts alleviated her discomfort, somewhat, and with that, she leaned slightly inward and shut the window.

A few moments later, Helen walked through the clinic's front gate and headed to the Post Office. She dispatched telegrams announcing her husband's death to Athens, Herakleion and Thessaloniki, to family and friends. She thought telegraphing the news was hard enough; *vocalizing the chilling words is harder, still,* Helen thought, as she placed a call to Agnes Roussopoulou, her trusted friend and lawyer.

Agnes was a feminist and trade unionist, a fighting spirit, daughter of celebrated chemist Othon Roussopoulos, the illustrious founder of the Academy for Trade and Industry and member of the Parliament. Her mother, Helen Naoum, who hailed from a renowned family of fur manufacturers in Kastoria, had been born in Leipzig and had been a close associate of the legendary feminist Callirrhoe Siganou-Parren, founder of the Lyceum Club of Greek Women, responsible for the publication of *Greek Woman* magazine.

Helen had not even considered which words to use in that phone call, and the voice of her friend on the other end startled her. It would be the first time she would acknowledge it, that she would utter the words.

"Agnes... we lost him..." she cried into the telephone, bursting into tears, as if hearing it herself for the first time. For a few seconds, neither could speak; when their sobbing subsided, Helen begged her to get there as soon as she possibly could, to be by her side.

"Of course, my dear," Agnes answered. "Please don't worry."

Her painful duty done, Helen set out aimlessly, walking about without a destination like a queen deposed through the medieval cobblestone alleys of Freiburg – the most sunlit town of Germany – with its austere geometrical colorful homes, the large windows and the impressive rooftops. Here and there, small water canals intersected her aimless stroll; the legend in those parts said that one would marry a local if one touched the waters, but Helen walked on indifferently, crossing the picturesque bridges, unmoved by the water's monotonously harmonious rhythm. She couldn't enjoy anything during this perfunctory Sunday walk. She tried to organize her thoughts and priorities, to foresee any troubles or issues that might arise, a process she had mastered by being constantly at his side.

To him she had been everything: lover, wife, his right and his left hand, manager, secretary, typist and nurse. It was she who had typed his *Odyssey,* the titanic opus of 33,333 verses – of which her husband had been so proud – seven times, on a small ribbon typewriter. It was she who had taken care of the tedious procedural matters: exchanged letters with publishers, arranged all legal issues, cooked, washed, cleaned house, and ensured that Nikos got his medicine when he was sick. It was she who would read all that he'd write and encourage him or dissuade him respectively, and she who had urged him to turn the stories he would tell her each night, so she could go to sleep, into written novels – those incredible stories about his old community, his town, the Crete he had known and was nostalgic for.

"She is my guardian saint, my St. George," he would write to his friends about her.

Yet now she stood before the unknown, unable to fathom how the Church and State – those institutions responsible for Nikos' self-exile and his longstanding enemies – might react to the news of his death. Still, it was Nikos' wish to be buried in the blessed soil of his homeland, Crete, so she would have to make arrangements with Agnes, who had helped him with his last will and testament.

Nikos had been hurt by many "friends", by people he had cared for and had loved, but who had indulged, over the years, in the guilty pleasure of the character assassination campaign mounted against him, seduced by a disingenuous friendship with pseudo-intellectuals and "world-educated" critics who loved to spread rumors about him. Each time the discussion turned to this topic, Nikos had only smiled; he would rationalize their bitter envy against him, even justify it. From his perspective, he had felt it was all too reasonable: their own work was not read, not even by Greek readers, who might have not even known they existed, and the very thought of international recognition was out of the question for them. They were only famous in their own backyards, and all that remained for them was to gossip and ridicule the works and choices of others. Among those in these "intelligentsia" cliques, sadly, was Galatea, his ex-wife and one of the main sources of those rumors.

Would she be at the funeral? Helen wondered, but just the thought caused her distress. Helen was not jealous of Galatea – perhaps, in those first years when Nikos and Helen's relationship was still young, but, as time passed, whatever jealousy she might have felt for her in the beginning had long subsided, despite the fact that Galatea had continued to use Nikos' surname. She had even received full credit for the grammar school textbooks that Nikos had authored, and had become rather famous, not just in Greece, but throughout the Greek diaspora as well, and all of it with his permission, his approval, his suggestion, even. While Helen, still unmarried, had struggled to save him from starvation and impoverishment, Galatea had been using his name as her own, all the while leading a faction of intellectuals at Dexameni district in spreading rumors about him.

Perhaps Galatea had been reflecting about all that she could have experienced at his side but was never able to, Helen thought, mirroring her husband's compromising and forgiving spirit. *Perhaps his rejection of her as a wife and a lover had hurt her so profoundly, so entirely, that it had given birth to an overpowering hatred.*

Suddenly, Helen felt awfully weak. She couldn't remember how many hours before – or was it days – she had last eaten. The mere thought of eating repulsed her, but self-preservation prevailed. She tried to orient herself, spying a sign about fifty meters away; guided by a black arrow, she reached a massive wooden door with over-sized hinges, and pushed it with her last remaining strength. Inside, the heavy baroque design, with brown and verdant green dominating the space, evoked a feeling of stability and safety inside her. Only a young couple were there, cooing under the mezzanine, looking as though they were in a cave all by themselves in the entire world.

Helen sat at a table by the window, anxiously avoiding the dark corners of the room. Convincing herself she would get something to eat a little later, she ordered tea. She let her eyes drift around the room and soon found herself unconsciously staring at the young couple; they were leaning toward one another, exchanging whispers, swift touches and smiles. She wasn't jealous, not at all; she felt happy for them. She had lived it all, wholly and completely with a man she admired, a man she was passionately and unreservedly in love with, who had gifted her with more than one lifetime, who had cared for her, elevated her and loved her.

Her mind gradually calmed, simmering down from its racing thoughts after the third sip of tea. She felt her eyelids becoming heavier, shutting themselves, and for a few moments she gave in to the temptation of keeping them closed, when a thought shook her awake.

I have to speak to Agnes again, as well as with Nikos'
publisher in Greece, John Goudelis...I need his help with all the
necessary procedures. How will we transport his body to Greece?
What will it cost? Will I even have enough time to return to
Antibes, to get some clothes?

There was a whole tedious process that had to be completed,
and she realized she had to move quickly, she needed to have all
the information by that afternoon, to organize her hectic schedule
for the days ahead. The only thing she felt with certainty in that
moment was that she needed to sleep as soon as possible.

She left in a hurry without finishing her tea, leaving behind
some coins on the table. From the corner of her eye, she stole a
glance at the couple once more; they were seated just as she had
spotted them about twenty minutes earlier – huddled over one
another, still exchanging smiles and caresses.

They have all the time in the world ahead of them, she thought
with a smile, as she let the enormous wooden door with the large
hinges close behind her. Her step had regained its usual
determined rhythm. She would return to the hospital to await
Agnes's phone call, and would see to it that all the procedures in
this – the toughest week of her life – were underway.

After a fifteen minute walk, she returned to the Clinic. Passing
through the hospital gate, Helen was met by a blond nurse with a
closely shorn hair and a noticeably masculine body and manner to
match, who informed her that a relative of Nikos' was going to
call again, apparently to learn the details of his passing and
matters relating to his funeral. Helen ascended the stairs to the
room. The sterilized environment made her want to flee, but this
feeling subsided when she opened the window and let her gaze
trail through the Black Forest. She leaned her elbows on the
window ledge, recalling all the lighthearted strolls she had shared
with her Nikos, all the teasing and laughter.

For long periods of their life, their world was never larger than
the dimensions of the bench they shared, and it had been the
dreamiest world she could have ever lived in. He would be reading

his ever favorite *Inferno* by Dante Alighieri, and she would just gaze at him, devoid of concerns, wants, fears or guilt.

The same nurse came to inform her that she had a phone call, and by the time Helen descended the stairs and reached the ground floor, she was once again the iron lady, the dynamic woman behind the eminent man. On the phone with Nikos' nephew, Helen answered all of his questions: his uncle would be interred in Herakleion – it had been his final wish, after all; she did not know in how many days that would be, though she estimated that the funeral would take place by the middle of the following week. It was fortunate that only a few seconds after she lowered the receiver, another call came through for her, one where she could speak more freely. It was Agnes.

"Helen, I don't have a passport. Today is Sunday and, since tomorrow is October 28, a national holiday, I would have to wait until Tuesday, when the public services will be open..."

Helen was almost overcome with despair, until she heard the "but" which quickly followed. "...But, finally, I located a friend of mine who works at the Ministry of Interior. I am on my way there now to be issued an identity certification so I can travel."

Helen felt warm tears rolling down her face.

"Thank you so much my friend," she said, trying her best, for the third time that day, to smother the swelling gratitude she felt for her friend's immeasurable generosity.

"I will call you again from the airport," Agnes assured her, and Helen longed to kiss her hands, to give her a tight embrace; she felt immensely grateful to that strong-willed and, at the same time, delicate creature.

Helen put down the receiver, utterly spent. Exerting every effort not to succumb prematurely to the fatigue that engulfed her, she managed to go up to the room where she collapsed just as she was, fully clothed, and gave in to sleep. She had no more strength, nor will, nor courage...

SUNDAY, OCTOBER 28, 1957

Athens

The memories of the Nazi occupation and the Civil War had faded to gray, supplanted by lavish polka dot dresses and massive Buicks. The majority of Athenian high society craved a westernized normalcy, though this was more true of the grand bourgeoisie, of course, since the urban lower classes had more basic issues to resolve, the primary of which was survival. That October of 1957, the focal point of interest in Athenian salons was the Orient, with the Soviets having launched the first satellite, Sputnik, which had successfully risen above the atmosphere and had entered orbit around the Earth.

The men wondered how the Soviets had managed to surmount the "mutual restraint" that governed the world, and placed bets on how impressive the response of their beloved Americans was going to be; the ladies, on the other hand, especially those well-versed in international fashion, were abuzz with the death of the French fashion designer, Christian Dior.

A common topic for both sexes was the impending arrival of Jane Mansfield, the so-called "atomic bombshell" – according to the press – in Greece. When these topics were suitably exhausted, the discussion would shift to the best transatlantic cruiser for travel to New York in view of the coming Christmas holidays, or, if anyone had finally seen their name posted on the national telephone company's roster, that much-coveted list of all those who met the requirements to obtain their very own telephone line at home.

Nevertheless, it was politics that always endured as the leading topic of discussion. People placed bets on when the Constantine

Karamanlis government would fall, or if the opposition led by George Papandreou and Sophocles Venizelos would win the elections. On Sunday, October 27, 1957, however, a speech by King Paul in Thessaloniki, commemorating the 45th anniversary of the city's liberation from the Ottoman yolk, had dominated all other political discussions for its highly offensive swipe at the people of Greece.

"The Greek people are ignorant of their civic duties," the King had said, to the chagrin of public sentiment. The assertion did not seem to bother the illustrious patrons of the Grande Bretagne or the King George Hotel, where the Athenian elite frequented, but twenty or so meters down the street, at the more progressive Zonar's Café, the complaints were quite vocal.

The unexpected news of Nikos Kazantzakis' death in Freiburg found the Athenians unprepared and quite hungry, anchored around several Athenian restaurants, about to order their Sunday lunch. It was the eve of a national holiday, the anniversary of October 28, 1940 – a highly coveted three-day weekend for public servants whose time off would span into the following Monday, as well. It was such a joyous compensation for every employee when national holidays fell on a Monday, even as many Greeks, as few as one in four, worked with their labor rights acknowledged in 1957. Unemployment was rampant, and petty crime followed in direct proportion.

There were those, however, who felt the holidays were an intolerable indulgence, an extravagance only known to them through the accounts of others; for such people, like journalists, the countdown to the next working day was akin to Chinese water torture. It was only natural, then, that when the news of the death of the Cretan thinker spread through the center of the Greek capital, journalists could hardly wait for Monday afternoon to return to their desks.

One of the first to receive the news was Peter Charis, a seasoned journalist working at *Eleftheria* newspaper and a native Cretan, who had enjoyed a friendly relationship with the deceased. In fact, almost a decade before, he had been called in by the Police Directorate to explain himself for having published Kazantzakis' subversive theatrical play, *Sodom and Gomorrah*, in *Nea Estia*, the magazine he was running at the time. Upon receiving the news, his journalistic instinct prevailed against his personal sentiments when he called his chief-editor, George Androulidakis.

"George, good afternoon. Peter Charis speaking."

"Can't this wait until tomorrow?"

"I'm afraid not. I'm guessing you haven't heard…"

"No. What happened?"

"Kazantzakis died in Freiburg. Complications from the flu."

"Are you sure, man? Have you verified this with anyone?"

"I'm sure. The news came out of Herakleion. His wife sent a telegram to his nephew."

"It can't be! No, damn it! But he was out of danger, isn't that what they said?"

"I guess it was something much more serious than the doctors had initially assessed."

"Call Goudelis for confirmation, and anyone else you can! I know it is hard for you, Peter, but I'm assigning this to you. I will tell the kid, Germanos, to call around and find out whatever else he can."

"George, you know what's coming, right? There may be tension, disturbances from the Church, from a handful of fanatics that will try to stir public sentiment."

"We will rise to the occasion with dignity, come what may. We'll talk tomorrow evening."

Androulidakis breathed a heavy sigh in an effort to cast aside the sadness that had accumulated in his chest and throat. It was now his professional and moral duty to relay the true measure of the man to the readers of his newspaper. When one reports constantly about death, loss, disasters and any news that provoke incalculable grief to an unspecified number of people, generally unknown to him personally, he develops a rare immunity when faced with the devastation of others. Loss, to a reporter is just another day at the office, it generates no emotion, only a series of considerations: where might the topic lead, what attention-getting title will provoke the readers' interest, will there be a good photo to draw the eye? In the case of the tabloid press, the event itself may not even be enough; a special twist of the brushstroke is required for the salacious headline, which will be accompanied by the necessarily disturbing photo.

The more serious and prestigious newspapers, however, set up their topics in keeping with their reputation, and with the right handling, a novel approach, a witty opening sentence and an evocative closing, the loss and grief of others may become a first rate success for the journalist and editor who cover the subject. Yet, when a tragedy's protagonists are not completely unknown to the journalist, his immunity weakens and all those human emotions rise to the surface, reminders of his own forgotten mortality. Readership appeal or personal advancement cease to be an end in itself, since the reporter becomes part and parcel of all the "others" who are impacted by the pain, who empathize, who experience the devastation, and in those moments, a journalist must struggle to reconcile his human vulnerability with a most basic level of professionalism.

Androulidakis did not weep for Kazantzakis. He honored him with an impulsive moment of silence at first, then with a rudimentary yet sensitive remembrance of the author's works and days, his ascending path through the raging decades experienced by the whole world. He felt like the indispensable lighthouse keeper, who prevented shipwrecks during the dark night but was forgotten in the morning; a hero and beacon in the darkness, yet invisible and useless in the light.

The sound of the telephone snapped Androulidakis back to the present, the irritating ring making him spring up from his seat. It was the publisher and general manager of *Eleftheria*, Panos Kokkas, who had heard the news from another source. It was really true, then, the facts checked out: beyond any doubt, Kazantzakis was dead! Androulidakis informed his boss that he had assigned the reportage to Peter Charis, who was the first to announce to him the tragic news. Kokkas told him he would call

John M. Panagiotopoulos to write the obituary for the Tuesday edition; he had been friends with the deceased and was the most appropriate person to write something worthy of the man's stature. Besides, Panagiotopoulos possessed the necessary background and Kokkas was certain he would read a memorable homage penned by his capable hands. The publisher went on to instruct his chief-editor to assign the research to a second person who would fact check everything that was circulating as an additional help to Peter.

"The kid, Germanos," Androulidakis suggested.

"Are you sure? Isn't it too soon for him?" Kokkas asked.

"He's ready," the chief-editor declared, with a certainty that precluded any further questions.

"I'm particularly worried about the Church's reaction," Kokkas went on, touching upon one of the most crucial factors of the whole issue.

"I don't think the Church has anything to be concerned with anymore; he is dead," Androulidakis reassured him. "Unless they fear his resurrection, of course."

"Death provokes extreme emotions, my dear fellow," the publisher replied. "I don't think it is that simple. We must be vigilant."

"Has Mitsotakis said anything to you?" Androulidakis asked, concerned.

"That's all for now," the publisher replied, and hung up before the chief-editor even had a chance to say goodbye.

The dark days of 1954 flooded Androulidakis' mind with a vengeance, those days when the Holy Synod of the Church had declared war against Kazantzakis in a hateful campaign that, by contemporary standards, was purely an assassination of character. Enemies of the author were recruited from all social circles: religious sect leaders and followers, Orthodox Church priests, politicians, journalists, artists – or at least, they professed to be.

Sadly, all this could repeat itself, he thought, and he had to prepare for that possibility. Androulidakis set aside history, swirling in the dizziness of her infinite recurring cycles, and wasted no more time as he placed a call to the newspaper headquarters, looking for Freddy Germanos. That twenty-three year old, he believed, was a man gifted with special qualities: a contemporary, unconventional and charming pen and a first rate sense of humor. The call reached the young journalist at his office, where he was on standby, even on a Sunday, on the eve of a national holiday.

"Freddy, how are you? I have some distressing news. Kazantzakis passed away in Freiburg."

"I know, Mr. Androulidakis. I am trying to verify. I was going to call you as soon as I fact-checked it."

"I have verified it myself. Try to gather any information. Call our correspondent in Herakleion. Find out how we could speak to a relative or a friend."

"Will I be covering this story, Mr. Androulidakis?" young Freddy asked enthusiastically.

"No, Peter Charis is covering it. You will help him."

"But, sir..."

"Not another word. Do what I told you. Finish your shift and get some sleep. And tomorrow afternoon be at my office at four. Do you understand? Goodbye."

Freddy hung up the receiver, dismayed. He wasn't at a loss because of his chief-editor's reprimanding tone; that was typical every time something important was taking place. Nikos Kazantzakis was one of his heroes. All his heroes were authors and actors, with Ernest Hemingway the foremost among them. He realized it was something he very much wanted to do, to assume the heavy burden of writing Kazantzakis' obituary. He took off his modern browline glasses and laid them on the black desk with the enormous grooves that reminded him of the face of an old wrinkled man. He brought his right hand to his face, rubbing his tired eyes with his thumb and index finger; this typical and recurring motion of his hands had begun early in childhood, as he had needed prescription spectacles from quite a young age. Reading Venezis' *Aeolia* – another one of his heroes – had greatly weakened his eyesight.

Pensive and depressed, he opened the balcony door and stood on his dispiriting little terrace, which measured no more than one and a half square meters. He was certain that if he were to admit to Androulidakis how much he wanted the story, the chief-editor would respond with the expected platitude, 'No need to hurry, kid! There's a hierarchy in place. You have many years ahead of you for that'. What frustrated him the most was that he was probably right. Freddy was no stranger to hard work; he had been the errand boy at an accountant's office, and then had worked as a fabric retailer and a door-to-door salesman for five years to put himself through journalism school, and for the last three years, he had been covering the column on overnight pharmacies at *Eleftheria* newspaper, even though he had made a few contributions to some articles of minor importance.

But here, now, he had advanced with each exhausting step, from the entrance to the upper floors, having earned his own office, his own telephone device, and his own sources – all things a respectable journalist ought to enjoy. And despite all this, he was about to miss out on the story of the decade. *What would Hemingway do now?* he wondered, thinking back to the years the American author had been a journalist. He dug in his heels. *I will do what I have always done.* He hurried in, leaving the balcony doors creaking open.

His determination had carried him this far, had offered him gifts that existed only in his dreams until a few years before, and this is how he would continue. He set his mind to waking up half of the slumbering city, whose weary residents were surely enjoying their siestas after their hearty afternoon lunches. He moved the black telephone closer to him, placing his little notepad right next to it and began making his calls, noting down every detail that seemed important.

"This is Freddy Germanos, a journalist from *Eleftheria* newspaper," he repeated with every call, never tiring of the frequent phrase, as if he were uttering the words more for himself and less as his introduction. Those words - "I'm Freddy

Germanos, a journalist" – were strung so perfectly together, resonating like the motif of a beautiful melody in his young ears.

Freiburg

Helen woke up, short of breath. Startled by the unfamiliar environment, she looked around her; realizing where she was, she laid her head back down on the pillow, trying to make peace with the new space and timeline she was now living in. She took a big breath; she could sleep in a little longer, for she still felt weak and drained – even though she had slept for four hours, which was far more than she had slept in the past few weeks. There were things she needed to see to; she needed to find a hotel for herself and Agnes where they could stay until all the details had been sorted. Still, she allowed herself to stay in bed for five more minutes. Three or four rays of sunshine pushed through the window, tinting the gray in the room with a soft yellow hue, whitening the walls. It was already five in the afternoon, that time of day when her Nikos would stop writing, leave the upper floor of their home where his office was located, and would descend the circular stairs to tease her and joke with her.

He had always been the same: waking up in the early dawn and effortlessly, tirelessly writing, taking a brief pause for breakfast, a break for lunch, and until five or six in the afternoon, filling pages, smudging them, rolling them into crumbled balls, throwing them around him... But she also had worked incessantly, for when she wasn't taking care of the house or cooking, she would type his texts or write letters, even if she occasionally misspelled a word or two.

"Nikos, dear," she would call from the ground floor, "how do you spell this word?"

If they were still at their home on the island of Aegina, this would be around the time he would be going out for a swim; and in Antibes, he would sometimes head out for a walk, as he had done the last twelve years, even though his health had deteriorated considerably.

"Where are you going?" she would ask him.

"I'm taking my walking stick out for a walk," he would reply, chuckling under his breath. And when he'd return, he would sit down to eat with such hearty appetite the greens, eggs, tomatoes, cucumbers, olives and fruits that were always on their table, though often, there was hardly anything else; and, in keeping with his Cretan custom, when he would chance upon an acquaintance on the way, he would invite them home for dinner, but only after warning them that the dream of a plentiful dinner was something that could not be fulfilled in his home.

No one could ever guess, of course, that the couple survived almost exclusively on greens, gathered by Helen herself from the sidewalks or the mountain sides, or olives and tomatoes, as if constantly living in a self-imposed fast. There were those rare times, on festive occasions or for important visitors, especially when they were living in Aegina, that Nikos would walk to the nearby tavern and order some pastrami or something even more lavish and expensive. He had even made arrangements with the local captain of a small boat that ran the evening journey from Athens to the island:

"If you have a passenger on board who is coming to visit me, sound your horn three times as you pass by my house".

When the couple would finish their usually meager dinner, he would read to her all that he had written, always asking her opinion of his works.

"Explain, explain," he would exclaim persistently, though one time, when she had pointed out to him a verse in the introduction to his *Odyssey* that had left her unimpressed, he had rejected her observation.

"Well, in this case, there is nothing we can do about that," he had replied tenderly but firmly.

Nikos had assumed the role of the story teller when they would go to bed.

"Come; let's talk about the neighbors," he would say and would take her in his arms, cradling her with stories of Herakleion, with customs, beliefs and urban legends he used to hear when he was growing up in Crete. And the next evening, when they would retire to bed once again, he would ask her: "Where did we leave off yesterday?"

She had always insisted that he write the stories he told her every night and turn them into novels, but he would give her the usual reply: "I don't have the patience to write something so large," to which Helen would retort, "If we had been recording all the stories you tell me each night, you'd have been rich and famous by now".

Helen smiled, recalling that one night, when he had timidly complained to her, adjusting his tone to sound all bashful and playful.

"I know of a man who began his work today without having any breakfast."

"Who?" Helen had asked, astonished, and her beloved husband, still coyly – as if it were his own fault, replied, "Err... well... that would be me."

"And why didn't you say anything?" she had snapped back, feeling guilty at her absentmindedness, while he had already burst into laughter.

Helen felt a glimmer of cheer at this recollection of playful memories, and rose from the bed. She began to fill just one piece of luggage with the bare essentials for the next few days. There was already so much clothing, so many books and items of every kind, including gifts from their extended stay in Copenhagen, where Nikos was first hospitalized right after their return from China, and then in Freiburg, where she had to carry them. With her luggage in hand, she slowly descended the marble staircase and saw Tapita, their favorite nurse, standing at the bottom.

"How are you, Mrs. Helen?" she inquired.

"I'm fine. I'm on my way to find a hotel," she replied. "Do you have one in mind? It needs to be as close as possible, so that we can come back and forth without much hassle, as we are wrapping up all the procedural matters."

"There is one nearby, just straight ahead from here, approximately four hundred meters away," the nurse answered courteously.

"Thank you so much," Helen said, and picked up her luggage once more and headed slowly to the exit.

She hadn't yet reached the door, when she heard someone call out, "Frau Kazantzaki, Frau Kazantzaki".

It was Tapita calling her, and Helen stopped and turned back; the elderly nun approached to tell her someone was on the phone for her.

"Yes?"

"Helen, hello! I found a plane ticket for Munich. I am about to fly in a little bit. I'll take the train from there and come to you."

"All right, Agnes, dear. As soon as you reach Munich, call again, here at the hospital. They will give you the phone number of the hotel where I will be staying."

"All right, Helen. Do not worry."

"Thank you, dear Agnes," Helen bid her farewell, but was unsure if Agnes heard it.

The sun permeated the evergreen courtyard of the hospital, adding its own brushstrokes of eccentric colors. Helen was in no hurry; she had already walked a small way when she spotted a secluded bench in the distance. She had always loved sitting on park benches, taking long walks – always with him. The notion of doing things they loved to do together appealed to her greatly; besides there was no reason to hurry, no one was expecting her. Sitting on the bench felt so familiar – as if she had returned home somehow. The sun, the garden, nature... It seemed like a century ago, since that afternoon when he had leaned in and kissed her for the first time; a whole century that lasted a second! There was nothing strong enough to replace that memory with any other! Helen closed her eyes, submersing herself completely, intuitively in that singular, everlasting moment, having held onto that kiss for thirty-three years.

For on that same night, she had written to him a letter, frightened as she had been, in which she had said to him, "This seems to be going too far ahead. From today, it would be better if we saw each other less frequently, more rarely," but it was the forty-one year-old's assertive reply, so hopelessly in love, that put her concerns to rest: "The opposite is in order. We need to see each other more often".

She had read that letter over and over, afraid she was reading into it her wishes and not what he had actually written. In the end, they had been both vindicated: Nikos who had persisted, Helen who had given in.

Helen looked in the distance, to the nurses sitting on benches, talking, and patients strolling in the courtyard, and it occurred to her that no one was as fortunate as she was. It was now her duty to honor this fortune. Duty. One of his favorite words. She got up and began to walk along the path Tapita had indicated. The streets were filled with German girls crafting chrysanthemum and heather bouquets in preparation of the Catholic All Soul's Day. Further down, Helen saw a sign with a large arrow, with the letters "Hotel Paradis". *Paradise Hotel? How Kazantzakian is that!* Helen thought instantly. She continued on, through its green yard with the large monastic tables, and climbed the staircase to the reception, which was a vibrant display of the color brown in its most popular shades.

"Good afternoon. I would like a double room," she said to the lady with the striking red cheeks and enormous blue eyes.

"Good afternoon," the receptionist replied with a smile. "For how many nights?"

"Two."

"Of course," the receptionist answered, leaning forward to consult her notebook for almost a minute, despite the fact that the hotel seemed to be only half full.

"Room 108, on the first floor. Are you waiting for your husband to arrive, or will you be going up now?" the receptionist asked politely, unsettling Helen.

"No... I don't have a..." she stuttered.

"My apologies! Please follow me," the receptionist said, as she took hold of the luggage and moved to the stairs, evading in this way the tears that were rolling down Helen's cheeks.

Once in the room, she immediately began to remove her clothes and her personal items from her bag, putting them away. She was almost finished when she heard a knock on the door.

"Who is it?" she asked, startled.

"Room service," she heard a woman's voice, and opened the door to the receptionist holding two buckets of hot water. Helen thanked her profusely, taking them from her hands and carried them into the bathroom. A warm bath at that particular moment seemed to her like the best idea in the world. The hot water washed away all evidence of her grief and suffering, as she submerged herself in a cleansing baptism of her body and soul. The tears and sweat glided off her body, all fear and mourning evaporated from her mind; she felt herself relax completely, engulfed in the cloud of steam that was inexplicably charged with wonderful memories of her life with Nikos.

She felt a chill and was jolted awake. The steam had dissipated. Refreshed, she emerged from the water, and looked through the closet for something to wear. *A black skirt and blouse will do.* She paired them with her more comfortable shoes and went down to the reception and called the hospital, informing them of her new address and phone number, should anyone need to reach her.

Helen found the weary receptionist huddled over a book, and explained to her briefly what she needed. The receptionist had realized the enormous blunder she had made earlier, when she had asked Helen if she was waiting for her husband. The guilt was readily apparent in her eyes when she offered to make Helen some tea; one did not need to know her well to see it. This was the second great idea for the night, and Helen accepted the wonderful offer, walking out into the courtyard to sit at one of the long wooden tables by herself.

The sturdy wood table had grown damp as the inflamed sun was bidding them farewell, setting off for other places, and soon, the receptionist was serving her tea and cookies. Helen sipped her tea gratefully, even sampling one of the cookies, which she thought was marvelous – when the receptionist let her know she had a phone call. Helen was certain it was Agnes; it had been hours since they had last spoken.

"Agnes?"

"Helen, dear, I'm calling you from Munich Airport. Unfortunately, they tell me here that due to works on the Augsburg railway lines, we will be running late. I can't be sure what time I'll be there," she said, disappointed.

"Don't worry, Agnes dear. I'm at Hotel Paradis."

"Paradise?" Agnes repeated, astounded.

"Yes, I know, the bitter irony," Helen replied faintly. "It's really close to the Freiburg University Clinic. Would you give me a call when you get here so I can come and pick you up from the station?"

"No, you don't need the hassle. I'll get a cab when I get there," her friend replied and said goodbye.

Helen returned to the courtyard and finished her lukewarm tea. She thought of Agnes with love, knowing full well the hardships she was going through just to be near her as fast as possible to offer her support. She had managed to elude her fatigue for a little while, but it was creeping up on her again. She reasoned Agnes would most probably arrive early in the morning, so she decided to retire to her room and get some sleep. A middle-aged man of fifty-five with gray hair, green, weary eyes and glasses that balanced on the tip of his nose had replaced the kind lady at the reception. She asked him for a morning wake up call at seven a.m., and retired to her room, exhausted. She opened the door to her bedroom, and barely made it to the bed.

Athens

The state radio was the first to broadcast the news of Kazantzakis's death in Freiburg, sparking an assortment of gossip and speculation that made the usual rounds. Journalists, publishers, politicians, government officials and ecclesiastical circles were all apprised of the fact, and, as it was to be expected, the initial assessment on how to handle this affair gave everyone a headache. The authorities had been dealt the proverbial hot potato that was being tossed around swiftly, heading with lightning speed into their hands. What would the people's reaction be? Who would they side with – the persecuted, now dead, author, or the authorities? Kazantzakis may have been living abroad for many years, but his undeniable presence was still felt in country through his works and the stir they had caused and the international acclaim he had received. For every one person who criticized his work as unpatriotic and un-Christian, there were a myriad of others who believed the exact opposite, and practically the whole of the Cretan population was bursting with pride for their fellow countryman.

Freddy was too young to know the many points of contention between the Greek status quo and Kazantzakis; he had to research, comprehend, and evaluate all the people and situations at play, to understand what had sparked the beginning of the state's efforts to trap the man, to comprehend the Church's persecution of him. Freddy had finished waking half of Athens with his phone calls, and now it was Herakleion's turn. He managed to locate a Cretan man who knew a great deal about the past and about Kazantzakis and was more than eager to share, which was quite fortuitous for Freddy, for when a journalist pokes around in the dark, he is essentially searching for that one enthusiast – a journalist in the making – who would be a willing participant in his effort to document History. It was such a man who recounted to Freddy the first episode in a series of incidents that stretched over twenty-two years, all with one victim – Kazantzakis himself – and one stricken nation, Greece.

It had begun on the evening of Friday, February 13, 1925, when Kazantzakis had been arrested as the main instigator behind mobilized protests in Herakleion and had been held at the police headquarters for twenty-four hours. Freddy's new friend, the Cretan, shed light on the matter, having the good sense to keep a newspaper clipping from the daily *Nea Efimeris* of Herakleion, which had documented, in a single column, the following concise report of the event:

"Kazantzakis, who has been suspected of leading the local communist subversive activities, appeared before the District Prosecutor yesterday, where his innocence was established, and whereupon he was released."

Freddy's "man in Herakleion" knew a great deal about the people and issues at play; he even gave Freddy the contact information for some of Kazantzakis' relatives, at least those who actually had a telephone number.

"I will call you again tomorrow as well. But I would like to ask you one last question. What is your personal view of Kazantzakis? Was he an enemy of the Church and State? Just your assessment..."

Freddy actually heard him smirk.

"As much as anyone who points out the errors of our government is an enemy, who writes about scandals and corruption and immoral politicians. That's my answer. Did you get that?"

"I got that," the young reporter replied, nodding emphatically.

The Cretan's viewpoint, especially one from Herakleion, was interesting, but it could hardly be considered an absolute truth; Freddy needed to know what the official Church had against Kazantzakis. Freddy had read *Captain Michalis* and *Christ Recrucified,* and neither work had raised any alarm about Kazantzakis being a "red agent," an instrument of the communists and, in particular, of the Soviet Union, as he had been branded by his enemies in Greece, naturally, for abroad Kazantzakis had no enemies. All that Freddy could surmise on his own was that Kazantzakis was more well read than the overwhelming majority of the clergy, and that he had most certainly lived a life more ascetic than the members of the Holy Synod.

However, a journalist should not dwell on a single view, especially expressed by a person whose origins, motivations or incentives are unknown to him. On the other hand, the motives of a "kinsman," could not be comparable to those of a politician, a career government official or a priest with hierarchical aspirations; the Cretan was familiar, after all, with the historical course of Nikos Kazantzakis, the author and the man, which meant that whatever he asserted was not to be dismissed. It was simply one perspective of the story. Freddy's pencil sharpener was on fire, and soon his notepad was full of notes. It was after ten p.m. when the janitor knocked on the open door to his office and asked him to wrap up for the night. He would read over his notes at home, would reevaluate his material and would then outline calmly the profile of his hero.

He stepped out onto October 28th Street – named after the national holiday – and realized it was almost midnight. Traffic had abated, and the parked cars along the road seemingly formed a barrier of steel from pedestrians. The night air was mild and Freddy began to walk down Panepistimiou Avenue, trying to enjoy his walk by casting all thoughts aside. The twenty-three year old tried to focus his thoughts on something other than Kazantzakis and all the things he had learned earlier, or even the Cretan kinsman, with whom he'd be speaking again, tomorrow, but it was no easy feat; the young reporter was caught in the eye of a storm, his mind surging with ideas, one after the other.

He turned on Ippokratous Street, and the gentle breeze blew through his hair, grazing his forehead.

All my friends are probably at a nightclub or somewhere having fun right now, he thought to himself, but the idea of joining them did not even cross his mind. Laying in bed at last, he opened his notebook and went through his notes, enumerating the gaps in the Kazantzakis story. It wasn't long before sleep tried to overtake him; Freddy was aware, the pencil still in his hand, but too exhausted to resist. He tried to fight it, but failed.

It's funny, if you think about it, how heavy a dozen strands of minuscule hair on your eyelids may feel sometimes, he thought, and succumbed to the weight of his eyelashes.

MONDAY, OCTOBER 28, 1957

Athens

The festive sun shone brightly, setting the tone, and the Athenians poured out into the streets as if part of a silent conspiracy for which they had long prepared, to commemorate the national anniversary but also to honor one of the truly last warm days of the year. Already at ten in the morning, the city's center swelled with the weight of the holiday; the townsfolk of the lower middle class were parading up and down Stadiou Street in their Sunday best, with Tsita's fully packed confectionery as their reference point.

Patriotic pride exuded in every coffee shop as Greek coffees were consumed alongside political discussions of the newest scuffle that had commenced between Constantine Karamanlis and George Papandreou in light of the notorious speech given by King Paul in Thessaloniki, just two days before.

The grand bourgeoisie had already taken their seats comfortably at Floka's Café, while the more progressives sat right next door, at Zonar's, and just across the avenue, in the uphill curve of Voukourestiou street, past Pyrsos Bookstore, the aroma of freshly ground coffee startled the passersby. It was here, at the infamous Brazilian Café, that Athenians were initiated in the joys of espresso, even if they soon betrayed it for the iced drink called "frappé". This temple of superb coffee – no more than a hole in the wall – was a celebrated meeting point for the Athenian intelligentsia, much like the Loumides Loft Café at Stadiou Avenue, the Dexameni coffee shop – a personal favorite of Nikos Kazantzakis and Kostas Varnalis – and the Vyzantio Café in Kolonaki.

That particular morning the usual haunts were mournfully silent. The royal blunder and the Papandreou-Karamanli tussle did not even concern the patrons that day, least of all, the impending arrival of the bombshell Jane Mansfield in Athens. The death of Kazantzakis hung heavy in the air; even his most vociferous critics were sparing in words and bile against him, while his friends and admirers of his work and his life stance, were inconsolable.

Sorrow was certainly not equally shared among the patrons of these intellectual hang outs, though the anxious concern regarding the position of the Church and the State was evidently affecting everyone.

"Will it be a state funeral?" someone would ask.

"Would a bishop find anything good to say about him?" another would inquire.

Freddy Germanos had put on his brown business suit, a gift from his grandfather, as he was still too young to own a groom's suit. It was a modern three-button jacket, and when it would get too hot he would replace the jacket with a cardigan. He began meandering from the city's center at Stadiou Avenue to the Loumides Loft Café, to get a feel of the atmosphere prevailing in the Athenian intelligentsia. He passed by Tsita's Confectionery for a taste of the average people's discussions, and then headed to his personal "command center" at Zonar's, to enjoy his regular cup of coffee and to glean any information he could from his more experienced colleagues that would surely be there at this hour.

He sat down comfortably at his corner table, which provided him with a very strategic visual angle of both Voukourestiou Street and Panepistimiou Avenue. At the very next table, Freddy recognized two of his esteemed colleagues – whom he knew only by sight – news reporters from the first in circulation newspaper, *Vima*, commenting on Galatea Kazantzakis' latest book, *Humans and Superhumans*, a title with a rather Nietzschean flair. The book had already been in circulation for a few months, and in it, Kazantzakis' ex-wife had presented her life with the author in the bleakest of colors.

"It's clear that Galatea is trying to expose him in a way that is, at the very least, vindictive with this novel. I say the truth is somewhere in the middle. Neither Galatea nor Kazantzakis is a saint," said the elder of the two reporters, holding his cup of Greek coffee in front of his lips as he spoke.

"But I can't help but wonder about Kazantzakis's reaction. There was none; not even an interview to defend himself," the other reporter replied. He was the younger of the two, dressed to the nines, with a blazer and a plaid pocket square, and quite eager to probe for an explanation he was certain was forthcoming from his seasoned colleague.

"But Kazantzakis knew all too well, that such a move – a direct confrontation with Galatea – would result in nothing more than splendid promotion for her book. He would have nothing to gain from something like that," the older reporter wisely intoned, and finally took that sip from his coffee which had grown cold.

Freddy was not just eavesdropping, he was hanging on the older reporter's every word. He had the audacity to take out his pencil and notepad, and proceeded to jot down the spicy discussion. The weathered newsman placed his cup down on its finely curved saucer, and continued in a display of thorough proficiency on the enmity between the former couple.

"And let's not forget, Galatea attempted something quite similar to this twenty-one years ago, too."

The young man in the fashionable suit and the white shirt seemed clearly astonished, even reverent, as he watched his esteemed colleague pull this tidbit of information from obscurity.

"What do you mean?" he asked exuberantly, his eyes bulging.

"Kazantzakis had published a truly perplexing article in *Kathimerini* newspaper in 1936, in which he had tried to excuse the Italian and German people who had allowed the rise of fascist regimes, by calling attention to the fact that fear and hunger of the poor tend to bring about such results. Galatea did not let the opportunity pass; she responded with a fiery article and sent it for publication to *Eleftheri Gnomi* newspaper. She really let him have it, the poor bugger!" the wise reporter concluded and lifted his cup once more to his lips.

"And how did Kazantzakis respond?" the young journalist asked.

"He didn't," the knowledgeable journalist replied, taking another sip of coffee and placing the cup back down on its saucer without the slightest noise.

Freddy listened on in absolute elation; he had to restrain himself from cheering out loud. In just ten minutes he had collected such invaluable information that, under different circumstances, would surely have taken him days to unearth. Another journalist joined the pair, a reporter of about fifty-five from *Ta Nea* newspaper. Even though both newspapers belonged to the same parent press group, the Lambrakis Company, the *Vima* newspaper journalists regarded those at *Nea* as slightly inferior.

"What do you think? Will Galatea attend Kazantzakis' funeral?" he interjected before he even sat down, in an attempt to offer a new perspective on the Kazantzakian issue.

His eyes were sparkling.

"Absolutely not," the old journalist replied. "Neither she, nor Markos Avgeris, her husband, will attend. And the fact that he was once a good friend of Kazantzakis' is beside the point," he added.

"But where's the rub? When did it all go sour between them?" interrupted the youngest of the group, effectively ignoring the "lesser" journalist of *Nea* newspaper, who had just tried to sprinkle their fine discussion with his yellow dust of intrigue.

"Galatea is a die-hard communist. Kazantzakis himself, despite having lived in the Soviet Union, or having been invited by the actual Soviet government to the ten-year anniversary of the October Revolution, was not, in fact a communist. He called himself a meta-communist. Truth is, he had been disillusioned quite early by the developments of the revolution. He came to realize that a great opportunity had been squandered for humankind to make amends for the poverty that had sparked the revolution in the first place, and the poverty persisted, despite the ascendance of the proletariat and the promises of its leaders. Therefore, from a point onward, Greek communists came to regard Kazantzakis as a conservative with right-wing views, not to mention a spy working for British intelligence, while the conservatives labeled him a communist. The poor man was neither!"

At this point Freddy realized that his notepad did not have nearly enough pages to capture the girth and breadth of this illuminating discussion. He decided to record the expert reporter's statements as concisely as he could to conserve space, and signaled for a second cup of coffee, as the case was getting juicier by the minute.

"Let's not forget, of course, how the antagonism developed between the former couple. They were both novelists. The word is that she was the one who hated Kazantzakis. And rumor has it that when she married her second husband, Avgeris, she was a virgin," the reporter from *Nea,* ever a fan of intrigue, leaned in and whispered in a conspiratorial tone.

"My esteemed colleague, I cannot help but be mystified by the ease with which you invoke urban legends that touch upon the pettiest of women's gossip," reacted the older reporter with an air of displeasure.

"But this proves so much about Galatea, who never actually bothered to put an end to any of these rumors, and in fact propagated this very 'urban legend' as you call it, by allowing it to merely hover, at first, and then to...crawl behind our prominent author," the journalist from *Nea* argued in his own defense – and in Kazantzakis' – though the only thing he accomplished was to confirm to the other two journalists from *Vima* that his brand of journalism was of the tabloid type.

"And what do you think the Archbishop's reaction will be?" the youngest of the group circled back.

"Well, I suppose he is a clever man. He won't fan the flames, and there would be no reason to," replied the expert, casting a sideways glance to his peer, in an effort to prevent a potentially sensationalistic yet completely inappropriate position on this matter as well.

"That's right! No one would want an escalation of any kind right now," agreed the youngest reporter.

"Well, yes, but wouldn't such a controversy be the perfect buffer to the King's blunder in Salonica? Wouldn't such a diversion give the Palace and the government a conveniently effective way to deflect public attention?" sprang up the audacious reporter from *Nea*, sporting a winning smile.

"Well what should the Church do, then? Ban his books? They essentially did that and failed miserably. He is now dead. If the Church had the power to resurrect him, then indeed, it would have the golden opportunity to get back at him, by resurrecting him and leaving him in the dirt. But now..." retorted the young reporter in the modern business suit.

The group fell silent for a moment, interrupted only by the sounds of the reporter from *Ta Nea*, who was taking vociferous sips from his coffee, when he attempted to draw all the attention to himself, and, perhaps earn the respect of his colleagues, by mentioning a piece of news he had picked up.

"Yesterday, a minute of silence was observed at the Kotopouli Theater, where Dostoevsky's *The Idiot* is playing," he said with pomp and circumstance, and, seeing that he was already accomplishing the first of his two goals, pressed on.

"During the intermission Katrakis took the stage – he is the Director of the Greek Popular Theater, you know, and declared it was a 'national loss, even though Kazantzakis's work will illuminate us forever and will guide us on the path for a better tomorrow'. And then he praised *Christ Recrucified*."

All three agreed that Katrakis was increasingly being acknowledged as a leading figure of the Greek Theater, and the reporter of *Nea* was all fired up, going on to say that Logothetides, who had been in the hospital, was now doing much better, was about to be discharged the very next day, and in about fifteen days he would rejoin his theatrical troupe in the show *Pros Theou,*

Metaxy mas [Between us, Naturally] by Dimitris Psathas, which had been met with great success the previous summer.

Ten minutes later, the journalists' clique, which had proven so unexpectedly useful to Freddy, was abandoning its table, as they started off for Christou Lada Street, where their newspaper offices were located. He remained at his small table, evaluating his valuable notes, unable to process the enormity of his good fortune.

Freiburg

They had been on Aegina island, laying in the sand, talking under the starry sky.

"You need to choose one of the big souls of this world and devote yourself wholeheartedly to that soul," Nikos had advised her. His advice had come at the time she had been writing the biography of Mahatma Gandhi.

"Then, when you are done with that, I will help you find another one," he had added. "And what about you?" Helen had asked him.

"Buddha won't let me sleep. I really would like to write a tragedy," he had replied. Suddenly, there was a loud noise, as though someone was knocking on the door.

"But I'm not in any hurry, I'm just letting the subject mature in my loins. What is important to understand is that we need to let ourselves be consumed by a great beast. This is the only way to get rid of all the lice."

The noise grew in rhythm and intensity. "Fräulein, Fräulein!" Helen opened her eyes wide and sprang from the bed. Someone was knocking on her door; she opened it to the bespectacled, middle-aged receptionist.

"It is seven, madam," he informed her.

"Thank you very much."

"Good morning to you," he bowed slightly, and retreated.

Helen washed up and donned her solemn, mourning suit of black and descended to the breakfast hall, to her favorite refectory table where she ordered tea with bread and marmalade. A demure yet expressionless blond woman around forty, petite, with milky white skin, brought the tray to her. The sun gradually revealed its intentions, leaving no room for the immense clouds and pesky winds. She had barely eaten her first slice of bread, when the middle-aged receptionist appeared at the threshold and informed her that she had a call. Helen thought for a moment who it might be, then got up quickly.

"Agnes, my dear!"

"Good morning. I'm at the Freiburg train station. I am getting in a cab and I'm on my way to you, Helen dear," she heard her friend say in quite the lively tone, given her lengthy and arduous journey.

"My hotel is very close to the station, Agnes dear. I'm here waiting for you," Helen replied, her anticipation mounting.

The train station was but a few minutes away from the Freiburg University Clinic; Helen knew this well, from that dreadful day she had pressured the Danish doctors to release Nikos so she could bring him to Freiburg from Copenhagen. His right arm, which they had injected with a vaccine to protect him from the pox and cholera, had been dreadfully swollen and the risk of gangrene was substantial. She could still recall how Nikos had passed out at that station, as soon as they had stepped off the train; it had taken everything she had to lift him up and help him sit somewhere, as she had waited for the ambulance to arrive.

"He's an awful mess! Is this how you bring him to me?" Dr. Herder had yelled.

That he had recovered from that had been the final miracle, Helen reflected.

She stood on the small terrace at the hotel's entrance when, at the end of the path leading to the pavement, she saw a car pulling over, and, after a few seconds, a woman marching towards her. *Agnes*, she thought, and began descending the steps as fast as her legs could muster. She threw out her arms when she saw the other woman, her arms outstretched, moving towards her, and they both fell into a tight embrace. Ensconced in each other's arms, their bodies connected, their heartbeats vibrating in each other's chests, their tears falling irrepressibly on each other's shoulders, they held each other firmly, like a single statue with a double, pulsating heart.

When a few moments later, their souls were appeased, Helen wiped the tears from Agnes' cheeks with her delicate fingers.

"It's all right, Agnes dear. All is as it should be. Nikos is fine now, he is no longer suffering," she whispered, comforting her. She was strong, like he would have wanted her to be.

"Yes, Helen dear. He is fine now," Agnes whispered back, her turn now to console her friend.

"Come sit for a bit, so I can see you. You must be exhausted," Helen tenderly suggested.

"No, not so much," Agnes replied, walking towards the refectory table, where the tea, marmalade and the bread were waiting. "I slept a bit on the train. It was comfortable, though we had a bit of a tough time."

"My dear girl," Helen said compassionately, "Wouldn't you like to eat something and then go up to the room to get some sleep?"

"No, I'm fine. Let's sit here for a bit and then we can get started on the procedural things. And before we start with that, I want to inform you, as your lawyer, that Nikos has left all of his—"

Helen raised her right hand, silencing Agnes.

"Let's not, I am not interested in any of those things right now. Besides, I know everything he wrote to you in that letter."

Agnes fell silent and took hold of Helen's hand and squeezed it lovingly.

"Tell me, what happened... how?"

"When we got here, his health had improved. He felt much better. The swelling in his arm had subsided. There were three more Greek patients in the hospital: Papantonopoulos, Iatrides and Mitsis. They all died before Nikos. He was devastated; he took it as a bad sign. He thought he would die as well, even though I kept reassuring him that they all suffered from a very different illness – they had cancer.

"Dr. Heilmayer was optimistic; he kept telling me to go back to Antibes, to bring back some warm clothes, and that, as soon as he would release him, we should visit the mountains so Nikos could convalesce. But the day before my trip, he developed a fever. That same night it went down, but then spiked up again, it just wouldn't drop. On Saturday, an Anglican pastor and a catholic priest came to see him. He turned his back to them; he didn't want them, and then....that same night, at ten thirty, he 'left'."

Agnes listened, squeezing Helen's hand tightly in her own in an effort to comfort her friend but also hold back her own tears. Helen sensed Agnes' deep turmoil.

"Come, drink some tea. It will be good for you," she suggested.

Agnes drank a few sips and bit a little slice of bread with marmalade that Helen had prepared for her.

"Could I ask something important?"

"Of course, my dear Agnes."

"The funeral will be held in Herakleion, right?"

"Of course. That was his wish. He used to say he wanted to return his body from whence it came, back to the Cretan earth."

Helen saw Agnes was welling up again; she calmly raised the teapot and refilled her cup.

"Would we need to inform anyone else about the funeral?" Agnes asked, regaining her composure.

"I haven't been able to get a hold of Goudelis," Helen answered quietly.

"Look, it's already eight thirty. Shall I go up to the room, take a bath and then we can head to the hospital?"

"Yes, Agnes, dear," Helen replied serenely.

Athens

The headquarters of *Eleftheria* newspaper at Panepistimiou Avenue were abuzz with life in the early afternoon, the time when most of its journalists came in to write their articles. By now, news of Kazantzakis's death had spread far and wide, rippling across in solemn waves, though not for everyone – for some, the heavy atmosphere was only because it was just Monday. This was not the case, of course for Freddy, neither for Androulidakis nor Peter Charis.

The three of them were in the chief-editor's office, discussing the way the newspaper would cover the topic. Behind the chief-editor, various iconic cover pages of *Eleftheria* newspaper framed the wall – a precise delineation of Androulidakis' resume – and were placed in such a manner that, if one was seated in one of the two chairs across from his desk, one got the distinct impression they were demarcating his very existence. The big window offered some relief to the heavy air that hung permanently in the room. The young reporter could never get enough of those covers; sitting in the hard, uncomfortable chair, he would cast furtive gazes at those frames, which had committed to paper, day by day, modern Greek history in its making.

"Peter, have you managed to find out how the Church plans to proceed in regard to Kazantzakis' death? Do we have any news from that front?" Androulidakis asked.

"Nothing. Not a clue of their position in all of this," Peter Charis replied.

"This silence worries me; no leaks from anywhere. I do hope they will at least show some respect for the dead," Androulidakis went on, while Peter cringed with disappointment, shaking his head.

"Show respect?... I'm inclined to think that the religious sects will exert pressure on the Holy Synod. And as we all know, there's more than a few bishops who will jump to take advantage of the situation, to gain publicity as well as new hardcore aficionados. There are always those who are simply terrified of sect leaders, and, even worse, those who owe them something," Peter poignantly observed.

"We must keep an eye out for everything that *Estia* Newspaper publishes, on the explicit accusations against Kazantzakis, and especially the implied ones. Other publications as well, even the rags. Our own stance must remain one of dignity and propriety without overreactions on either side," the chief-editor intoned, speaking firmly and calmly, unlike the reporter who had let his overflowing passion for defending Kazantzakis get the best of him.

"What do you mean by 'dignity and propriety'? Do you not recall Melas' tirade against Kazantzakis? Calling him a Commie and a Bulgar?"

"Could someone please explain to me so I can make some sense of what you are talking about?" Freddy, who until then had sat quietly, broke his respectful silence, stunned by the torrent of information.

"Of course. Peter, please explain," Androulidakis exhaled in an almost paternal tone.

"When Kazantzakis' novel *Captain Michalis* circulated in 1954, Emile Hourmouzios, a close friend of his, and then editor-in-chief of *Kathimerini* newspaper, wrote a raving review of the book. That's when Spyros Melas intervened with an article of his own, in *Estia* newspaper, in which he targeted Kazantzakis with the most insulting remarks, and concluded that he was left wondering how 'the Cretans had not yet smashed the storefront windows of bookstores where the book was being displayed', while at the same time provoking the Holy Synod and the Public prosecutor to step in and take measures against him.

"Hourmouzios responded with another editorial in *Kathimerini*, underlining that whatever had been mentioned by Spyros Melas was nothing short of McCarthyism. The feud did not end there, however, since a very rabid Melas retorted yet again with a new article, in which he randomly attacked Henry Miller with a few choice words, and wrote that he much preferred McCarthyism to 'Scum-of-the-earth-ism'! Kazantzakis, scum of the earth! Are you getting this?!"

"But isn't Spyros Melas a man of letters? And as a matter of fact, an esteemed member of the Academy of Athens?" asked Freddy, causing the other two to burst into laughter.

"Spyros Melas was in fact using his articles at the time to call out to Greeks to collaborate with the Nazis," Androulidakis informed him. The only reason he became a member of the Academy of Athens was that he was a fierce and vociferous advocate of the Metaxas dictatorial regime, long after he declared himself a supporter of the Left, and later, a staunch supporter of the liberal Venizelos. So, as you can see, he has endorsed the entire political spectrum!

"It was Melas who was dispatched as an envoy by the Palace and Queen Frederica of the Hellenes to Sweden, to prevent Kazantzakis from winning the Nobel prize. He stayed there for a whole month, and together with the Greek ambassador in Stockholm, they tried to take meetings with members of the Swedish Academy to slander Kazantzakis, accusing him of communism – right in the middle of the international anti-communist craze – of being a menace to democracy, an atheist and a threat to youth everywhere.

"They warned that a potential win for Kazantzakis would cause irreparable harm to the stature of the Swedish Academy. And as you very well know, Kazantzakis was never awarded the Nobel Prize. They were successful in influencing the members of the Swedish committee. Kazantzakis was nominated for the Nobel Prize nine times. Have you ever heard of him winning? Well now you understand why."

Freddy simply stared, aghast, trying to process the maelstrom of information coming his way. He stared at his mentors and fellow colleagues, searching their faces, expecting the moment at least one of them would burst into laughter in their joke at the rookie's expense; but the moments dragged on, and Freddy realized this was not a joke, after all, that everything he was listening to was the plain, undiluted truth.

"He really has the nerve to—" Freddy began to say, but Androulidakis interrupted cut him off.

"Of course he does! Why wouldn't he have the nerve? But let's take things from the beginning. With the Church, the first episodes broke out right after the circulation of *Saviors of God* in the *Anagennisi* [*Renaissance*] literary magazine by Dimitris Glinos in the autumn of 1927. The ensuing uproar was quite massive, and the author, along with his publisher, were called in for questioning by the authorities. Finally, they were both indicted on the charge of 'irreverence to the established religion' and their trial was set for June 10, 1930. Only, this trial never came to pass, yet nonetheless, the charge itself was never actually voided," Androulidakis said with a mischievous smile.

"But why all this?" Freddy asked innocently.

"So that they would feel unsafe constantly and limit their activities," Peter Charis asserted. "I should also tell you, Freddy, that these particular two people, Kazantzakis and Glinos, were arrested again, about a year later."

"Another charge?" the young man inquired, astounded.

"It's a bit confusing, trying to unravel it all, but I will give it to you in chronological order. Early in 1954, Pope Pius XXII, included *The Last Temptation of Christ* in the Index of Forbidden Books of the Roman Catholic Church, the notorious and widely feared Index Librorum Prohibitorum. Kazantzakis was irate and responded with a telegram to the Index Committee with just one phrase, a quote by the early Christian Church Father Tertullian: '*Ad tuum, Domine, tribunal appello,*' which means: At your own Tribunal, Lord, I make my appeal."

"But why would he react this way? Being included in the Index, with the likes of Voltaire, Descartes, Copernicus, and Galileo, is, at worst, the most splendid promotion for his book, courtesy of the Pope himself! Why take it so hard? Wasn't he an atheist after all?" Freddy asked once more with sad naïveté, his disillusionment deepening.

"An atheist? Kazantzakis had one quest: the meaning of existence. He was better versed in the Bible and the Scriptures than most priests; he had studied them in depth. He was searching for answers. In no manner did he insult religion in his *Last Temptation,*" Peter countered.

"Back to our issue," Androulidakis curtly interjected, steering the discussion.

"After the Pope included the book in the fearsome Index, our own religious fathers went into a frenzy: they proclaimed his *Captain Michalis* offended the state and religion; they condemned *The Last Temptation*, quoting parts of it out of context. Naturally, they did the same with *Christ Recrucified*. The Archbishop of America attacked *Captain Michalis* without ever having read a word of it, basing his attack on an article by *Estia* newspaper."

"Remember, Peter, what a remarkable article that was?"

"Absolutely. We had taken a stand, as a newspaper; the occasion had demanded it of us. What a farce! The Archbishop of America himself had denounced *The Last Temptation* without having bothered to read it first. There were many metropolitan bishops exerting all kinds of pressure as they tried to come up with a strategy to manage the issue. That's when they decided to condemn Kazantzakis' books and demand that they be officially banned by the government.

"The matter reached the Parliament, following an official inquiry by Cretan parliamentarians belonging to the Center-oriented parties, who wanted to condemn Kazantzakis' persecution by the Church that kept demanding to have his books banned, on the grounds it was nothing more than a 'persecution of Culture'. The Church's decision was also openly opposed by the City of Athens, and the City of Thessaloniki followed suit with a similar vote."

"And how did Kazantzakis respond to that?" Freddy asked.

"Ah... that was the best part, the most brilliant part. He sent them a letter, stating, 'You gave me your curse, Holy Fathers, I give you a wish: I wish you that your conscience is as clear as mine, and that your morals and your faith are as deep as mine'," Peter quoted with a satisfied smile, as though he had authored the letter himself.

"Well, what was the outcome after that? When was he excommunicated?" Freddy asked impatiently, completely spellbound by the chronicle of Kazantzakis's persecution as it was being laid out before him.

"Never happened!" his two colleagues replied in unison, and Androulidakis took over to explain.

"The Holy Synod could not just take a decision of such magnitude; besides, it wasn't even in its jurisdiction. Kazantzakis was Cretan, and the Church of Crete does not belong to the Orthodox Church of Greece but is rather, a self-governing entity, subject to the Ecumenical Patriarchate of Constantinople. Furthermore, Kazantzakis lived abroad, not in Greece. The only recourse the Holy Synod had was to write a letter to the Patriarch Athinagoras, asking him to proceed to an excommunication."

"And did they?" Freddy asked anxiously.

"Of course they did. Though I bet the Patriarch shoved that letter in some desk drawer, for he never dealt with the issue."

"Yeah, if it wasn't immediately thrown into the waste paper basket," Peter added with a snicker.

"But Kazantzakis' reaction was limited to that one letter?" the young Freddy asked again, whose curiosity made it clear he had a brilliant career in journalism ahead of him.

"He did give an interview to *Nea* newspaper, where he said he was saddened that the Church had fallen so naively into the mire created by two of its senior representatives. And then he stated that the publicity generated by this persecution far exceeded any promotion he himself could have paid for to advertise his books."

"And who were these two senior representatives mentioned in his interview?" Freddy asked.

"The first was Metropolitan Bishop of Chios, Panteleimon Fostinis, who hadn't even read *The Last Temptation of Christ*, since the book had not even circulated in Greece – he admitted as much himself. The second was Archbishop of the Greek Orthodox Archdiocese of North and South America, who didn't even know the book's title. He condemned it as 'Captain Michalis...Mavrides'. Well 'Mavrides' happened to be the publisher's surname, which was placed far below the title on the book's front cover!" Peter concluded, bursting into peals of laughter.

"The way you've explained everything only confirms my suspicion, that the Church will attempt to further tarnish Kazantzakis' reputation," Freddy said, a shadow clouding his face.

"Let's not rush to any conclusions," Androulidakis interrupted him.

"So! To your stations. Freddy, you will assist Peter with the research; you are to do nothing else. I want you at your desk, gathering data, fact checking, and helping Peter with whatever he asks of you. And Peter, I want the objective report from you."

"I would like to add a personal touch to this," Peter Charis replied.

"And so you will," Androulidakis agreed. "You were friends with Kazantzakis. We want a story originating at a memorable moment of your friendship, that establishes his way of thought, his daily life, his life's stance. What will your introduction be?"

"When you read it, you can tell me if you agree with my choice. My personal experience will actually serve as my conclusion, after I have laid out my report and the important milestones of Kazantzakis' timeline," the seasoned journalist replied.

"Is Panagiotopoulos writing the obituary?"

"Yes, he is," Androulidakis replied. "Kokkas wants it and I think Panagiotopoulos himself wants it. Any objections?"

"For God's sake, no! In fact, I think he's a great choice," Peter Charis acknowledged and stood up.

Seconds later, the two journalists exited their chief-editor's office, and Freddy could no longer hold it in.

"Peter, I want to hear everything about Kazantzakis," he said in an almost conspiratorial tone.

"Of course, Freddy, but not today. You understand, right?" Peter asked with a wan, almost fatherly smile.

"Yes, yes, I do," the young man contentedly agreed.

After his brief conference with his newspaper director/publisher, Androulidakis had begun to form a general idea of the cover page. The article on Kazantzakis' death would dominate the upper right side; directly beneath it, J.M. Panagiotopoulos' obituary would fill out the right side of the page. Freddy took his notes to Peter Charis, but seeing that the seasoned journalist had already completed his research and had everything he needed for his article, drew up a chair and sat next to him.

Freddy observed Peter as he structured his text and began to write his article:

"Nikos Kazantzakis, one of the most prominent Greek authors and one of the world's greatest novelists, passed away in the early hours of Sunday morning from complications of the influenza virus at the University Clinic of Freiburg, where he was being treated for the past month. The news was announced in Athens on Sunday, and was met with intense grief, for few authors' are as widely read and familiar to the public as Kazantzakis."

Freddy did not linger for long; he got up silently from his chair, and a few moments later was seated at his weathered desk with the wrinkled surface, trying to process all that he had just learned. The discussion had had an overwhelming effect on the young journalist; within the last hour he had earned a greater respect for both, Kazantzakis as an author and a man. He leaned deeply into the chair, and felt it give way gently as it tilted him backward; he looked up as though trying to decipher the cracks on the ceiling, his eyes searching the murky trail of yellowed rivers formed by decades of smoking, those markings on a map left by his stressed-ridden predecessors.

He sat down to his task mechanically, trying to complete his overnight pharmacy column, but his mind was still processing everything that Peter Charis and Androulidakis had told him. When he was done with his column, he delved into the his newspaper archive to discover all he could find on his new hero, Nikos Kazantzakis, his arch-enemy Melas, and the rest of the shady cast of his sad story – the Holy Synod with its decisions, the religious sects. He placed another call to his Cretan; Kazantzakis' past trials and tribulations had captured Freddy's imagination so completely that this story now took priority over everything else.

Freiburg

At the park outside the main gate of the Freiburg University Clinic, three nun-nurses in white uniforms with their folded, starched white caps were casually conversing with each other. As soon as Tapita saw Helen, she got up and hurried towards her. She greeted her warmly, introduced herself to Agnes and led the two women to the appropriate office to take care of all the procedural issues arising from the death of a man. Agnes gathered all the necessary documents which needed to be submitted to the Greek Consulate in Frankfurt; only after the procedural requirements were met, could the body be transferred to Crete. As the day of the burial loomed far away, however, the head nurse suggested embalming, but Helen adamantly refused.

"No, I do not want his heart and his organs removed. It was his wish that he be buried in Crete. 'I am made from Cretan soil and that is where I will return' he used to say and that is how it will be done," Helen insisted.

"I understand that, madam, but the ride in the car will be long and the body will have to be preserved somehow," the nurse calmly responded.

"All right, what can we do about this? What else would you suggest?" Agnes asked, whose practical mind had helped save the day many times.

"Well, we could place the body in a metal coffin, which will then be placed inside the wooden one..." the nurse replied as Helen nodded eagerly, and it was clear to the two women that this was a solution with which she felt comfortable.

The helpful nurse informed Helen that their luggage had been put aside and would be dispatched to the address she would provide. Everything was falling neatly into place; still, Helen struggled hard not to let out the storm that was brewing within her heart as she quietly observed Agnes coordinate all the remaining pending issues with the nurse with expert efficiency.

"I... I will be outside waiting for you, Agnes," she gasped, and pushed the ward's door open, rushing out to the corridor, desperately in need of air. Her pace was quick and steady as she headed straight towards the main exit, and made it out like a diver who had barely managed to reach the surface only a moment before drowning. Her face ashen and her eyes brimming with tears, she crouched over and breathed hard.

The life-saving nurse Tapita Swetcher appeared once more, seemingly out of nowhere, without a magic wand but with something far more useful: a glass of water. Helen took three sips and the thoughtful nurse poured the rest of the water on her handkerchief and wiped the sweat from Helen's cheeks and forehead.

"Come, dear," she said tenderly, guiding her to a nearby bench.

"Thank you, Tapita," Helen said a few moments later, when she had recovered her composure.

"I'm sorry, I didn't mean to—" she tried to continue, but the woman interrupted her. "Why are you apologizing? You didn't do anything wrong. Relax...." she said to her calmly, and gave her a steady embrace.

Agnes appeared at the door a little later, holding an envelope which doubtlessly held all the necessary documents for the Greek Consulate.

"I just couldn't allow for him to be buried without his heart," Helen said to Agnes softly, almost in a whisper, as they turned in the alley away from the University Clinic. "You do understand, right?"

"I understand this is not some whim on your part, but the desire of your dead husband. And so this is the way it must be. I think you mustn't stay here any longer; you should go home, to Antibes. You've been gone for more than five months and you need to regroup," Agnes recommended.

"So I should just leave him here on his own?" Helen asked, surprised.

"I'll be here. You must get clothes, prepare, see what you will need for the funeral. You understand..."

"Yes, you're right. Let me think on it..."

They arrived at the hotel.

"Helen, I need to make some phone calls. Would you like to sit outside, in the courtyard?"

"Yes. We should go over the funeral. We need to find a proper coffin..." Helen replied, as the two of them sat once more at their familiar, and, by now, beloved refectory table.

"Don't worry about that. I have that under control."

"I trust you, Agnes," Helen said with a smile.

"Did you ever feel you were losing him?" asked the lawyer.

"Just once. It was the winter of '32. Nothing was going well for us then. We were in France, but no matter where we turned, the doors were closed. I was forced to sell all the jewelry I had. Nikos kept writing; he had completed the translation of Dante's *Divine Comedy* in the demotic Greek when he decided to go to Spain."

"Would you like to order?" the waitress interrupted them. With their order out of the way, Agnes eagerly pressed for the rest of the story.

"He went to Spain, where he was going to meet with Jimenez and other intellectuals. We had no money, but he always knew how to find cheap yet beautiful boarding houses. He only ate fruit, and those were plentiful and well-priced there. He held his meetings and everything seemed to be going well, until November 10, when his mother passed away. He loved her dearly; perhaps he never loved another person as much as he did her. And, as if this was not enough, only a month and a half later he lost his father as well. I was so upset... though not more than him. It was all an immense ordeal. And, by the end of January he had written me a letter which he asked me to burn."

"Why?"

"He detailed his feelings about the loss of his father. He wanted me to burn it because he believed no one would understand the deeper meaning of his words to me."

"Meaning?"

"I'll tell you because I trust you. In that letter, he had written that this death had liberated him. 'The loss of my mother', he'd written, 'was a bitter pain, like the bitter pain of the inconsolable child who is left in the dark and feels the beloved hand slip from his grasp.' The loss of his father, however, he described as heart-rending relief. 'I am lighter, liberated, my soul will now thrive.'"

"Incredible!"

"If one considers how demanding his father was, and considers Nikos' own disposition, always feeling the weight of obligation to his father whom he never wanted to disappoint, then one realizes the constant pressure he felt and can understand the unexpected liberation which came, albeit following his mother's death that weighed on him so terribly."

"And what did you do?"

"I tried to encourage him. I wrote to him constantly. It was the only time I felt such fear; not that I might lose him to another woman – I never feared that. I understood right then that he was a man who believed what he said. 'Blessed is the misfortune which allows us to weigh our spirit and find it worthy', he'd say of every obstacle."

"That was him, yes. Fearless!"

"And you know what else, my dear Agnes? I loved him for a reason more, for something much more trivial than all these things. Even when he'd see someone cower, he never embarrassed him. You never felt his scorn. He always imagined you to be better than you actually were. And for this reason you could follow him blithely in the harsh upward ascent."

"I never met a person who meant every word he spoke; who followed so steadfastly his principles."

Their discussion was once more punctuated by the waitress placing the large tray with their order on the table.

"Even when he knew there was no harm in a slight deviation, he would obstinately insist on his own ascending path. He had this unrelenting belief in integrity."

Athens

He hadn't checked the clock on his way out of his office, nor had he seen his colleagues who were still in the building. He wanted to go home, to eat a home cooked meal and to sleep. He stood for a little on the entry stairwell and turned up his collar. The street was empty due to the cold that followed the sunset – or came before sunrise. He began to walk down October 28th Avenue. His mind flooded with all his "source" had relayed to him – his newfound friend and compatriot of Kazantzakis from Herakleion – the "Cretan," as he called him. They had spoken at great length on the telephone and he had related pivotal moments in the life of the great thinker, the events that shaped Kazantzakis' thought, his ideas and his fears from childhood, and the role played in all of it by his father – that terrible and mighty descendant of pirates – Captain Michalis. Freddy, at this point, knew a great deal about the author's childhood, that delicate time when character is forged and the ideals of the future adult are molded.

Kazantzakis had feared his father. Captain Michalis was the archetypal Cretan, constantly brooding and ready to snap, without any discernible weakness and still without any desire to contemplate anything outside his own orbit. One would have to think long and hard before disagreeing with him – or not consider it at all. He hailed from a village outside of Herakleion called Barbaroi – where the name alone evinced its origins. He had always singled out Nikos, who was his natural male heir, though he had two other daughters, and a fourth child, George, who had died in infancy. He had tried to raise Nikos in the manner that he himself had been raised. When he took Nikos to school for the first time he had told the teacher, "His meat is yours, his bones are mine. Have no pity; make a man out of him".

Nikos must not have been quite eight years old when the Turks throttled yet another attempted Cretan uprising. That night, while the conquerors had been out on group patrols, killing indiscriminately, Captain Michalis had been ready for everything.

If the Turks broke down his door, the father would slaughter his own wife and children to keep them out of enemy hands; he had come to this decision consciously some time before. The morning of the aftermath he had taken Nikos by the hand, dragging him through the empty, blood-soaked, terror-stricken streets of Herakleion.

"Are you afraid?" he had asked.

"Yes," the young boy had answered.

"That's fine, you'll get used to it," the father had replied.

They had come upon the Lions Square, and there, up on the plane tree Nikos had seen the corpses of three Cretans, barefoot, their tongues hanging out as they themselves swayed to and fro. The son had tried to avert his gaze but the father had grasped his head and turned the child around to face the hanging martyrs. The father had asked if the boy could touch them.

"I cannot," the boy had cried.

"You can!" the father had insisted. He had taken the child's hand and placed his fingers on the foot of one of the dead men.

"Bow!" he had ordered him. The boy had tried to flee, but the father had caught him under the arms and held him before the hanged man, bringing his head before the foot so that the child's lips pressed against the cold skin.

"So that you get used to it," he had said. When they had returned home, Nikos' mother had been furious.

"We went to pay our respects," the father had answered gruffly, thus ending the argument.

Despite his efforts, Captain Michalis recognized early on that his son resonated at a different frequency than his own. There was no way for one to reach the other; there existed no intimacy in which this could take place. The world of the father smelled of gunpowder, sweat, blood and revolution, required sacrifice, nurtured hate for the Turk oppressor and admiration and respect for the freedom fighters and heroes. His son was enamored with this world, but only as an observer; instead, Nikos' world had spiritual battles, cumbersome quests, exhausting ascents, dialogues with gods and super-humans. They could only have understanding between them. Nikos never made a joke to elicit a laugh from his father – though the young Kazantzakis had humor both plentiful and unique. No one in Herakleion remembered Michalis Kazantzakis ever laughing. His only smile came the day Crete had been liberated from the Turks.

Freddy's mind turned back to Kazantzakis' childhood. Captain Michalis had once grabbed his son by the hand and had begun to run ahead, with the young boy struggling to keep up with him, out of breath.

"Christ is Risen, Captain Michalis," a passerby had greeted him enthusiastically. "Crete is Risen," he had answered.

"Where are we going?" the boy had asked.

"To your grandfather," Captain Michalis had replied, determined to reach his destination.

Once there, before the grave of his father, Captain Michalis had dug the ground with his bare hands. He had cupped his fingers, shouting of Liberty into the mound:

"Father, She came! Father, She came! Father, She came!"

He had then poured wine into the pit, a libation.

"Did you hear?" he had asked his son.

The boy could not answer, overwhelmed as he was.

"You didn't hear?" the father had asked again, angrily. "His bones rattled!"

The only common point of reference between them, where their values intersected was the unrelenting fight for freedom: the father's fight for Crete, the son's fight for the spirit. Even so, the son felt the weight of the responsibility to make his father proud, to justify all that his father had invested in him. He recognized that to this belligerent, frightful rebel he owed his impressive education; that his father had offered it to him in the hope that he would one day see him become a lawyer, and span that career even to parliament. Either that, or an abbot – after all, this was the prophecy decreed by the midwife when she had helped birth Nikos into the world.

The young Kazantzakis had learned to survive in this particular environment especially from the moment he had agreed with his father that his purpose was to excel in his studies, and he never stopped honoring his father. Until the day he surrendered himself to the unusual charm of Galatea, who had been two years his senior and whom Captain Michalis had rejected because he did not think she was worthy of his son, for he could not see a way in which she could help him achieve his lofty goals.

When Nikos returned from his travels in Italy, he had called on Galatea to leave Herakleion and join him in Athens. They had rented a small apartment on Knossos Street, in Patissia. He had already begun to earn a living from writing and the translation of foreign works, but he soon found himself in the crush of opposing forces: on the one hand, his father's rejection of a pivotal life choice, and on the other hand, Galatea's family, which had pressed for the formalization of their union so as to repair their daughter's tarnished reputation.

Though the Alexiou family was a progressive one of the sophisticate middle class of Herakleion – her father, Stelios, had been owner of an historic printing press which had printed, in 1911, the seminal first literary edition of *Erotokritos* by Stephanos Ksanthoudis – they had been adamant about the marriage. It was the gossip in Herakleion that had fanned the flames of the whole matter – it was, after all, 1911.

"They shacked up in Athens, with her two years older than him and unwed!" – that was the talk of the housewives in all the little neighborhoods of Herakleion at the time.

At that time Nikos had to choose between his father and the security that he provided, and the seductive nature of the adventure promised to him by love. He was thirty and completely given to the thirty-two year old Galatea, to her progressive nature, her fighting heart, her unconventional mentalité and her feminist spirit. "Galatea and a hut," he had written once in a notebook in answer to the question, 'What do you dream of?'

He couldn't bear the thought of losing her, yet he had no hope of talking his father into acceptance, and so, only one choice remained. His wedding to Galatea became infamous in the city's recollection, in part owing to the unfortunate decision to have it at Saint Constantine's – the little church in the cemetery of Herakleion – on a Friday evening, with only a few guests from the Alexiou family and George Fanourakis, his old classmate and university contemporary, as his best man.

When it had gotten dark, they had crossed over tombs, stepping on a few brittle carnations that had come undone from the traditional red and white funerary wreaths, and had arrived at the little church to become husband and wife in a murmur, in the dark. This decision, beyond whatever symbolism one might draw from it, also had had a practical purpose: to ensure that Captain Michalis never learned where the wedding was taking place, for fear that he would have intervened and call it off.

Freddy let out a long sigh. What an amazing story, he thought as he explored a detail from the story that made him identify strongly with Kazantzakis: the almost pathological love that Nikos felt for his mother, Maria, or *Margio*, as was his affectionate name for her. Such was the relationship the journalist had with his own mother, the person who had built the dream for him and had helped him to inhabit it, the woman who, owing to her youthful tryst, had given him a name that made everyone wonder whether they had heard it correctly the first time he'd introduce himself, and would ask him again to confirm.

That woman had convinced him to write, to write ceaselessly, from the time he had been eight years old. For it was together, after all, that they had set up his childhood newspaper, which they produced in twenty copies using carbon paper, and with which profits Freddy secured his weekly chocolates. She had chosen the fiction piece her son had submitted, when he was nineteen years old, to the Pan-Hellenic Literary Contest instituted by Babis Klaras at the *Vradyni* newspaper, where he had won the second prize. It was she who had taken him – secretly from his grandfather, who had been determined to send his grandson off to study finance, but also from his father, who had wanted his son to become an officer in the Navy – to journalism school.

She had raised him, divorced as she was from her military husband whom she had married at age eighteen. She had loved Admiral Andrew Germanos, but she never forgot the indelible first love of her youth on the island of Mytilene, her own native land, never forgot her brief love with a British officer that had ended poorly. When she had become pregnant, she had eloped with Germanos and had asked him, if the child were a boy, to give him the name of her first true love. He had accepted and a few months later they had held Freddy in their arms.

When he finally crossed the threshold of the blue apartment building in Exarchia, across the street from the Vox movie theater, Freddy felt so tired that he dropped to the bed with his clothes on. He fell asleep immediately; he did not wish to think any more.

Freiburg

They had separated the beds, and Helen took the one near the window, while Agnes took the one closest to the door. Neither was tired, though neither of them spoke. Both were absorbed in images that sprang forth from the past to remind them of their obligation to the particular man they held in common. It was Kazatzakis who colored the harsh, monochrome past, and his absence now was slowly draining, day by day, the color from the present.

"Is it true you had a stipulation, that he could see his ex freely so long as you were present?" Agnes asked, guessing that Helen was still awake.

"It's true," Helen replied, smiling softly.

"And also that, in his fifteen years of marriage to Galatea, they never made love?" Agnes continued.

"Nonsense," Helen answered nonchalantly.

"And yet, this is what Galatea told everyone," Agnes insisted.

"Well clearly, the inconceivable part is not that Galatea would imply such a thing, but that so many people rushed to accept it. That is the true absurdity!"

"He had plenty of detractors. Many were the friends that turned their backs on him, but the way he treated them never gave the impression that he had been deceived by them, but that they had lost out."

"The only thing that bothered him was Sikelianos' absence. That was yet another time that I had seen him truly miserable. And how could I fault him? He had no peace and would mutter to himself for months. It was inconceivable to him that his beloved friend was left alone, sick and helpless. The very Sikelianos! His generation knew no one brighter. And still, this greatest of the greats died forgotten in a hotel with his entire left side paralyzed, having drunk a liquid laxative instead of his medication by mistake. Nikos had been inconsolable and had written a letter to his friend, the Norwegian Knös: 'They proposed to hold his funeral as a public expense, but at first the government refused, stating that Sikelianos was an anti-nationalist, a communist, an enemy of the state. This is what we have come to'."

"Always the same story," Agnes commented.

"He'd become ill! I remember that letter, because I'd never seen him in such a state; 'I cannot hold back my tears as I write to you. Tears of pain, rage, and disgust. I wish I would die, to not have to endure these shameful times in my country now'."

"And this is nothing compared to what you endured."

"I will never forget, my dear Agnes, this one event, not ever: we had gone to our embassy to request a visa. They would not give us a passport, you know that. We had gone for the visa and they kept us standing for three hours. Standing! They didn't even offer us a chair! And that same night, at the Chinese embassy that was hosting a gala in honor of Nikos, the Greek ambassador was there and tried to have his picture taken with Nikos! Never in my life have I known such galling impudence. I will never forget it."

"At some point, Helen, these things need to be said. All the Greeks need to know who Kazantzakis was and who these people truly are who profess this 'national pride'. But rather than delve into all of this with you now, and make you upset, it is best that you sleep. Tomorrow will be yet another difficult day. Goodnight, dear Helen."

"Sweet dreams, my dear Agnes. And....thank you for being here. I don't know what I would do without you."

TUESDAY, OCTOBER 29ᵗʰ 1957

Athens

He woke up at ten a.m. and sprang from his bed like a child that had already missed the first hour of school. Certainly, he'd much prefer to stroll around the center of Athens if that first hour was indeed math; how he hated that subject. Splashing his face with his hands full of water, he returned to the present and remembered the historic front page of the day's news. He dressed hurriedly and ran out.

The sun shone as though it were a bright September day; clouds were gone, clothing was light. He walked to the kiosk to see the front page of the *Eleftheria* newspaper, which was hanging on the wire like freshly washed linen. The first headline to the left focused on the expulsion of Field-Marshall Zukov in the Soviet Union. The central headline was about the speech of the king in Thessaloniki, which had provoked several reactions, and read, "The government leaves the monarch without cover". To the right, a picture of Kazantzakis, with the headline, "N. Kazantzakis dead following complications of the flu in Germany," and further down, in smaller print, "His last wish: to be buried in Herakleion, where his remains will be transferred." Directly beneath that headline was an article by J.M. Panagiotopoulos, one of the few, true friends of the late author. The title read, "Kazantzakis, the Great Desperado".

Freddy turned the newspaper and positioned himself so as to keep himself from the sight of the kiosk vendor, and began to read hastily, curious to know what the formidable reporter had to say.

"The death of Kazantzakis came as we expected. Suddenly. From one moment to the next, that great heart that held inside it heaven and hell stopped obeying, stopped serving. Now Kazantzakis is dead. And this nation, which attacked him, cursed him, denied him, has, as its ultimate duty, to bow before his cold face and to reflect on whether or not it has misjudged him."

Freddy breathed deeply to soothe the burning in his chest. He could not get enough of the article.

"For I fear that with Kazantzakis the same story has played out, all too familiar in the history of the Greeks, from antiquity to the present. The Greeks excommunicated Laskaratos, condemned Pope Joan by Roides, left Theofilos Kairis to rot in prison, politically assassinated Charilaos Trikoupis in a tragic general election, and anathematized Venizelos..."

Panagiotopoulos was relentless. Yet who could argue with his point?

"Most modern Greek monuments of great men are confessions of guilt, grand stones of regret. We murdered Kapodistrias and then wrote books about him, so that we could ascertain how truly right he was, and then we set his marble effigy everywhere, even in front of our University..."

Passersby stopped next to Freddy, pushing him out of the way so that they could read the other newspapers, but he held fast, immobile, utterly swept away by the bitter truths in the unrelenting criticism of J.M. Panagiotopoulos.

"There is no other contemporary thinker, I believe, nor prose writer nor poet, who utters more frequently from his lips the word 'God' than Kazantzakis. Moreover, he struggles with God at his side, with God across from him. In his letters to friends he was never remiss to say, 'God be with you'. At times in quotation marks, to denote his own quest of God, while at other times without quotation marks..."

"Hey, Freddy, what will it be? Would you also like some coffee so you can read the entire paper in peace?" yelled the kiosk owner in a gruff voice, courtesy of unfiltered Assos cigarettes. "I wouldn't say no to a sweet hot coffee, Mr. Fotis," Freddy quipped.

"Hey you little - !" the vendor growled but the young journalist interrupted him.

"Alright, already, I'm going to see it at the office anyhow! Does this mean you're trying to get out of the coffee?" he continued, teasing him.

"Get done!" Mr. Fotis yelled again, turning his attention to his other customers.

Freddy had reached the end of the obituary, which concluded as follows:

"Nikos Kazantzakis – the man who, following post World War II Liberation, had momentarily shown interest in politics, having served for a brief time, in 1945, as Deputy Minister of Education in the Sofoulis administration, was the most widely translated contemporary Greek author, with some of his works making quite the stir in Europe and the United States, and had been nominated repeatedly for the Nobel Prize. Now his work The Last Temptation of Christ has found enormous success in northern and western Europe in the film of the same name, shot on location in Crete by Jules Dassin. It must be noted that the Greek state, which at no time conferred upon him a single honor, finding him unworthy to be inducted into the Hall of Immortals of the Academy of Athens, limited itself to simply award him last year's prize for best theatrical work."

"Mr. Fotis, I'm going elsewhere for that coffee," Freddy said as he left, not waiting to hear all the gruff vulgarities the kiosk vendor had in reply.

At the Zonar's cafe courtyard, the usual suspects were in play: journalists, politicians, businessmen, loitering entrepreneurs, academics and armchair scholars, breadwinners and scions – all were ready at the battlements. The newspapers they held in hand afforded them a convenient hiding place to avoid the prying eyes of passersby and shielded their discussions with whomever they liked.

"Freddy," a voice came from behind an *Eleftheria* newspaper.

It was Mr. Fotis, a fifty year old failed author and failed critic, though very successful heir to his Egypt-born uncle's fortune. His was the classic example of a man who, unable to create art himself, kept occupied with the hapless reproduction of gossip concerning the arts; in short, a person that every journalist could use.

"Good morning," the young man returned.

"Sit," the reclusive patron beckoned.

"I'm simply overwhelmed by the death of Nikos Kazantzakis, one of the greatest European thinkers of his generation," he said with the kind of pomp required of someone making an official statement to the press. With one difference, of course; at that particular moment, no one had asked him for anything of the kind.

"Tragic news," Freddy commented. "What did you think of our articles on him?"

"Oh they were exceptional," he replied, maintaining the pompous tone, having fully embraced his role. "There are, of course, certain elements that weren't fully developed," he hastened to add, wanting, at the same time, to accentuate his very own proficiency on the topic of Kazantzakis.

Naturally, Freddy did not let this moment go to waste.

"It's reasonable that not all aspects of his life could be explored in just a few articles," he began with an excuse, so as to probe the burning matters that interested him the most.

"But perhaps you, with your effortless flow through the artistic and scholarly landscape, having spoken with so many of our great thinkers – perhaps you could tell me what you know about Kazantzakis' marriage to Galatea?"

"Oh young man," the middle aged heir said with a smile, "these sorts of things are more or less already known."

"Well, I certainly know them too, but I'm asking you for confirmation."

Mr. Fotis drank some water and raised his hand to signal the waiter who was taking an order at a nearby table.

"Hot coffee, sweet," Freddy ordered, and delved straight into the heart of the matter. "How is it that after being so in love, the two ended as bitter enemies I'll never understand..."

"It is in the nature of people, and especially the nature of the female, to compete, to be irrationally jealous, to seek revenge. Naturally Galatea expected something else when she married Kazantzakis. You must know that the young author at that time had gone against his father's wishes and married her, knowing full well yet caring little that he would suffer the financial suffocation of marriage without his father's assistance. Galatea went from a life of means to a life of financial penury, living with a husband who cared more for books than he did for her."

"That is well known," Freddy answered, though admittedly to him this information was not known in the least, as Mr. Fotis rushed to supply him with every detail to impress him.

"Oh but of course! Who could believe what was once talked about, that theirs was a 'white' marriage? That Galatea had never slept with Kazantzakis and that her first experience was with Mark Avgeris, who was a friend of the couple before ultimately becoming Galatea's second husband?"

"Well, no one, I'd hope," the journalist answered with a smile, trying hard to contain his joy over his good fortune.

"And yet, Galatea was beloved by many. It wouldn't trouble them in the slightest to believe it," Mr. Fotis said with an air of utter authority.

"Kazantzakis had many critics who hungrily devoured this kind of gossip and happily reproduced it. Success is a difficult mistress, my dear boy Freddy. Everyone loves her and everyone hates the man who sleeps with her," he said pursing his lips, wondering if his young listener had fully caught his truly inspired analogy.

"You put it so eloquently!" Freddy replied, knowing full well he needed to play along.

The waiter had just brought over the coffee and the young man had caught it practically in midair in his effort to enjoy the first sip of the day, which was a loud one.

"Young man, slow down! At this rate you'll inhale my newspaper," Mr. Fotis said with a measure of displeasure.

"So, where were we? Ah, yes, of course Kazantzakis had mistresses. Many were the young ladies who admired him, and, if I am not mistaken, he had many amorous experiences all over the nation with his best friend at the time, Angelos Sikelianos. Though, from what I am in position to know from the friends of the deceased, he also enjoyed great successes with the opposite sex abroad. To sum up, where you hear incredible tales, keep only what you find reasonable."

Freddy decided to summarize the points to ensure he'd understood them fully.

"The financial hardship in their marriage, the rivalry....these are all well documented, as are those unbelievable rumors about a 'white' wedding. But, do tell, why would she keep his last name?"

"This too is well known. She had consented to give him the divorce he so desperately wanted on the condition that she keep his last name. You see, at the time Kazantzakis had already met Helen, his future wife, and he was fully aware of Galatea's relationship with Avgeris. Galatea wanted his last name because this was the name in the books at the public schools, and she took credit as their author! Though I must say that Kazantzakis always forgave her and thought kindly of her. Even when she wrote her book, *Men and Supermen.*" Freddy did not know what he was absorbing with more anticipation and pleasure, the coffee or the words of Mr. Fotis.

"Yet you give all the right to Kazantzakis and find all the fault with Galatea," Freddy opined, playing the devil's advocate.

"Well I think, young man, that I know the female sex better than you. I don't blame Galatea. Her actions speak for themselves, as does Kazantzakis' inaction. If one were to judge what followed their breakup as isolated, unconnected events, one might think that Kazantzakis' silence harbored some guilt. But if one examines the events cumulatively through the passing years one finds a repeating motif: Galatea would attack, and he would remain silent. Thus, you come to understand, young man, who was the angered party, who desired to lash out, who wanted to denigrate the value of the other, and who respected the past and his feelings, and decided to sidestep it and move on."

Freddy was also ready to move on, but he couldn't contain himself and posed one final question, by way of a compliment.

"What a lovely way to state things. Do you perhaps have a new book in the works?"

"I don't think I am cut out for writing, my dear fellow. It requires effort to turn your writing hobby into your second nature. So let that be a reminder to you to practice it every chance you get."

The time had passed and the heir folded his newspaper in three short moves with grace and style and placed it in his right jacket pocket.

"Young man, this was a lovely and illuminating talk about women who stay in the shadows and feed the dark, and about other women who step out into the light and are set aflame. Good day."

Freddy smiled at these words as the man withdrew with his head bent low, his huddled frame hinting at the slightest hump forming atop his back.

Freiburg

"Helen, the Prime Minister has sent his condolences for Nikos' passing," Agnes said as she came down the exterior balcony stairs of the Hotel Paradis.

"Really?" asked Helen in surprise as she drank her tea idly at the refectory table which had now become a trademark of their fellowship.

"Yes, Karamanlis. The funeral will be a public expense. Please don't worry, I will make the arrangements. My people told me about it just now on the telephone," Agnes explained animatedly as she reached for the teapot. Helen looked at her with concern.

"What's the matter?" asked the lawyer.

"I am not sure if I should accept that. I'm not sure if this is what Nikos would have wanted," Helen said in a reserved tone. Agnes thought about it for a few moments.

"Helen, it is the last honor they can give him. The final farewell to Nikos. And furthermore, we shouldn't provoke things. Nikos belongs to all the Greeks. The state is only doing this to show it recognizes his great worth, but it doesn't negate everything it did to him..."

"Yes, I know."

"We should not stoke the fire, then. His funeral should be on par with that of Kostis Palamas, or Eleftherios Venizelos."

"Yes, you are right, dear Agnes."

"Well then, I need to drop by the hospital and then leave straight for the Greek consulate in Frankfurt. I need to file the required documents for the transfer."

"I'll come with you. I won't let you go there alone."

"I don't want you to tire yourself, Helen. Your schedule is about to become even more hectic as the days go by."

"I am fine. My schedule was always hectic, Agnes."

"You know, I was thinking about what you said yesterday... why Kazantzakis never called out Melas for everything he'd done to him in the press."

"Well, because that would have legitimized him in the minds of all fanatics. I'll tell you something funny..."

"Do tell," Agnes prompted, smiling with anticipation.

"From about 1950, when Nikos' name started circulating in Europe, various reporters would come looking for interviews. Nikos would receive them, speak with them, but none of these interviews were ever released. At some point, we were informed that the people who came to interview him weren't really journalists, but undercover police! So, you see what I mean..."

Agnes did not find this story funny at all, even though Helen seemed quite entertained in telling her. She was beyond such troubles now.

"How many times was Nikos put forth for the Nobel Prize?"

"Nine," Helen said thoughtfully as though she was counting them based on the sorrows they had suffered with each nomination.

"The first one was in 1946. I'll never forget his joy, because he had been nominated together with Sikelianos. A year before that, just for one or two votes, he was not inducted into the Academy of Athens. The Greek most famous the world over was never invited into the highest academic institution of the nation. That's what it came to," she said as she sipped her tea, perhaps to clear her palate of the bitter tale she was revisiting.

"I remember that double nomination...That was when *Estia* newspaper came out with the headline 'An International Scam,' calling out Kazantzakis and Sikelianos as frauds," Agnes recalled angrily.

"That's right! You remember it well."

"But the president of the Academy, Mr. Melas, had the nerve to go to Sweden with our ambassador there to visit the king and members of the Swedish Academy so they could slander Kazantzakis in the vilest way. And naturally, with the blessings of Queen Frederica. Our friend, Knös related to us exactly what Melas did in Stockholm: word for word, he told the king and the members of the Academy that Kazantzakis was a communist and that he was guilty of corrupting the Greek youth, and that Greece would be ridiculed if he was honored with the prize!"

"How shameful! And to think he fancies himself a man of letters..." Agnes noted with disgust.

"Each year, Agnes, that Nikos' nomination for the Nobel Prize was announced, the Academy in Stockholm received hundreds of letters, all of them naturally against him, all driven by Melas. No one wrote anything positive. Not a single person!" Helen repeated bitterly.

"That scoundrel, Melas!"

"You see what individuals hold the highest positions of authority in our land."

"That explains why Minotis calls it Mellas instead of Hellas! The land of Melas and his cronies!"

"Nikos would call these people pseudo-Greeks."

"Instead of fighting alongside him for the glory of Greece on the international stage, Melas and Ambassador Pindar Androulis roamed from office to office, slandering Nikos while Queen Frederica sent letters to her 'confrere', the King of Sweden, to ensure the prize was not given to a radical."

"It was sometime around 1952, I think, that Knös suggested to Nikos that he acquire Norwegian citizenship. This way, the path to the Nobel prize would be unobstructed by the likes of Melas or Frederica. Nikos, though, wanted the Nobel prize for the Greeks. He refused to even consider it."

Agnes stirred her tea, deep in thought over the unimaginable events that the widow of Kazantzakis was expressing to her. Helen, however, felt freer than ever to discuss these things. She had come to realize that the circumstances were now ripe for the whole world to know the deplorable behavior of the official state toward her husband, and, by extension, to herself. *And now I have become his apostle,* she realized with a secret smile.

Athens

Freddy drank yet another coffee and, having chatted a bit with various idle patrons about the Panathinaikos football team and the arrival of Jane Mansfield in Athens that Thursday, promising them a date with the "atomic bombshell" at the Tropicana nightclub as well as a social coffee with the footballer Linoksylakis, he settled his bill and started his way downhill to the newspaper office. It didn't bother him in the slightest that the sun had set, and he was little perturbed by the fact that he hadn't seen his friends in almost a week. He was enthused to be in the center of developing stories, to be learning first-hand the great events taking place in the history of his country. His euphoria reached indiscernible heights when an idea came to him just before entering the apartment building that housed the newspaper offices: *I'm going to request to cover Kazantzakis' funeral in Crete!*

The thought filled him with joy, realizing that he actually had quite a good shot at it since Peter Charis was already swamped with work.

Androulidakis can't say no to me forever, he thought. *If necessary, I'll do whatever he asks.*

He had an unwarranted confidence that he would succeed. He walked in, and, after greeting the doorman, dropped off his precious notepad on his desk and went to the chief-editor's office with the blissful ignorance of every young person shortly before he is met with defeat. Still, Freddy was quite mature for his age.

"Good morning, Mr. Androulidakis, how are you? I wanted to ask if you needed me for anything," he said, knocking on the open door, being careful, however, to not cross the threshold of the office.

"Freddy, my boy, come in. Yes, I need you for something. Sit," beckoned the ever busy, ever huddled over stacks of papers on his desk, Androulidakis.

Freddy had often wondered if he should check those papers to see if they were the same as last week's or last month's, to make sure they weren't just props in service of the role of a chief-editor.

"You are going to Hellenikon airport tomorrow afternoon," the editor said bluntly.

"Yes, sir," Freddy said quietly.

"You will meet Jane Mansfield," the chief-editor continued dryly.

"Could we perhaps..." Freddy began politely, but faltered.

He looked down at the floor, then up again. His gaze had changed.

"Mr. Androulidakis," he began, then stopped in a dramatic pause, before blurting it out.

"I would like to be the one to cover Kazantzakis' funeral in Herakleion." Androulidakis jotted some notes on a piece of paper and did not lift his head; he replied after an entirely undramatic pause of his own.

"Yes, you will go. But get me a good piece on Mansfield. And take this on your way out, it needs to be typed. It's by Ploritis and it is going to print the day after tomorrow, understand? It's for Thursday."

"Thank you so very much!" the young reporter cried out, enthused. "I will give you the best story, the best article, don't you worry."

He turned to leave, only to hear the chief-editor thunder after him.

"Freddy, the paper!"

The young man turned back sheepishly, his forehead beaded with sweat; Androulidakis' stern look reminded Freddy that a professional journalist never reacts like a schoolboy.

He walked to the typist's office, glancing casually at the paper as he went. It was an article on Kazantzakis. He immediately changed course, opting to go to his office to read it before passing it along to the typist. He left it on his desk, opened the balcony door, not caring that the sun was majestically bright, and sat in his chair. He realized his seat tended to lean to the right, of late, and found it the most inopportune time to deal with the stability of a seat, which he reasoned, was, at the very least, as old as his desk. He took his glasses off momentarily, rubbing his eyes before putting his glasses back on. He read the title: "The Last Meeting with Kazantzakis".

Ploritis described to the readers how he'd met with the author some three or four times that past May, which was five months ago.

"[...] Many reviled him, attacked him, stoned him - Greeks, naturally, against the Greek prophet. Blinded by their passion, their envy and their prejudices, or, willfully shutting their eyes to his Truth. None of these people must have ever truly met him – not even a little – in person; otherwise, their contempt would have dissipated before the Man. Kazantzakis, the ever fervent, the ever hermit – had a gift to overpower you."

Ploritis wrote in censure of the enemies of the late thinker, caring little for how his criticism would affect his career in the theater. Enthralled, Freddy rubbed his eyes once more and continued to read.

"If one knew Kazantzakis in person, however – oh how dangerous and, for the most part, how disappointing it is to meet your idols – but if you met him in person, you could see that the ordinary Man was wholly consistent with the Spiritual. His word, committed to paper, was not just talk for consumption but the very cry of his blood and his mind. The incarnate Kazantzakis never betrayed even an iota of his spirit."

Freddy oscillated between drinking the water from a forgotten glass atop his desk and drinking in the text. He could feel both servings take root in his gut.

"Perhaps the most notable, and most attractive aspect of the text was its simplicity. Not his long term thought, not even his tireless battle with himself, nor even still the international fame he had achieved, so late in life, ever set him apart from people or gave him the slightest conceit.... Greece figured continuously in our talks. So did his distant friends, and sometimes, his outrageous enemies. Kazantzakis did not despair. He withstood the stoning. Only once, did he sadly say, 'Why do they yell? I asked for nothing, I wanted for nothing, not from anyone. Each person goes about his own work, as best as he thinks he can. Each person tries to subdue the tiger riding on his back. My entire life I have battled, as has everyone else. I did what I believed in, so should other people do as they believe'."

Freddy read on in ecstasy; Ploritis was revealing the human Kazantzakis before his eyes, the one whom Freddy had no hope of ever meeting, and his profound gratitude turned between Ploritis, for writing this article, and Kazantzakis, for his literary and moral stature. He read on, about the author's dream to go to South America. "It is a world I have never known and it has always excited my mind," Kazantzakis had said to Ploritis, while at the same time longing to return to China and Japan, finding that the two countries had changed significantly since his first travels there.

"'And what of Greece?' I asked him. 'Greece is the Great Mother,' he replied animatedly. 'It does not matter if I am far from her. I carry Greece inside of me, and Crete even more so…. Even here, in Antibes, we are in Greece. Wasn't Antipolis built by the Greeks, by Ionians? Whether I am here or elsewhere, Greece follows me everywhere, always. But I want to die in Crete,' he added in a hushed tone. 'It is my land, there at the Castle in Herakleion. Even if I don't make it there in time, I want to be buried there. Cretan soil gave rise to my blood – and it is Cretan soil that should claim it back.'"

The article ended as follows:

"A little while later he was walking me out to the garden gate. I shook his long, slender hand for the last time. 'God be with you', he said, as was his custom. And he added, 'Be joyous that you were born a Greek.' When I reached the bend in the road, I turned back to glance at him. That unassailable silhouette of Mount Psiloritis stood stalwart, almost biblical at the threshold. And I never saw it again."

It's really good. I must write something as good as this, better, if I can.
Freddy reconsidered; *no, just as good as this*, he settled. The idea that tomorrow he would have to go to Hellenikon airport to cover the arrival of Hollywood bombshell Jane Mansfield agitated him. Who would take him seriously? He exited his office and started to wander aimlessly to the desk of Peter Charis. The

journalist was there trying to write something, unsuccessfully it seemed, though he appeared exceedingly good at basketball, with all of the balls of paper he had shot into his wastebasket.

"Peter, can I bother you a moment?" Freddy asked with feigned shyness in his voice. He was not timid in the slightest, but he needed to keep up appearances every now and then.

"Go on Freddy, tell me. As you can see I'm not in the best shape for inspiration."

"Yes, but you're a great shot!" the young reporter replied with a smile, looking at the wastebasket.

"The never-ending gifts of failure. You get to be good at various useless things," Peter answered with a smile.

"What's on your mind?"

Freddy took a chair that was facing the wall and sat himself squarely before Peter. The brown desk was so clean it dared you to seek out its flaws. The books, literary ones mostly, lined the bookcase behind him and were ordered by height, with the short ones on the right and the tallest on the left. Everything in the office was aligned symmetrically, including the journalist himself. Had he been of a different height, for example, the office balance would have been lost. Freddy made these observations in the time it took for him to move the freshly varnished chair from the wall and place it in front of the experienced reporter. They were observations he had made some time ago, but he always liked to confirm them each time he entered his colleague's office, and, having confirmed his observations anew, he began to explain the nature of his problem.

"Mr. Androulidakis told me I'll be covering Kazantzakis' funeral. It's something I really wanted." He paused, wanting to gauge how intently Peter was listening to him.

"Good. I'm very pleased for you, Freddy. So what's the problem?" Peter asked earnestly with his spirited voice.

"Well, tomorrow I have to go to Hellenikon, to cover the arrival of Jane Mansfield. Do you think I won't be taken seriously if I cover Kazantzakis' funeral just two days after that?" he asked with obvious concern.

"Of course not!" Peter scoffed with utter conviction. "These are your words," he continued carefully.

"But if our readers see my name on the byline of the Kazantzakis funeral piece and then recall that I've also written about the arrival of Jane Mansfield, won't that immediately tarnish my credibility as a reporter?" insisted the up-and-coming journalist.

"For the last time, no."

"How come?"

"I'll tell you how... A reputable reporter is judged by his every report, whether it's political coverage or a charity ball or a boxing match, or even the list of overnight pharmacies or an interview with a movie star. If a reporter is serious and does his job correctly, it shows and he stands out. Write what you see, ask questions, investigate, and no one will ever question your value even if you feel the topic you are covering is not worth the effort. So then, I as your reader, Freddy Germanos, expect to read a solid article on this Jane Mansfield, to see if all the talk about her is warranted. And I then fully expect to read a rich article that relates all the events that unfolded at Kazantzakis' funeral. As a reader, I have expectations about you and your newspaper!"

This short speech by Peter Charis rang like a Christmas carol in Freddy's ears, who was utterly besotted with his experienced colleague's inspired words.

"Thank you very much," he said somewhat awkwardly, trying hard to refrain from hugging and kissing Peter with joy. He got up from his seat and moved his chair back to its original spot. On his way out of Charis' office, he stole a glimpse out of the corner of his eye, as Peter picked up the pencil once more, and soon after heard the sound of paper being crushed and tossed back into the bin.

Freiburg – Frankfurt – Freiburg

Deep in thought and exhausted, Helen took in the sights of the German countryside as it flowed past her train cabin's window. Agnes sat next to her, lost in her own thoughts, having succumbed to her own fatigue. Helen did not care for their visit to the Greek consulate in Frankfurt; she had felt a disturbing sense of déjà vu when she realized that nothing had changed in the way the Greek state dealt with her. The reluctance to assist her, the constant obstacles they kept coming up with for the sole purpose of giving Agnes a hard time were so familiar to Helen, that she grew bored and tired of them. No, her rage had left her years ago, for rage is the prerogative of youth.

"At least this time they offered me a chair, so that I didn't have to stand as though in punishment simply because I chose Kazantzakis to be my husband," she had answered Agnes as to whether or not she was outraged, as they exited the consulate.

What would it matter? She was proud of herself and her choices. And more so than that, she was proud because, from the moment Kazantzakis had assured her of an impoverished life at the beginning of their relationship, she had never felt the slightest qualm in how to proceed. Here was a reason for a person to be proud: she had chosen so consciously and had fought so valiantly that she never allowed herself any self-doubt.

Her discussions with Agnes over the last few days actually had made Helen feel that the value of their life together by far outweighed any price she had paid. Everything she had experienced – which could fill three or four lifetimes – made fatigue or poverty pale in comparison. *You tricked your fate, Helen,* she mused. Her guardians, to whom her upbringing had been entrusted, had been monstrous to her. "Orphans don't do this, orphans don't do that, orphans don't play, orphans don't go to the university," were only some of the usual phrases she had learned to anticipate whenever she tried to ask for the slightest thing. How had this orphaned girl – the daughter of a professor of the National Technical University and Chief of Forestry at the Ministry of Finance, the child of the man who forested the entire Ardittos hill where the Panathenian Stadium stands today – how had this girl managed to become the stormless harbor to the most persecuted outcast of modern Greece? How had she become the woman on whom leaned the most erudite Greek after Homer, Plato, Socrates, Aristotle and all the others of their ancient kind?

Perhaps it was their common thirst that bound them; a thirst for life, for learning, for justice, for freedom. Perhaps, instinctively, people reach for each other and are drawn to those with whom they feel they have common needs. Not interests, but needs! At the side of her Nikos she had satisfied all of her needs in a life beyond any and all expectation. And to think that she hadn't wanted to meet him initially, having been influenced by all the rumors she'd heard at Dexameni – the meeting place of young progressive intellectuals, of which Galatea was the core.

Everyone spoke of the young philosopher in the most contradictory terms; yet in the eyes of her dear friend, Marika Papaioannou – who would go on to become a celebrated pianist – she had never met anyone more charming than Kazantzakis in her entire life. It never became clear whether or not Marikas' insistent urging for Helen to meet Nikos sprang from some deep instinct that a potential meeting between the two would be fateful. The same nagging question would raise itself over and again in Helen's mind, how Kazantzakis chose her when she herself believed there were others more far more worthy. First and foremost, her friends, Marika and her sister, Kaity Papaioannou, who were her dearest friends, and whom she felt were far superior to her.

She watched the meadows sprawling before her through her train window, and tried to calculate how many evenings they had eaten wild greens that she had picked from some field or mountain top, cooked with only a handful of rice or whatever other humble offering they had at home. Poverty and hunger had long ceased to bother her; at any rate, she could not recall a time of true abundance by his side. Still, she had known this from the very first day they became a couple.

"You will never be bored by my side," he had said to her, and he had kept his promise to his very end.

Helen recalled every word, every letter and every scribble in that message she'd received in France, where she had been working as a correspondent for *Kathimerini* newspaper, in which Nikos called her to be with him in Russia. They had known each other for two years and had already traveled together to Palestine with the Papaioannou sisters.

"Our life will not be easy, as you already know how dull life can be with me for the socially minded. I will work all day, and will see You only in the evenings – sometimes I will be sad and laconic, other times emotive and joyous, with correspondence and letters that may be unpleasant for You with persons I love. Our material life shall be simple, necessitous, as it has been since I left my father's house. But You are not worldly; You are uncomplicated and heroic."

Six months later, while Helen was still contemplating whether or not to take the 'big step', he had written to her again: "May it please God that with me you will experience great joys and great sorrows but never mediocrity or boredom." And his prayer was answered and fulfilled to such a degree that not even he would have believed it. As she had prepared to leave behind her promising career, to leave Paris and the life she had built for herself with great difficulty, to live the unconventional life he proudly promised her in the Soviet Union and anywhere else – not even he could have known then where they would end up – Nikos had asked of her something completely brazen, not only for their time – it was 1928 – but also by today's standards: to first go to Düsseldorf and find his first lover, Elsa Lange, to stay with her and to learn everything about him, and then to decide for herself if she truly wanted to continue her journey to Moscow or to return to Paris.

If she continued her path to him, it would be a path with no return – that is what he had written to her. Another woman in her place might have seen this as a humiliating indignity, but to her it was an honest test. She loved him deeply even if she had experienced him mainly through their correspondence. Perhaps this frightened her; how much more could she love him, if the intensity she felt without his physical presence was already too much for her to bear?

She had stayed with Elsa for a week. She had been very kind to Helen and one needn't more than a mere half hour of conversation to see the pure adoration she had for Nikos. There was no doubt that she still loved him, but in the purest, most consummate form of love: ready to do as he asked for the sake of his happiness, demanding nothing in return, as though one might do anything not simply to please the person one loves but rather to honor one's own love for them.

On the third night of their unconventional cohabitation she had spoken warmly to Helen.

"Yes, that is it, yes, yes...you can trust him. A fire burns him from within and yet he does not lose his sense for life even for one second. Balanced, perfectly normal. And, no matter what happens, please never regret heeding his call. I will be with you in my thoughts, I will stand by your side in your difficult times. He is as naked as Saint Sebastian. Please, protect him from the arrows."

Those words had bolstered Helen's confidence. She mused whether or not this was the portrait of a saint's life, when Elsa's gentle voice interrupted her thoughts.

"He has his vices, of course. He is the first to recognize them and to resist them. He could be selfish, but he is not, save for his work. He could be cruel, but he is not, save only to himself."

That is when Helen confessed the fear of a woman so in love she would cross all of Europe on her own to get to the man she so desperately loves.

"He is on his way to ruin! The way I saw him – he will self-destruct in his effort to reach the highest peaks. And yet, it is so odd! By his side I feel rested, all problems seem to find their solution or to disappear, I feel refreshed as though I am resting beneath the shade of a large oak tree or sitting next to a cool stream."

Helen had then made her decision.

Onward to Moscow, to Nikos!

Athens

Freddy wrapped up the section on the overnight pharmacies, and headed for the office of Peter Charis. Each minute of conversation with the experienced reporter was akin to countless hours training on the job for the young journalist.

"Good evening, gentlemen," Androulidakis said curtly as he entered the office moments later. His agitation was evident in his nervous gestures – but he retained his composure when things became difficult, for it was one of his defining traits.

"Be in my office in half an hour. I want to know where we are on the Kazantzakis article. The information I have at this moment is quite disconcerting. Please get started on phone calls to his friends and family, but also to people you trust and who might know persons in the church hierarchy."

Nothing more was said; Androulidakis exited the office and silence remained, demanding and vengeful. Heads bowed low, and fingers complied to the dictates of the mind. The order concerned the young journalist as well though his odds of breaking the story were less than zero. Freddy had no delusions, but instead had the steadfast spirit of a newsman – an absolute necessity in his field – beyond his obvious talent in writing, which was undeniable. Still, he knew the only way for him to make a name for himself among his colleagues – which would be the first step in securing his broader recognition in any field – was to hunt down the news and to secure exclusive stories that would stimulate the public sentiment. This is what separates the journalist from the mere clerk.

He called the Archdiocese, not because he knew anyone there, but because it was the obvious point at which to start... It was afternoon, and no one answered. He insisted, but to no avail. A few moments later he saw Peter Charis standing in the doorway; he was clearly excited and impatient.

"Come, Freddy, let's go..."

Peter stopped adroitly in front of Androulidakis' open door, but was motioned to wait. A few moments later, the voice of the chief-editor boomed in the hallway.

"Are you certain?" they heard him ask, as though what was being said to him on the telephone defied all credulity.

Freddy crossed into the office hesitantly – as though he were an uninvited guest at a party – unlike Peter Charis who stormed in, clearly with the story in hand.

"You were right, George," he said before he had even sat in his seat. "There are voices in the hierarchy that would rather see the Church not bury Kazantzakis."

"I'm being told that parareligious organizations are exerting pressure. Did you hear about that?" Androulidakis asked him.

"Yes, I heard the same thing," the reporter told his chief-editor.

"I even got the name of the man behind it all," he continued.

"Is it Kantiotis?" Androulidakis asked, as if he already knew the answer.

"The one and the same," the reporter confirmed with a chill.

Freddy realized that he was about to experience another déjà vu moment in yet another high paced lesson in modern Greek history, as the name 'Kantiotis' seemed laden with a significant story, and none of it benign; his name certainly wouldn't have been so well known in the newsrooms otherwise. Freddy had many questions, and Androulidakis answered all his unspoken queries as he pressed on.

"Kantiotis is an overly ambitious hardcore cleric who moves in the shadows. He's the head of the parareligious organization "Zoe", which counts fanatics and zealots in its ranks. His activity is well documented. His name has been whispered steadily since 1945. Suspicious individuals of questionable motives spread the idea that he ran food kitchens during the Nazi Occupation in Kozani, but no one was ever able to ascertain the source of his funding. He was a military physician who would hear the confessions of the EAM National Liberation Front and the ELAS Greek People's Liberation Army captives, and was later accused of divulging those confessions in the court-martials."

"Imagine, in 1952 he protested obstinately against the beauty pageant," Peter Charis supplied sarcastically. "He took some of his zealots with him and tried to attack the venue. Mitsotakis was there at the pageant and so were many other front line politicians."

"Ah, is this when Mitsotakis met his wife, Marika?" Freddy asked triumphantly, for he did know something after all.

"We'll talk about it some other time, if you think it's that important," Androulidakis said, steering him back.

"At the time they'd attacked the home of the sculptor Iliades, screaming 'break it all!' and 'Christ is risen!' because the judge's committee was deliberating at his house on the new Miss Hellas. At the trial that followed, Kantiotis presented himself as president of the anti-pageant organization called Saint Athanasios. It's so ridiculous you don't know if you should laugh or cry," he said, shaking his head.

"The truth, however, is that no one wants to make an enemy of this man, especially when it is rumored that he operates under the auspices of the Palace. And of course you know that Archbishop Theoklitos was only elected three months ago – in a process that was anything but amicable. He will certainly not want to find himself at odds with the fanatics, and there's no shortage of those in the Holy Synod."

Freddy took this all in with his well known, by now, surprised look as the chief editor continued his story.

"For the religious fanatics Kazantzakis is enemy number one. Kantiotis, Melas and all the rest see in his face a stark threat. And it is precisely for these types of situations that they have overtaken the positions that they hold...to launch a dirty war, to dirty their hands where the official state cannot," Androulidakis said.

Freddy understood that things were indeed serious.

"The faithful in Crete have been outraged for quite some time at the way their beloved kinsman has been treated," Androulidakis continued. "I fear that there will be riots if Kantiotis does not stop. That's what the publisher just said to me. It was relayed to him by a trusted source, a friend of his who is a member of parliament."

"Who would that be, sir?" Freddy asked naively.

"Come on, lad, use your brain. You're a journalist! Which member of parliament from Crete visits our paper often?" Androulidakis asked with a smile.

"Mitsotakis," Freddy replied as naively as before.

"There you go," Androulidakis laughed. "Have you been keeping up with the other newspapers? What are they writing? Or are you going to attend this funeral without doing your homework first?" he asked as Peter Charis chimed in with laughter.

"The *Vima* newspaper writes about the articles in the newspapers of France that deify Kazantzakis and his work. And, although I've gathered that he will be buried in Herakleion, no one seems to know when that will take place. And, given what I've heard just now, let me add that no one can be sure the funeral will be held at all," the young man responded in halfhearted jest.

"Do you think the Church would accept such a burden? To not bury him? What do you think, Peter?" the chief-editor asked.

"At this point no one can be certain. Kantiotis will surely try to flex his power to the new archbishop, who only got thirty-one votes out of the total fifty-seven, which means that only three metropolitans need change their position and the archbishop loses his majority. So, I think he'll wink a little to the hardliners, trying at the same time to appease the faithful. On the other hand, I want to believe that political pressure, and especially from Papandreou, will yield some results. Though I fear that, if Frederica wills it, Kazantzakis will not be buried."

Peter Charis had made an astute summation of the fluidity of the situation, which smelled of gunpowder, basil and myrrh. The three of them stood silently, each of them assessing the situation according to their experience.

"I was thinking of what you said yesterday. I've concluded that the Church has not excommunicated Kazantzakis," Freddy said, troubled.

"Well that is one elaborate trick. Officially no, they have not excommunicated him. Officially, the Church has asked the Ministry of Justice to obstruct the circulation of his works. So, technically, it has succeeded in cultivating the idea in the faithful that Kazantzakis is an enemy of the Church. And don't forget, the Church is political. It wouldn't want to turn its thinking faithful against it, but it does want to allay the fanatics. And so, the excommunication lingers. To you 1916 might seem a lifetime ago, but believe me, to a historian forty-one years is nothing at all."

"Why, what happened then?"

"The anathema of Eleftherios Venizelos, that's what. The Archbishop Theoklitos gathered the faithful at the Field of Ares Park, where they had dug a pit and had placed in it an effigy of Venizelos. The newspapers at the time wrote that hundreds of thousands of people attended. The church bells had been ringing since noon, and when Theoklitos stood up, it was sheer pandemonium. He proceeded to recite the curse in his deep voice: 'To Eleftherios Venizelos, who imprisoned high priests and conspired against the monarchy and the nation, anathema!' Then he tossed four stones into the pit. The people, who had gathered from many districts in Athens, even the farthest ones, proceeded to pass by the pit and toss a stone into it, repeating the curse. It wasn't long before four tall mounds had formed from all the stones."

"Two metropolitans were also there hurling even more detailed curses, remember, Peter?" Androulidakis asked.

"Yes, yes, of course I remember. The metropolitans were Ambrosios and Nikephoros. It was they who anathematized him and cursed him to suffer violently the following list of torments: to suffer the rashes of Job; to be swallowed whole by Jonah's whale; to suffer the scourge of Jehovah; to wither as though dead; to feel the death rattle of those perishing, to be struck by the lightning of Hell; and to know the curse and anathema of his people."

"All this in the heart of Christianity??" Freddy asked, taken aback.

"Years later, Penelope Delta recalled how her mother had been so saddened by this situation," Androulidakis said, his eyes half closed.

"She recalled how the sheer volume of the stones had turned into something grotesque. And it wasn't just stones from Athenian soil, no, they had brought stones in from various cities across the land, and piled them up in the pit. At night the Venizelists would leave flowers over the pit, but of course those were all gone come morning. At some point Venizelos had come to Athens, and Virginia Choremis-Benakis, the wife of the former mayor of

Athens, Emmanuel Benakis, and mother of Penelope Delta, had asked him to reach out to the Church to lift the anathema.

"He became outraged. 'I most certainly will not, Mrs. Benakis. I will never do that,' he retorted. 'That anathema will stay, and beneath that anathema we will win, we will liberate Macedonia and crush the Bulgarians. Not only will I not ask for the repeal of the anathema, but those stones will stay right where they are, in their huge piles, so that people can always remember that I was anathematized and yet I still prevailed.'"

The narration held the two men spellbound in their seats as they listened to the chief-editor. The only thing in motion in the entire room was the smoke wafting from his cigarette; Androulidakis even changed the timbre of his voice when he related the dialogue of those involved, so lively was his account! After a pause and a puff of smoke, he realized, quite content, how captive an audience he had, and so continued.

"Then someone informed him that at night the mounds were gradually growing smaller because people were taking the stones. Venizelos shouted, 'This is not what I meant! I do not want to lose the proof of this anathema! I will post guards! I mean that these stones should remain where they are, so that people can see them every day and know how utterly foolish and futile the Church's curses are!'

"Then it was Emmanuel Benakis who tried to change his mind; 'It is an unsightly thing in the park, Mr. President', said the former mayor of Athens. 'We will have to live with this ugliness, Mr. Benakis', Venizelos replied resolutely. 'We will endure it for the edification of our people, who must learn to evaluate an ecclesiastical curse as much as a blessing, when the Church becomes a blunt political instrument.'"

"So what do you say, lad? Do you think Venizelos got the church or the people to reconsider their stance?"

"No, I don't believe that at all, sir," Freddy replied with such disappointment as though he himself had been betrayed by the clergy and the people.

"The issue is that Kazantzakis is dead. If they feel he is an overrated author and nothing more, not an intellectual nor a philosopher, then logically they will take the higher ground, show decency. They will attend to the dead with all the honors and rites deserving of any baptized orthodox Christian. Nothing more," Peter Charis noted.

"Its not even decency; it is the least they can do," Androulidakis scoffed, and went on, "I heard, also, that Onassis has offered a plane to transfer Kazantzakis' remains from Freiburg to Athens, though the arrangements had already been made and his remains are now en route from Freiburg by hearse."

"And what about what you heard, courtesy of our parliamentarian from Chania, Mr. Androulidakis?" Freddy asked with a smile.

"That too, young man, that too," he replied with a smile of his own. "Now lets get going. And keep your ears open."

The clouds hung low above Athens, highlighting the comings and goings of pedestrians as night fell upon the city. Freddy walked his usual course, sensing colossal and conflicting feelings within him. These days had changed him in an undefined way; there was no point in speculating he was becoming harsher, that he was losing his faith in people, in institutions, in meritocracy, for which he thirsted as a young romantic – after all, every young man of humble beginnings longs for meritocracy.

And after the battle – a battle for life! - all that remains are those things that keep a man awake at night, that steady him each morning, making every cell in his body desire to experience them desperately. Those defeated souls we call dreamers. He tried to think of an elegant way to phrase it. *Well I am not a dreamer*, he said to himself with a measure of anguish. And, truly, he wasn't.

He entered his home lightly, without making the slightest noise. He laid down immediately, taking off his glasses carefully and setting them on the bedside table, and, after tossing and turning several times – for if one were to view him from above, one might think he was rehearsing some rock and roll moves instead – he turned on the lamp next to him, put his glasses back on and stretched out his hand under the bed. As soon as he looked at the cover of the book *The Old Man and the Sea,* his ragged face, which bore the strain of his daily stress, at once softened into calm symmetry.

Freiburg

It was quite late when they returned to their "Paradise", tired and disappointed from the cold reception they had received at the Greek consulate in Frankfurt. Despite their fatigue, the two women agreed to dine before going up to their room. The light breeze was refreshing and enticed their appetite. When dinner was finished Helen found herself taken with an impudent black cat, a poor imitation of a puma. She tried to find something it might like to eat, but it made it clear it was a cat of particular tastes, and opted to simply smell everything the likable lady tossed its way.

"Helen, did you have a lot of cats?" Agnes asked.

"We always had them in the house. Only this last year… Nikos didn't want them anymore," Helen answered, and continued to toss morsels of food to the paunchy black cat who was enjoying the olfactive experience with his tail pointed high in the air, as though it were a submarine periscope.

"Why not? What happened?"

"Nikos loved cats a great deal. He trained them, he taught them to play….but that last one, Popouli, left us three years ago, without us knowing what happened to him. We both loved it so very much. Each night I'd prepare some cream and leave the bowl in the window. It would come to the windowsill and we'd let it in. It would eat and then it would come lay down with us. Nikos was so distressed after it disappeared, that he decided he'd never take another one in."

"Did you ever have any complaints for him?"

"Only one – that he never complained. He would accept it all, no matter what happened."

"You know what I admire in you, Helen? Above all of the things for which others may admire you – and Nikos, first of all – is that you stayed with him without marrying for many years. That shows how much you loved him."

"I never asked him to marry me..." Helen said softly. "I always wanted to see how long he could go *without* marrying me," she continued, and the two friends erupted in laughter.

"Well how did it happen? How did he propose then?"

"Simply, purely, without gifts or fanfare: '*Want to get married?*'. There never was a truer sample of a Kazantzakian sentence."

"Sometimes that is the best way."

"Well I never expected anything else. If it hadn't happened this way, it would mean that he didn't hold fast to what he believed. The funny thing was, that at our wedding at Saint George Karytsis church, he had forgotten the wedding rings, and so we were forced to use the wedding bands of Angelos and Anna Sikelianos. Our wedding rings literally read, 'Angelos' and 'Anna'."

"That's incredible," Agnes yelped and broke out laughing, so much so that they frightened the faux wildcat away.

The evening was quite cool and still the two women were wrapped up in their stories of Kazantzakis. Agnes could not get enough of these accounts regarding the man she so respected and loved, and Helen never tired of telling the great and small tales, from the juiciest to the bluntest events of their life together.

"And you continued to speak to each other in the plural until the end?"

"Until the very end!" Helen confirmed, then paused for some time. "It began as a joke and it lasted a lifetime. It was only when he would be sick that he became my darling, 'my child'."

"Yes, I remember what a terrible ordeal you both went through with his eye.... What torture that was!"

"We went through a great deal, that May of '53! He was on the brink of death in Paris, owing to a doctor's mistake in Antibes. In his delirium he thought Saint Francis of Assisi was in the room with him. Later he confessed to me that he could see him sitting next to him, telling him stories."

"He came so very close to death then, didn't he?"

"So very close. After that ordeal, which cost him the vision in his right eye, he changed his stance on some things. This was the second time he was 'rescued' by his beloved Saint Francis. You see, he came quite close to death once before," Helen began, as though speaking to his biographer.

"It was during the Occupation. In Aegina people were dying of hunger. Nikos became infirm and wasted away, having exhausted his body with years of his own ascetic living. To understand the depth of his frailty, I must tell you that a decade later, when a doctor examined him in Paris, he asked me if Nikos had ever been in a concentration camp. Our friends tried as best as they could to help us, but things were terribly bad. And, naturally, the authorities made sure to exacerbate the misery. When one of his theatrical plays was about to be staged, the Censorship committee rejected it. And, on the other hand, there were affluent publishers who were buying his works for a literal piece of bread."

Damn them!" Agnes yelled, enraged, momentarily interrupting her friend.

"Now just imagine Kazantzakis, who never cared at all for sales or percentages, to not want to give his works for publication. 'If I were not in such dire financial straits I would perhaps tolerate being taken advantage of. But not now, not by any means,' he wrote to his dear friend, Pantelis Prevelakis, in 1941. I was forced to go to the food kitchens at the prisons to fetch some food. After many ordeals, it was the Catholic monks who saved us. They asked Nikos to translate the life of Saint Francis of Assisi, and gave us food in return. And this is how Kazantzakis survived the Occupation."

Helen paused briefly. She held her gaze steadfast, and it seemed as though her last words hammered the silence and echoed back to her.

"Would you like to turn in for the night? I'm starting to get cold," she said as she realized she had grown tired.

They settled their bill and proceeded to their room. Helen had resolved earlier that morning to ask Agnes for a favor but kept putting it off. She had waited for the cover of night to shield her face so that she could muster all of her courage and ask it.

"Agnes, my dear, would you do me a favor?" she asked, about five minutes after saying goodnight.

"Of course. Tell me..."

"I....I would like for you to go choose his coffin," she managed to say before her voice cracked and her tears flooded her pillow.

"Of course," Agnes replied, as though it were no matter. It took quite some time to fall asleep; it came only after they had dried up and had no more tears to shed.

WEDNESDAY, OCTOBER 30, 1957

Athens

In the morning his grandmother found him immersed in deep slumber, his bed side light still on, a book lying open on his chest, his glasses still held loosely in his left hand. Freddy was only forced awake by her persistent yet tender nudges.

"You know you need your rest, child," she whispered gently while he was already leaping out of bed. In under ten minutes he was out the door. After a quick good morning to their next door neighbor – the mother of his much older – by ten years – and budding leftist politician, Leonidas Kyrkos – he rushed down the stairs. He was wearing a suit and a long coat; how he loved to wear a coat! It made him look older, a greatly craved advantage in a profession where status and experience were of vital importance. He was, of course, going for coffee, to find out what news he could about the Kazantzakis story.

He thought he heard someone call his name as he was crossing Stadiou Street. Reaching the pavement, he paused and turned, trying to determine where the voice was coming from. Only a few steps from the entrance of Zonar's, an elevated arm caught his eye in the sea of tables at one of the most cosmopolitan cafeterias of Athens. A few steps away, still waving at him, sat his new middle-aged friend, Mr. Fotis, the failed author, successful heir and talented money-earner, dressed like a dandy, accompanied by a friend with matching sartorial preferences.

"Freddy, my dearest and most talented young journalist! Join us!" he beckoned excitedly.

Freddy smiled.

"Gentlemen, good morning to you. Freddy Germanos," he introduced himself, extending his hand to the still unknown person across from him.

"Dinos Makris. A pleasure!" the man responded without getting up. "Please, do tell, is this a *nom de plume*?" he inquired, curious.

"No. It is my actual surname, just like it says right here on my identity card," Freddy answered curtly, trying to show his distaste for any further discussion on the subject, that was frankly getting a little old. But Dinos' curiosity was more intense than subtle.

"But, really, how...?" he retorted.

"As you are neither the first, and I'm sure, not the last to ask about it, I will indulge, as succinctly I can. So, here goes: My great grandfather studied in Germany. When he came back, everyone began calling him 'the German,' which ended up being his surname."

"And wasn't that a problem for you, during the Nazi occupation? I'm sorry to be asking; I am genuinely curious," Dinos rushed to explain himself.

"Yes, it did. How could it not? It was a hideous surname for that time. I must have been in the eighth or ninth grade, during the occupation, when my classmates wrote in my textbook: 'Kick the German out of our classroom!' and other such niceties..."

All three laughed.

"I must have been the youngest German sympathizer in Greek History. I do hold that dreadful record, to be quite honest."

The laughter only increased; Mr. Fotis wouldn't let the subject go.

"And I, for one, would love to meet the priest who consented to baptize you with what the name 'Freddy'," he said.

"Well, it's really not something that peculiar and I will of course explain why. On the island of Mytilene, where I was baptized, we had to 'oil' the hand of the priest to allow this name, if you know what I mean. But what can you do? Oiling is part of the whole baptismal process, anyhow," he laughed even harder this time, making everyone at the nearby tables turn to look.

"And what made you decide to become a journalist, Freddy?" the ever curious Dinos asked again.

"I wrote a lot as a child, and read a great deal. Every night. I wanted to become a writer. Journalism is the closest thing in the writing profession. This way, I'm following in the footsteps of my favorite author, Ernest Hemingway," Freddy began, but was interrupted by Fotis.

"He's already won an award, when he was nineteen, in the Young Author's Competition."

"The second place award," Freddy was quick to clarify.

"That worked out in your favor. Had you won the first prize, you'd have thought writing was over for you. And how did you celebrate?" Dinos asked.

"I danced the tango with my grandmother," Freddy said as the others erupted in laughter.

"That wasn't a joke, I was being serious," Freddy said, somewhat annoyed.

"And were you a good student in school?" Dinos insisted.

"Oh, the worst. I still know nothing about mathematics, algebra, trigonometry. In elementary, I changed schools every year, like I was wanted and on the run. At the Varvakeios School, my math teacher never saw me, didn't even know what I looked like, nor I him. I was always gone, because I always had something more important to do."

"Like what?" Fotis beat Dinos to the question as though they were competing in a curiosity contest.

"Keeping up with my cultural education was very important, and I did that at the cinemas on Patission Avenue – at the *Hellas*, the *Roseclair*, the *Alaska*," the young reporter replied, making the group break out in laughter once more. Freddy's demeanor suddenly changed, and his tone became deep like an old smoker's voice. "Can we give it a rest now, because this interrogation has tired me out? And I haven't even ordered coffee yet," he said seriously.

"Of course... and, sorry," Dinos said apologetically and raised his hand to signal the waiter.

The coffee came with enviable speed. In the meantime, Freddy – who had learned that Dinos was, in a manner of speaking, an aspiring colleague of the aspiring author, Mr. Fotis, without so much as a single work of his published, however – wanted to know what their ever informed social circle, forged in daily gossip, might know about the Kazantzakis affair.

"The city council of Athens has decided to name a street after him," Dinos was first to say.

"And the Literary Society sent a condolence telegram to Helen Kazantzakis in Antibes," Mr. Fotis chimed in.

"That's all the news you know? And you brag that you're in the loop..." Freddy goaded them as he lifted his cup to sip a bit from his coffee.

"Well, of course not..." Fotis replied, insulted.

"You should be the one telling us what you know. After all, you're the journalist," Dinos retorted.

"You go first, and then I'll tell you," the twenty-three year-old smiled, as though he knew the entire back story and all the secrets that were usually withheld in articles, or that, when written about, were phrased in such a way that a reader would have to read between the lines to flesh them out.

"I was told the hearse will depart soon from Freiburg. It will arrive by car. It will make a stop in Athens, for the public wake, and then continue on to Herakleion," Fotis delivered the tip.

"But why is it taking so many days?" Dinos queried.

"The doctors recommended they embalm the body because the funeral would be several days later, but Helen declined. So they needed to order a custom casket lined with iron," Mr. Fotis explained. "Now when it will actually get on the road and when it will get here, nobody knows, though it should be here by Sunday."

"Logically, yes," Dinos agreed.

"Your turn, Freddy," Fotis said with a smirk.

"Well... it appears that various religious groups plan to cause disturbances in an effort to besmirch Kazantzakis' memory," the reporter began with a somber, measured tone, as though he was reporting the evening news.

"But that's just tragic! Go on... or wait, before you do, answer me this: is the person behind all of this Kantiotis?" Fotis asked with anxious anticipation.

"Yes it is." Freddy answered pithily.

"I knew it!" Fotis shouted excitedly. "Now go on."

"Everyone in Crete is in an uproar, because they've heard that the priests in Athens are up to something. Of course, no one knows what, exactly, so everyone is on edge," Freddy continued, adding to the suspense.

"But that is tragic! He's dead! What more do they want?" Dinos burst out.

"Pay no mind, Dinos. These are the rantings of the religious zealots stirring the pot. They wouldn't dare do anything," Fotis assured. "It would make no sense for the official Church to be led on by a bunch of fanatics."

"But what if this bunch of parareligious fanatics had such power as to harm the Archbishop?" Freddy asked in a conspiratorial tone.

"Oh, you know a lot more than you are telling us," Dinos exclaimed, agitated.

"I'm telling you all I know. Now the rest is just conjecture on my part," Freddy repeated with the same wily tone.

"At any rate, we will see," he said, and rose from his seat.

"Don't you even think of paying, Freddy. Go on, find out more, and come back here tomorrow and fill us in," Fotis stopped him. "By the way, the *Vima* and *Nea* newspapers have left you guys in the dust. They've been writing about Kazantzakis nonstop," he teased.

"Get a copy of the *Eleftheria* tomorrow and read the article by Ploritis. He'd met with Kazantzakis a few months ago. Goodbye, gentlemen," he bid them farewell with a smile and set down the hill towards his office, walking with the confident stride of a successful journalist.

Freiburg

When she awoke, Agnes was nowhere to be found. The sun was lodged high in the sky yet another day, far higher than her normal waking time. She would have slept in if she hadn't peered at her watch; it was already ten o'clock. She got up worriedly, splashed some water on her face, donned on her black clothes and hurried down the stairs. The clerk informed her that her friend had left earlier, at eight thirty in the morning. She realized then that Agnes was out on the favor she had asked of her the previous night. She took her breakfast in the garden. She had to order her next steps: arrange for their things to be sent to Antibes, go to their home and make the necessary preparations, and go to Herakleion for the funeral. Sipping her tea, she noted the names of all the people she needed to call – Nikos' nephew in Crete, his friend John Anghelakis, Pantelis Prevelakis, John Goudelis and Marika Papaioannou.

The previous day flooded her thoughts; she could not get over how she had been treated at the Greek consulate. She had thought, rather erroneously, that the Authorities would respect Kazantzakis, even at this late stage, now that he was dead. The disdain they had shown, most likely by order of the Greek embassy, meant that there would be no ceasefire on their part. *On the other hand, Karamanlis had sent his condolences and had announced that the funeral would be a state expense,* she thought. There was nothing, however, no announcement that could reassure her. She wasn't the romantic girl who had faith in people any more; the only person she'd ever believed in lay dead at the University Hospital morgue, just a few hundred meters away.

Athens

Freddy had left the noisy, bustling cafes behind him as he walked to his office. He couldn't fathom how fulfilling his profession would be, and especially now, that he was about to witness an historical moment that would be retold over the coming generations. Still, he was well aware he didn't factor into anything with too much importance just yet – otherwise he wouldn't be spending the next two hours writing the column on overnight pharmacies!

Once back at his desk, he opened the drawer and pulled out a new notebook; it smelled of crisp, fresh ink. *This is where I'll write down my questions for Jane Mansfield,* he thought to himself, questions beyond the typical clichés. He didn't want to be like the other reporters, who were clearly fans of the American star. How could he even utter questions like, 'What do you think of Greece?' as though he were a professor of Geography, which he both loathed and knew nothing about? He only managed to jot down a few questions before setting it aside so he could focus on what was truly on his mind. He had to speak to his source, the Cretan. It had already been two days, which meant that the Cretan was sure to have plenty of fresh information and would doubtlessly relay the atmosphere in Herakleion as things developed. He opened the drawer again and pulled out his old notepad.

"Who is it?"

"Good afternoon, Cretan. I'm calling from Athens. It's Freddy Germanos, the reporter from *Eleftheria* newspaper. Do you remember me? We talked the day before yesterday."

"Oh sure. How have you been, friend?"

"I'm fine. I'm calling to see how things are down there."

"We're fine, but troubled. We're waiting for Mr. Kazantzakis to arrive."

Freddy smiled a fleeting smile as he heard the formality in the Cretan's voice. He was tempted to correct the mistaken convention of calling the deceased "mister," but decided against it. He didn't want to offend the Cretan who was making every effort to be worthy of being the "source" for one of the largest newspapers in Athens.

"Well? What's new?" Freddy asked with a lofty air.

"Mr. Freddy, we don't know when the funeral will take place," the Cretan replied in his ever formal tone as he went on, "we're expecting Mrs. Kazantzakis to telegraph ahead. And we still don't know where he's going to be buried."

"Why? Won't he be buried in the cemetery?" Freddy rejoined, having struck a good bit of information.

"Nothing is certain. We're hearing that the Church won't allow him to be buried in the cemetery, but that he'll be buried somewhere on his own, as a tribute. We've been told George Papandreou and other politicians and parliamentarians and officials will come down for the funeral."

"Yes, yes, the announcement has been made, I think," Freddy pretended to be aware.

"And many unions and organizations will come from Chania to attend the funeral."

"And I will be there too, to cover the whole thing," Freddy informed him with a bit of a pompous air.

"Come find me when you do, I'll buy you a round of raki," the Cretan replied, enthused.

"It will be my pleasure," Freddy said, suddenly keen to hang up the phone so he could speak with Androulidakis. "I'll let you go now, and I'll call again soon. If you need anything, call the paper and ask for me. Germanos. I'm repeating my last name."

"You sure you aren't no German?" the Cretan asked him somewhat emboldened by their talk.

"We've been over this. It's a nickname given to my great grandfather, and it ultimately became our family surname. My father is an officer of the Hellenic Navy."

"Alright, alright. Bye for now, bye."

Freddy hung up the phone and went straight to the chief-editor's office.

"What is it my boy, do you want something?" he asked, stooped over his papers and notebooks.

"Good afternoon, Mr. Androulidakis. I just spoke with Herakleion. No one knows when Kazantzakis' funeral will be held. They just know that George Papandreou and other members of parliament will be in attendance."

"Yes, I'm aware. Let's see who goes to represent the government. Anything else?" he asked, this time raising his head to look his protege squarely in the eye.

"The man I spoke to, he also said..." Freddy faltered for a moment.

"Yes...?"

"That they don't know where he's going to be buried," Freddy managed to blurt out.

"I see. He doesn't know. I imagine you think this might be related to the Church and to everything we discussed yesterday," the chief-editor echoed Freddy's thoughts, though Freddy was uncertain whether he was being commended or reprimanded for it.

"Yes," he said slowly. "That is what I'm thinking. That the Church could be behind this delay. The Cretan hinted as much, but I'm not sure," he finished, hesitant once more.

"It's a good thought, and a good place to start for some phone calls," Androulidakis mused, which pleased Freddy immensely to have secured this small success. "You should know, of course, that the Church of Crete administratively belongs to the Patriarchate in Constantinople, not the Church of Greece," he reminded him, but it was not enough to erase the smile from Freddy's face.

"Of course I know that," Freddy replied confidently. "I just thought I should let you know."

"Alright, my boy. We should get an article in from our reporter in Herakleion for tomorrow's edition."

"But I brought it to you first...Shouldn't I get to write it?" Freddy protested.

"Freddy, please. Go finish your column on overnight pharmacies and get your questions in order for Mansfield. I'm sending you to the funeral, isn't that enough?" Androulidakis raised his tone enough to get the young man to retreat.

"Of course, Mr. Androulidakis," Freddy said, lowering his head in respect, disguising his disappointment.

"Keep making those calls when you have time. Keep at it, bravo," the chief-editor encouraged him.

Freddy returned to his desk and wrote down a few more uninspiring questions for Jane Mansfield, when he was rescued by Peter Charis, who entered his office.

"Good job, Freddy. Androulidakis told me it was you that found out everyone is in the dark in Herakleion about Kazantzakis' funeral."

"Thank you."

"Are you writing your questions for Mansfield?"

"Mostly erasing them," Freddy replied, and they both laughed.

"Did you go anywhere yesterday?" he asked but his colleague had already left without a word, only to return moments later, holding a chair which he set on the other side of Freddy's desk.

"I was at the set of Cacoyannis' film. It's being shot at an old manor on Voulis Street," Peter said as he reached into his white shirt pocket and retrieved an Assos tobacco case. He put his cigarette to his lips and kept the case open, offering one to Freddy, but he declined with a shake of his head, pulling a glass ashtray from the third drawer in his desk.

"Who's in it?"

"Lambeti is the lead. She's really good, Freddy."

"Oh don't I know it! And what's it called?"

"*The Final Lie*. A drama with some comedic elements."

"Shall we go see it when it premieres?"

"We sure can, Freddy. I'll arrange a double invitation for you, so you can bring your girl along."

"You know, Peter, I'm not seeing anyone now."

"Well don't be all dramatic about it like it's one of Cacoyannis' next films!"

"No, of course not. It's just that everyone keeps telling me I should be in a relationship and other such clichés for my age."

"Well, that goes for every age. And you're not the cliché type anyway."

"Of course not!"

"Look, I don't mean to pry, but, since we're on this particular subject….is it true you were with a woman who was much older than you, who worked in a cabaret, when you were seventeen?" Peter asked hesitantly.

Freddy smiled at the question.

"Yes it is!" he replied with enthusiasm.

"But how?" Peter wondered, fully aware he had crossed the line he'd set for himself.

"I was pretty wild when I was seventeen. Not that I've settled down now, but anyway, I was out walking one night when I saw her and a bunch of soldiers going into the Ritz. I followed them because they were foreigners, Americans, and I wanted to know what they did for a good time."

"But you knew it was a cabaret..."

"Of course. It said so on the sign outside," Freddy admitted as they shared a laugh. "So in I went, they saw me young, I asked a couple of cute questions and they liked me..."

"And how did your mother take it?" Peter pressed on, absolved of any guilt in asking the questions, enthralled by the charm of the misdeed.

"She didn't, because I made sure she never found out."

"Come on, where did you tell her you were going all those late hours?"

"I didn't say. She trusts me completely, she knows I'm very mature for my age. And curious, of course."

"And how long were the two of you together?"

"Enough. It was fascinating for a time, then I grew tired."

"Fascinating how?"

"It was like I came out of my fishbowl. I'd been very sheltered, with my mother, grandfather and grandmother; they would tell me about what went on in the world, but I couldn't really grasp it. I really saw the world as it was there: women who had lost their husbands in the Civil War, trying to charm drunk American soldiers who were missing their farms and ranches back home; silent, brooding men, drinking to forget the things they had seen; unsavory characters waiting for the night to come so they could leave home and remember they were still alive; lovers out of luck; married men with a long, insufferable married life ahead of them; unsuspecting young men, unaware that youth is a curse..."

"Could you really live a life like that, Freddy?" Peter asked thoughtfully.

"Only if I'd hoped for something. Hope makes people persevere. If you have hope, you can hold out. When hope runs out, that's when you can be saved. That's when you take the first ship out of Piraeus and don't bother asking where it's even going. That's what I would do, that's how it should be done, if you want my opinion."

"That would make for a great book."

"I'm already writing it," Freddy replied proudly, though with a tinge of restraint. He always felt that self-restraint when he said something about himself that could be seen as overconfident or arrogant.

"Bravo! Bravo!" Peter exclaimed. "Will you publish?"

"That isn't up to me. I'm in the process of editing it now."

"Do you have a title?"

"No, just a thought for now. Perhaps *Wet Nights*."

"I'd like to help you. Let me know when you are ready," Peter said with a wink, prompting a spontaneous smile from Freddy over this unexpected vote of confidence.

"Thank you very much, Peter."

"Alright, back to work now. Back to Jane Mansfield," Peter Charis exclaimed triumphantly, shot up from his chair like a spring, and was gone. Freddy watched him go quietly, feeling obliged.

Freiburg

"Nothing. They say they don't know anything at the consulate. I called the embassy, too, but it's the same," Agnes explained in desperation.

"Don't get worked up, my dear child," Helen said, remaining calm. "Haven't you figured them out by now? They're doing everything they can to infuriate you, and it's working."

"But it's just a piece of paper, a formality," Agnes replied, having calmed down.

"Nothing is just a formality for the Authorities when it comes to Kazantzakis," Helen rejoined, as she sat at her beloved table, scribbling on a piece of paper.

"But we're just sitting here, waiting for them to start moving when we should be transporting him to Greece...This is just unacceptable!" Agnes fumed, then stopped suddenly.

"What are you writing, Helen?"

"Just the things I need to get done," Helen replied as she continued writing.

"Well, now that we've taken care of the coffin and the transport, I wanted to ask you something else, Helen. What will you wear?"

"Black, of course," Helen replied naturally.

"We'll need to buy a dress and a veil tomorrow. You won't be wearing a black kerchief but you'll need a veil," Agnes counseled her.

Helen raised her gaze from the paper to give Agnes a pensive look.

"Yes, you are right, Agnes. I must not allow any talk at the funeral."

"As you know, every eye and every camera will be on you."

"Rest assured, I will not disappoint," Helen said with determination. "Though there is something else that is troubling me, and you just confirmed my concerns, Agnes."

"What is it?" Agnes asked, alarmed.

"I'm worried either the Church or the Authorities will have an ugly surprise in store for us," Helen uttered suspiciously.

"If they did that to a dead man, they would insult their very existence."

"Well I know that, but are you sure they'd agree with you?" Helen asked wisely.

"No. No I'm not at all sure," her friend replied.

They sat quietly until the waitress arrived to take their order. The two friends enjoyed schnitzel and sausages, while Helen asked one more question, this time aimed not at her friend and supporter, but rather at the lawyer who had seen to all the legal details governing the collaboration of two creative minds.

"Did they tell you, Agnes, when Dassin's film, *He Who Must Die* will premiere in Greece?"

"End of November, probably."

"I'm so glad he had a chance to see it."

"It was one of his crowning moments in Cannes, wasn't it?"

"How could it not be? It was sheer pandemonium when it aired. The photographers were all calling out, "Nikos, Nikos," just to get a shot of him, journalists, film critics and politicians all waiting in line for a handshake. And our Melina, of course, who was brilliant in it, and our Dassin, who had been converted by Nikos into a proper Cretan!"

"I remember the reviews when it came out, in *Time*, in the *New Yorker*, and you, with that elegant print dress in the photograph, standing next to Nikos and Dassin, all dressed up in their black tie smocks, and Melina looking radiant. I've kept those newspaper clippings." They both laughed.

"Oh you should have seen Jean Cocteau, who was president of the committee that year. He ran straight into Dassin's arms, very moved. I will never forget the expression on his face as he shook Nikos' hand. And who wasn't at that movie screening! Imagine, even the French President, Coty, attended the premiere in Paris, which was on the same day as the screening in Cannes. So many journalists stopped Nikos for a statement, from America, France, Germany, Sweden, and it was always the same.

"Nikos would set himself aside to glorify Dassin, describing him as a genius. 'I am moved by how faithfully and how true to the local color Dassin has delivered the book *Christ Recrucified*.' He'd said it so many times I simply can't forget it. I can hear him now, saying 'Dassin is a great director.' Of course, along with Nikos' voice, I also remember the protests of the members of the Turkish cinematic mission, who demanded that the scene where the Turkish Aga of Lykovrysi executes Greeks for his pleasure with legendary brutality be cut. But their voices, of course, were not heard by the French organizers."

"Wow!"

"Do you know how long they worked on that script in Antibes? Jules and Melina were crazy about Nikos' Cretan stories," Helen reminisced with a taut smile on her lips. "And after, Dassin invited him to the set in Crete, but he refused. He didn't want to go. He sent me."

"Why didn't he want to go?"

"He never did tell me the real reason, just some ridiculous excuses that only furthered my belief that he would never tell me."

"Was it his trouble with the Church?"

"It had upset him. He couldn't stomach how *Captain Michalis*, a work in which the entire Cretan spirit reigns, was charged as an unpatriotic work. He'd write to Knös: 'I sit here in solitude, quiet, dedicated to my duty, to work as hard as I can on the Greek language and the eternal Greek spirit'. How could he fathom what his enemies would come up with each time to slander him?"

"Our own priests almost excommunicated him."

"The Patriarch came to their rescue. You see they wanted to outdo the Pope, who had placed *The Last Temptation of Christ* in his Index of Forbidden Books. Can you imagine, asking for books to be banned, as though it were the Occupation? Only the Nazis burned books, and our own priests almost followed suit. Melas riled the people, calling for bookstores to be smashed, remember that?"

"I sure do... Come, Helen, let's go to our room, it's time to rest. We need to finish with the formalities tomorrow."

"Let's go, Agnes dear."

They paid their bill and retired to their room. *This is the best time of the day*, Helen thought; the time when Nikos would come to her thoughts and she could relive all their little, every day moments from Aegina and Antibes. How he would tease her and she would chuckle and then they would go on long walks together, in parks or museums, and would play their favorite game, guessing which country they would visit in a year's time, or how he would detail to her his next matchmaking endeavor, for he truly loved matchmaking.

THURSDAY OCTOBER 31, 1957

Freiburg

The streets around the University Hospital of Freiburg were bedecked with celebratory wreaths crafted by the local women. October might have been ending, but the stubborn morning sun had made its appearance for the third consecutive day, affording Agnes and Helen a brief moment of warmth before they turned left at the hospital entrance, where they suddenly felt the same tightness form in their insides, as though it were a prerequisite for entering the building.

Tapita Swetzer, Helen's favorite nurse was not on shift that day, and so a fellow nurse offered to lead them to the office to complete the paperwork. Everything had been seen to in half an hour, and all that was missing were the accompanying documents from the consulate. Helen felt a dangerous knot form in her stomach when she followed the nurse to the room where their luggage had been kept. The nurse asked if she wanted to take any personal effects, and Helen began searching desperately for his pipe and his glasses. She might have even brushed her hand over them as she rummaged through the luggage, and not have known it. Who could blame her? Certainly not the nun, who surely had witnessed many such moments.

She offered to search for Helen, and two moments later Helen tenderly held in her hands the paper bag with her beloved's personal effects. She left the room and quickened her pace to the office, where Agnes and a hospital administrator were waiting for her. Agnes had already consulted with the funeral home regarding the transport, and figured she would secure the transportation license and the remaining documents the next day. She requested to make a phone call from the hospital office to the consulate, in order to press matters and make things go faster.

Helen went out for the last time. She lifted her gaze up to the room where she had spent her final days with him. The image of him at the window, waiting impatiently for her filled her thoughts. She did not hate the building or anything in it – if anything, it had been here, with Heilmayer and his treatments that Nikos had received each year, that he had gained five years of life. Helen clutched the paper bag closely, as though she held something priceless; the possibility of losing it terrified her.

"Come on, we have work to do," Agnes said as she came hurriedly down the stairs.

"What's happened?" Helen asked, alarmed.

"Nothing. I asked the hospital staff where we could find women's clothing fit for a funeral and she suggested a good store a few blocks away from our hotel."

"Please, Agnes, I know it's important, but I really don't feel up to it right now," Helen said softly.

"I understand that, but it must be done. By midday tomorrow you'll be on your way to Antibes. When will you have the time to find something decent to wear? We talked about this..." Agnes insisted.

"I know, you're right."

"Good, that's what I wanted to hear. It isn't for fun, it's an obligation," she said, linking her arm through Helen's.

"Agnes, it's the money, too. You know that my financial situation doesn't allow me to spend a lot," Helen tried to excuse herself, having learned to be frugal at the side of the best teacher.

"I know that too, Helen. I repeat, you don't need to worry."

The two women walked on with the secret hope that they would meet with the soothing sun once more where they'd last seen it, at the hospital entrance. They were in luck. Fifteen minutes later, they walked into the women's clothing store. To their good fortune, it was as serious and modest a store as the hospital staff had described to Agnes, and the owner hastened to accommodate them. A modest, wide black dress with light fabric drew Helen's attention for its simplicity. After all, she'd be wearing a veil; she didn't need anything else, only to strike one more item off of her macabre to-do list.

They exited the store, with Agnes holding the bag with the dress and Helen clutching her precious paper bag. When they returned to their hotel by early noon, the kind receptionist informed Agnes that the consulate had called. *The papers must be ready*, Helen reasoned. Her thoughts were confirmed a few moments later.

"Helen I have to go to Frankfurt to get the documents. They are ready. I think I'll have enough time to leave with the hearse for Athens tonight."

"Are you sure, Agnes dear? You'll be traveling all night!" Helen asked her lovingly.

"Absolutely," she replied, steadfast.

"Then I'll get going as well."

"Yes, and by tonight you'll be in Antibes."

"Let's go pack, then," Helen said.

Half an hour later they were at the train station, getting tickets. They agreed to meet in Athens on Saturday, and arranged every detail, even exchanging phone numbers of their acquaintances should something go wrong. When it was time for Agnes to board the train, there was no internal strength, no command her mind could issue that could force Helen to withhold her outburst in her friend's arms.

"Thank you," she managed to utter before breaking down into tearful sobs.

Agnes broke down with her.

"My Helen! I will always be at your side. Never forget it," she whispered, unsure if she had heard her, but words meant nothing to Helen in that moment; what mattered was that her friend had put all her words into action.

Athens

If one were to view Hellenikon airport from above, one would think it was a contemporary island surrounded by antiquated structures from centuries past: stone houses, dry fields, pens filled with flocks of hungry goats and sheep. But that last weekend in October of 1957, at half past six in the evening, there was one more flock – this time, of young men, more than two hundred of them – which had besieged the building as they waited impatiently for the arrival of the American sex symbol, Jane Mansfield.

Wearing his favorite coat, Freddy looked out of the waiting room window at the scenes below, sometimes in awe, at other times in disgust. He waited in the practically empty waiting room with his colleagues – journalists and photographers from other newspapers – who were also there to cover her arrival. Freddy had spoken earlier to the manager whose firm was responsible for bringing Marilyn Monroe's competitor to Greece. He had informed him that the flight would be arriving late, and had entreated upon Freddy in a manner that made it impossible for him to decline.

"If you would, son, please write something about her schedule."

Freddy pulled out his notepad and a small pencil from his inner coat pocket, and turned his attention to the manager.

"I'm listening."

"Tomorrow night we'll be going to the Attikon club at ten p.m. After that, dinner at the Kastron. Then the day after tomorrow, she'll be at Asteria, at the dinner hosted in her honor by Olympic Airways and Skouras Films, which has brought her to Greece."

Freddy repeated the last words quietly, so that the manager might be convinced he was faithfully recording the statement.

"Naturally, we'll give her a tour of the ancient sites in the city," the manager added, making it clear he wanted the list of restaurants and clubs to feature in the article, instead of her tour of the antiquities.

"Well of course she would want to see the ruins," Freddy remarked with a hint of sarcasm, having recorded nothing from the last statement.

"I'd like to speak with her for fifteen minutes," Freddy said.

"Fifteen? Out of the question! What about three?" the manager negotiated.

"Well then you'll only get a single column in our paper," Freddy replied with a confident air of power.

"I'll try for more, but I can't guarantee anything. Maybe seven minutes," the manager rejoined before walking away, apparently seasoned in these types of negotiations.

Freddy opened his notepad to the section he had jotted down his questions for Jane Mansfield. He had done his research well; he had tracked down an interview she'd given with tantalizing information on her habits. An hour passed, and he decided to stretch his legs; it was already eight thirty and there wasn't a plane in sight, much less a plane on the horizon carrying a sex bomb. All he could hear was the occasional bleating commingled with the sounds of other livestock grazing around the area.

The carmine sun had receded into the waters of the Argo-Saronic Gulf some time ago, leaving behind a darkness which had spread over the well lit contemporary oasis. Freddy felt warm and started to take off his coat, when he realized it would ruin his crisp image of the austere journalist, and decided against it. He stood to the side of the reporters who had gathered, and, staring nonchalantly through the window, listened in.

"I'm telling you, even the *Times* wrote about Kazantzakis. We got a call from our readers in New York, and they told us about it. We're publishing it in our paper," one of the reporters from *Vima* said.

"What's happening is a tragedy. This past March everyone was talking about Kazantzakis, about Dassin and Melina Merkouri, in Cannes, everywhere. Everyone but us, here. He wasn't even admitted to the Academy of Athens. All of it the work of Melas and his cronies, because he's a communist, you see," commented another reporter.

"Why, wasn't he a communist? Serves him right!" came another voice, obviously a reporter of a populist paper.

"What are you going on about? Did you know that insanity withheld a Nobel Prize in Literature from your country? And that, to achieve it, the Palace sent Melas to Sweden, to slander Kazantzakis there with the help of our ambassador, saying he's a corruptor of youth and shouting that he's a communist? Isn't that a shame?" thundered the reporter from *Vima*.

"He was a communist and godless. He wanted to corrupt our children, to bring the Reds to Athens. He was a communist Slav, not a Greek!" the other reporter retorted, practically screaming.

"Who are you to judge who loves his country more? You and all those who think like you couldn't do what Kazantzakis has done for Greece, not even in five hundred years."

"Go on, tell that fanatic!" another journalist prodded.

"And what about your children? Are they such fine Christians that you fear a simple book can turn them godless? And not even a religious book, but a novel! Which, if we're being honest, they probably would never read," the journalist from *Vima* continued as everyone burst into laughter.

"Sure, fine, make fun. When the Russians are stepping foot in Greece, then we'll see what you have to say, you brainless bunch. Why would I respect someone who disrespects the Christ, who reviles our priesthood?" the fanatic reporter retorted.

Freddy turned around sharply, ready to respond, but controlled himself and turned back. *This isn't your fight, Freddy, yours is coming in a few days*, he thought to himself. He stayed near, however, waiting to hear what would come next. He had never heard any of Kazantzakis' detractors in person, and was curious to know how the man would support his argument.

"Who says Kazantzakis doesn't respect Christ? The opposite is true! And why respect a fallible priest, when he is worthy of our scorn due to his own actions? Come on, you turd, admit it," the reporter from *Vima* grinned as he paused slightly. "You really haven't read any of his books have you?" he asked, and the whole room shook with laughter.

The disparaging reporter was livid.

"You don't even know how to have a conversation. Go on, worship your communist corpse now," he screamed, and left the exit as he lit a cigarette.

Freddy felt so pleased with this moral victory as though his favorite soccer team, Panathinaikos had scored the goal right in Karaiskaki stadium!

"What's all the fuss?" sounded a voice from the offices. Everyone turned to see a police officer walking toward the group of reporters in his taut stride, assessing the situation with a look of power and authority.

"What is going on here, gentlemen?" the officer asked with an austere tone in his perfectly pressed uniform.

"It's nothing, a small disagreement," answered one of the reporters.

"What kind of disagreement?" the officer insisted, his gaze probing and inquiring.

"It's about Kazantzakis," the journalist from *Vima* replied.

"I will not allow that communist drivel to pollute my airport, do you hear me?" he raised his voice which managed, nonetheless, to retain its bass timber and its austerity.

It was clear he'd rehearsed this tone countless times before.

"Any disagreements are to be resolved outside of this room," he continued in perfect high Greek, while the reporters watched him, unperturbed. Then, in a sudden crisp move he turned and walked triumphantly back to his office.

I shouldn't be celebrating, Freddy thought as he watched the officer close the blue door to his office. He repeated to himself that his job was to be a neutral observer of events, that he could not give himself over to subjective judgments. *But dammit, freedom of speech and of expression is the first thing a journalist fights for! Of course I'm celebrating,* Freddy mused with a big grin. His euphoria lasted a brief moment, undercut by surprise as a loud booming noise rattled the window and shook the entire room.

"She's coming, she's coming!" he heard an enthusiastic voice exclaim, which was soon followed by many others until they commingled in a single chant: "She's coming, she's coming!"

The police poured out, swiftly forming a human chain with their hands, as though in position for some type of traditional dance. The white Olympic airplane seemed dauntless with its beak tilting upward as its hind quarters lowered gradually, as though it was something shameful to give up the air for land. Its wheels flirted momentarily with the ground, as if to resist, then gave way completely to the landing. The fans on the ground were in such a frenzied state that they broke through the police cordon while the airplane was still taxiing on the runway, and the police didn't seem to make any other effort to repel them. The young men were now besieging the airplane, running alongside it, like dogs chasing after a car, as it tried to reach its designated stop. The police followed suit behind them, trying to regain control of the situation.

When, at last, the stairwell was affixed to the plane and the door opened, an even wilder scene ensued: shouting and pushing, fans pressing against the police barrier while a medium height figure with infamous curves stood out in the shadow of the door frame, uncertain whether she should step out on to the stairwell amid this hearty Greek welcome. The reporters gathered to one side and began to record the desperation of the fans as they tried to worship their goddess, the police as they tried to corral the bleating mob, and the stewardesses as they tried to convince the sex bomb to disembark. Her manager tried to approach her as she looked out, astonished at the gathering crowd.

When things began to settle down, she eventually stepped out on to the stairwell, hesitant and platinum blonde, innocent and explosive! Her green blouse glistened in the dark and her tight tweed skirt highlighted her lively, restless and all too famous curves. She held a bouquet of flowers in her right hand, and a small white dog, which seemed miserable from all the shouting, nestled in her left hand. The police managed to form a barrier between the mob and the actress with her associates and her Greek manager.

All around them, fans were shouting her name, trying desperately to touch her, perhaps to make sure they were not dreaming, perhaps believing that if they could only touch her it would cure them of something terrible, though this seemed unlikely. The star seemed to asphyxiate in the police cordon, the dog seemed to asphyxiate in its owner's bosom, and the flowers now seemed more like wilted wildflowers and less like a bouquet. The traveling mob was making its way to the Foreign Visitor's Lounge, though at an abysmally slow rate; the journalists ran parallel to the crowd, entering the building on their own as they tried to not lose sight of the suffering star, even for a moment. The chaos continued for a few more minutes, until the police successfully kept the raving crowd at bay and the star slipped into the building.

The famous visitor retreated to a corner of the lounge, trying to freshen up. Her manager informed the reporters that the interviews would have to be brief; the reporters protested, but he was unyielding.

"She's far too shaken up, you all saw what happened," the manager said in his determined tone, and went back to check on the actress, who had by then regained her normal pallor and had slipped back into the role of being a star. After several minutes, the manager presented his illustrious guest to the press, and camera lights flashed across the room, something she seemed to enjoy.

"Alright, fellas! Freddy, you go first," the manager cued him, and the young man stood before her with a small smile and began his series of cheeky questions.

"Is it true that you sleep on black sheets?"

"Of course! Black sheets, black blankets."

"Why?"

She smiled.

"I feel more comfortable."

"And what do you think of marriage?"

"I'm not married."

"What do you think is the secret to your success?"

At this point her manager intervened with the requisite response.

"Her wit, of course, what else?" he said, thus ending what had been up to then a very promising interview.

Freddy did not complain; he almost enjoyed this premature ending to an inane conversation. He wanted to get back to his office and hand in his article as quickly as possible.

Freiburg

She leaned her head against the cold glass, and it was almost impossible, even for the most keen observer, to distinguish between the raindrops that fell on the window from outside and her tears that flowed on to the window from her sunken cheeks. She had been traveling for two hours, but in those last ten minutes the clouds had rained upon the German countryside much as her tears had rained upon the window. She pulled out a handkerchief from her purse and wiped her eyes.

A little girl with carrot-like hair and green eyes sat across the row from her, peering at her curiously. Helen tried to calm down. She thought about all of her childhood dreams when she was that little girl's age. How many lifetimes had she and Nikos experienced together? Three, perhaps four. Agnes' question came to mind once more; she wasn't sure which moment she had most feared that she might lose him, for he was always stalwart, detached from mundane things, slipping through the traps of death, invincible. She remembered the incident with the German soldier who had ransacked their neighbor's house in Aegina, in 1944. Helen had witnessed it and had come downstairs to report him to his superior.

Helen had been convinced that the soldier was responsible for one other theft in the area, and had gone to see the German garrison commander about it. He had gathered the soldiers so Helen could point out the culprit, and oh, how she remembered that moment, when the soldier had practically hid himself, last in line! One by one, his compatriots had snickered and made sarcastic comments, and when she finally singled him out, the commander had entreated her to not make a formal complaint.

"He's a good young man, he only took a lamp so he could light up his bunker. If you insist on this, our laws are very strict, it will ruin his future."

But Helen had been certain, and was proven right a short while after, when the soldier in question had tried to unload his stolen wares down a dried up well.

One night, not long after, while the couple had been sitting in their garden they had heard a whistling noise from afar, which although curious, was given no further thought. Nikos had suggested they go in so he could read to her from his latest manuscript, when they heard a sharp sound. He had turned on the light, then, and they had looked around but couldn't find anything out of the ordinary. It was only the following morning, when Helen had discovered the shattered jar of jam in the kitchen cupboard with a bullet lodged in it that she realized what had happened: the Germans had shot at them in the night, an act of vengeance for her actions.

What atrocities they had endured, and how many more they had only heard of! In the summer of 1945, the first one after the Liberation, Nikos had gone to Crete with professors John Kakrides and John Kalitsounakis on a fact finding mission to report on the state of Crete during that period. Even the greatest pessimist could never have expected to read the things listed in their report: desolate villages, bereft of the male population, ghost towns filled with ruined structures that signified civilized beings had once lived there.

When Nikos had later described to her what he had seen, Helen had shuddered. The unwarranted mass executions of the Cretans was just a historical fact to students, but what had come before and what followed after was a crescendo of savagery that Kazantzakis had documented in his report. The frenzied Germans had ransacked villages, pillaged everything of value, defecated in the cookware and then had moved on to the executions.

He had heard countless stories from Cretan girls about how their husbands had been shot in the head by the Nazis, how the women could only tell their dead apart by their clothes. "I scooped my son, ounce by ounce and put him in a bag so I could go bury him," a mother had lamented about her son who had perished in the slaughter of Amira.

There had been instances when the Nazis wouldn't allow the women to approach their dead, leaving their exposed bodies to the dogs. Other women had told him that, after the executions, the Germans would take pictures of them as they wailed over the corpses of their husbands and sons, and would make fun of them while they writhed in utter devastation. Each dead man was marked by a cross on the door of his home, and there were many houses that had four, or even five crosses marking the door.

Nikos had always felt moved when he recounted the words of an old woman he had met in one such village.

"I had five sons and none of them remain," she had told him.

"And why were they killed?"

"Because I was harboring the British."

"And why were you hiding them?" Kazantzakis had insisted.

"Because I thought of their poor mothers," she had answered.

What horrors they had survived, escaping alive and spiritually unscathed! They had escaped, and they had triumphed. She missed him terribly already; it was easy to retreat into the refuge of her memories when the present and the future seemed so uncertain. Alas, she was used to all of that. *I learned at the side of the master,* she thought to herself, feeling a measure of release from the Kafkaesque scenes upon which she had been reflecting.

Athens

It was about ten at night when he left the airport, Jane Mansfield with her little lap-dog and her flock of fans behind him. This time, he didn't see any elderly women clad in black, riding a donkey, as he'd seen just four hours ago when he had been en route to

Hellenikon; only tired carriages drawn by sleepy horses were out and about at this hour.

A few kilometers outside of the city's center were tantamount to a hundred years or more back in time. Freddy was a city boy, and not at all accustomed to what he saw on his travels beyond the city. He was out of his comfort zone, literally and metaphorically. The sights around him were truly remarkable, but Freddy focused on the structure of his text. He would first write about the whole "champagne in the bathtub" affair, then about the comical events that took place on her arrival, and would conclude with his interview. He imagined Androulidakis would not give him more than a single column for the article.

And even that's too much space, he mused.

Back in Athens, Freddy felt more at home. The billboards atop the Palia Athina club caught his eye: Tony Maroudas, Marika Nezer, Trio Belcanto, Martha Karagiannis, Beba Kyriakidou – the dream team of the age! He pondered how many days it had been since he'd last seen his friends, who were surely out somewhere having a good time. Curiously, it did not seem to bother him much that for yet another evening, he wouldn't be joining them.

Further down he saw an advertisement for the next day's premiere at the Idéal theater: "Lady Katherine presents, for the first time to the Athenian audience, the masterpiece *The Chalk Garden* by the famous author Enid Bagnold. Directed by Marios Ploritis. Starring: Lambros Konstantaras, Christos Tsaganeas, Aliki Vougiouklaki, Pamphele Santorineou, Aleka Paizi," he read aloud.

I should see that Vougiouklaki actress, too, he thought, *to see what all the fuss is about.*

A few moments later he was climbing the stairs to the newspaper offices, tapping his shoes on the steps as he went, trying to shake off any dusty remains of the journey he'd just had. He stopped by the chief-editor's office first, and lo and behold, he found him in his usual seat, pouring over stacks of paper on his desk. Thrilled to be back in his normal environment, Freddy knocked on the door and went right in.

"Good evening, Mr. Androulidakis," he said in an even voice.

"What's up, Freddy, my boy? How did it go out there? Is Mansfield really the sex bomb everyone says she is?" he asked without lifting his head from his papers.

"Not really," Freddy replied.

Androulidakis looked up, surprised, as Freddy smiled at him, full of innuendo.

"So you mean, she wasn't a sex bomb?" he asked again with a hint of sarcasm as the young reporter laughed, raising his eyebrows in the negative.

"Well what are you waiting for? Go write it! A little column, three hundred, four hundred words, tops."

Freddy happily obliged. As he sat at his rickety old desk, ready to write about his experience at Hellenikon, he felt out of sorts. Slumped over the empty page, he felt his eyes grow heavy.

C'mon, Freddy, write something good! Wake up! He could hear his thoughts, trying to force him awake.

What had impressed him the most? He wondered. Surely it was the whole affair with the champagne; *so I'll start off with that,* he mused.

An hour passed, he finished the article and took it straight to his chief-editor. Some of his colleagues from the political desk were in the room; Androulidakis cast a side-eyed glance at the article, and must have been pleased, Freddy thought, because he had that look he got when the outcome had proven him right.

"Gentlemen, what do you think of Jane Mansfield?" he asked the political editors. They shook their heads and shrugged, demonstrating they didn't know much about her.

"I see," he continued thoughtfully. "We don't seem to have an opinion, but we will certainly have one after we read what our correspondent at the airport – Mr. Freddy Germanos – had to say," and with that, Androulidakis began to read the article aloud.

"'Yes, it is true that I take a champagne bath. How much champagne? About fort-five bottles worth. French, naturally.'"

The other editors cracked up to the pleasure of their chief-editor. The article was garnering positive reactions from the very first lines.

"Such was the statement given to me last night by Jane Mansfield, the Hollywood siren traveling through Europe. At twenty-three years old, with platinum blonde hair and blue eyes, the result is entirely tolerable. Is the excessive furor surrounding her name justified? As with anything excessive, of course not. Jane Mansfield is a stunner, similar to all those other stunners produced by Hollywood each year. Beautiful? No. Cute, perhaps. The make-up doesn't leave much to be desired. I think if one saw her in a movie serving coffee to the protagonist, one would say, 'What a cute waitress'. It is possible that some ardent fan will disagree: 'Fine, sir, but what do you have to say about her body?' I admit I can not say anything. Mansfield's curves are abundantly clear – so clear that any clarification is unnecessary.

The Olympic plane that flew her from Rome landed at the Hellenikon Airport with a two-hour delay, at 9:16 p.m., where a crowd of her raging fans broke through the police chain – of course - rushed the aircraft, besieged it, and would certainly have carried Mansfield off had the police not countered at the last minute. The whole affair was reminiscent of a Greek-Turkish football match.

When the indecipherable cries had subsided and a relative calm ensued, Jane was finally convinced to appear on the plane's steps, where she emerged with an enormous bouquet of flowers in one hand, and a tiny, fluffy white dog in the other. Though she tried hard to hide it, it was clear that the intensity of her welcome had unnerved her.

She wore a glossy green blouse and a tight-fitting – naturally – tweed skirt. Slowly regaining her composure, she descended from the plane with her eyes half closed. But the route from the airplane to the foreign visitor's lounge proved to be an even more dramatic adventure for Jane Mansfield, more so than she had ever experienced, and one I hope she does not soon forget. Crushed to asphyxiation by an aggressive mob – a fandom absolutely starved for her, who at all costs wanted to talk to her, touch her, caress her hair, even tear a piece of her dress – she fought a heroic battle and finally made her way to the foreign visitor's lounge, sweating and exhausted.

Once there, she answered a few riveting questions during the course of our short discussion.
'Is it true that you sleep on black sheets?'
'Of course! Black sheets, black blankets.'
'Why?'
She smiled.
'I feel more comfortable.'
'And what do you think of marriage?'
'I'm not married.'
'What do you think is the secret to your success?'
At this point her manager intervened with the requisite response.
'Her wit, of course, what else?'"

The political editors, who had been laughing hard by the end of the article, erupted in congratulatory cheers and patted him on the back in praise. Androulidakis smiled as well.
"Bravo, Freddy. Go turn your article in."
Twenty minutes later he was sitting at his desk again. He did not know what time it was, but he did know he wanted to relive the experience he'd had in Androulidakis' office, over and over, with every chance he could get.
You can't simply wait for the opportunity, however, you need to create it, his young, impatient mind concluded, and the next chance lay right in front of him. He had already created it.

Antibes

The taxi dropped her off at the square. The entire neighborhood was in the throes of fall: trees bare, trunks weathered, mourning their nakedness, just as she was. To her right, the troubled Mediterranean reflected her turmoil. Darkness descended upon the stone-paved streets that were punctuated neatly by the fences of country home gardens. She paid the driver, who said something to her though she didn't hear him. She was lost in deep thought; four months before they had left this place for China. Nikos had been ecstatic at the chance to see all those things that had fascinated him, to speak to the wise men of the Far East, who would offer him the respect and the honor he deserved. He had carried on like a man returning to an old military post, with countless stories to tell about little streets and parks and friends he hadn't known before then and would never meet again after.

She remembered the day they left so intensely, each and every step of it. She approached the house with the number 9 on Rue de Bas Castelet – their home of a mere 559 square feet, which Nikos had called 'the coccoon' because "this is where the caterpillar becomes a butterfly". She gazed at the large iron ring handle on the garden gate, and hadn't crossed the threshold but ten minutes when she heard the sound of heels clanking on the cobblestone. She turned to see her beloved neighbor running towards her, arms outstretched. She dropped her luggage, waiting to fall into her arms. The two women broke down in tears, sobbing in each other's embrace. They were silent for a short moment, until Helen spoke.

"It's Nikos, Chrysoula, Nikos," she managed to utter.

"Cry, Helen," Mrs. Poiariet whispered, crying with her.

They sobbed together for several minutes, until the affable neighbor – a Greek woman from Smyrna in her sixties, prone to speaking fast and plenty, excessive in all ways – pulled out a plaid handkerchief and began to dab Helen's cheeks and then her own.

"Give me the suitcases," she said and grasped them without waiting for a reply. She stopped at the front door while Helen pulled her key out of her purse and turned it in the lock. The door made a terrible creaking sound, betraying how long it had been out of use. It also foreshadowed Helen's new lonely life.

The two women sat at the table, facing each other. Mrs. Poiriet had survived one of the darkest pages of contemporary Greek history. Married to a Frenchman, she had escaped the destruction of Smyrna at the last moment. When she had boarded the French ship that would carry them away from her burning homeland, she had implored the French to help her fellow countrymen. A Frenchman had approached her then, handing her a gun, and had instructed her to shoot at the people in the water, the people desperately trying to latch on to the ship's ropes. *Her* people. "You dogs!" she had cried out.

"I kept telling him, remember? Do you remember?" she asked, her teary eyes widening. "I'd seen it in the cup one day before you left, and I said to him, 'I see a grave.' And he just smiled..."

Helen nodded.

"And I remember what he answered you: 'To see a grave means a marriage. Just like in dreams.'"

"And that night before you left, I had terrible dreams. I told you both, but he just laughed."

Chrysoula's insistence had made Helen consider canceling their trip to the Far East at the last minute, and she had tried to talk him out of going. "Hold fast, now, my co-captain. You're not just going to give up now, that I am so excited to show you Peking?!" he had answered with a smile.

That incident bore into their thoughts, until Helen recalled an event Mrs. Poiriet did not know. At the end of August of 1926, Nikos had traveled from Athens to France by ship, and from there had taken the train to Spain, to cover the Spanish Civil War as a correspondent. While still aboard the ship, he had met an old Armenian woman who read his fortune in the cards.

"A great danger will soon come your way. Beware. You're life's purpose will be fulfilled, but it will come late in life."

Some days later, when his train suffered an accident in the Pyrenees, with several cabin cars overturning in the heavy rains, her words had come true. He had been pleased then, not because he had been fortunate to escape death, but because it meant that the second part of the old woman's prophecy was bound to come true: even at the end, his life's purpose would be fulfilled. *Had he ever forgotten?* Helen wondered. *Or perhaps he had been waiting patiently for that moment all his life?*

She shut her eyes, seeking out the dark in order to better frame that moment: it had been at this very house, eight months before. He had called her in one night, with his customary command. "Read to me, Lenotska. Let's see if there's anything worthwhile!"

That is what he called her whenever he wanted her to read one of his works; yet what Helen had read that night had been so unpleasant that she had struggled greatly to restrain her tears before him.

"I collect my tools: sight, smell, touch, taste, hearing, intellect. Night has fallen, the day's work is done. I return like a mole to my home, the ground. Not because I am tired and cannot work. I am not tired. But the sun has set."

She had yelled at him then, expressing her displeasure at the premature acceptance of his death. He had stood there unperturbed, as always.

"Calm yourself, dear companion," he had reassured her. "We've been through this. When I reach eighty-two is when you need to start worrying."

Then he had gone upstairs to write a letter to his dear friend, Pantelis Prevelakis. "I work hard, and in a few days I'll be done with *Report to Greco*... Helen did not want to copy it; she began to cry because it focuses on my death. She will have to get used to it, though, as must I."

Mrs. Chrysoula could not stop wiping her tears with her kerchief the entire time Helen spoke. The hour grew late; the tension that had been keeping Helen upright had started to fade and Mrs. Chrysoula offered to keep her company and sleep on the couch. Helen accepted the offer with a very warm embrace, trying to hide her tears.

She stopped by his office on her way to the bedroom; the silence was unprecedented, unrecognizable. She glanced at the bookcase, at the myriad of stacked books, and felt as though she were in a sanctum, a holy of holies. She walked out of there with the sudden certainty she would see him in her dream, with his jokes and his vibrant laughter. Their bed was no longer her bed. Their bedroom was a cold, rejecting wasteland. Her eyes closed and she began to drift before she even had a chance to see him in her dreams...

FRIDAY, NOVEMBER 1 1957

Antibes

Helen felt as though she had only closed her eyes for a few moments when she felt a light, repeated touch, stirring her. She jolted awake to her neighbor gazing sweetly at her.

"I let you sleep in a little while. It's nine in the morning," she said tenderly, and Helen jumped up, like a soldier on alert.

In just ten minutes she had pulled on her black clothes – that uniform – and, without taking breakfast, went to arrange the airline tickets that would take her to him, with her friend at her side. She would be returning to Greece alone, two years after the last time she had been there. Chrysoula told her of the countless letters and telegrams that had arrived and how she had seen to all of it.

They crossed the little square and Helen's gaze turned upward to the palm trees. It wasn't so long ago that she would wait patiently for their fruit to drop, she recalled. She would gather them and take them home, wash them well and then paint them different colors. Then she would thread them and transform them into necklaces and bracelets which she would sell to tourists.

"Helen, this gentleman wants to know when you'll be traveling," Chrysoula said for the second time, nudging her gently out of her reverie.

"The soonest possible. Antibes to Paris by train and then Paris to Athens by airplane."

"Okay. There's an available ticket for tomorrow afternoon at four."

The two women returned, arm in arm, back to the house. Chrysoula, ever the practical one, kept the quiet at bay as she suggested, "You should make a list of the things you'll be taking with you. It's not just the black clothes you're wearing – you'll need pictures of him, and something of his that he would want to take with him, too." Helen paused to consider the advice. She couldn't think of anything, not because she didn't know his treasured things, but because there were so many.

"You'll need three, maybe four black dresses and skirts. The press will be there, everyone will be looking at you. You must take care, Helen dear," she continued, wanting to protect her and prepare her for everything.

They parted at the gate of Helen's house. Chrysoula asked Helen to get some rest, telling her she would be by later in the afternoon to keep her company. They would take their tea together and prepare Helen's luggage for her trip to Athens.

Alone once more, Helen tried to decide which beloved artifact would escort Kazantzakis on his journey to immortality. It was that word, 'immortality' that flashed in her mind: "The first edition of the *Odyssey*, of course!" she cried triumphantly, wanting all of Antibes to hear her brilliant idea, one that would have made her husband proud.

She ran to find it in the bookcase with childlike enthusiasm. Her fingers brushed along the countless books packed on the shelves, as though she would find the book by touch alone. Her right hand trailed across to the middle shelf on the left edge of the bookcase, and, reaching up with her left pointer finger, gently pulled the *Odyssey* from its place.

The monumental composition was her husband's grand opus, with its 33,333 stanzas in 17-syllable verse. As unique as this work was, so too was the incredible story of how it was published – one that had left its indelible mark on Helen's memory since it first began, that first month of 1938. At the time, a rich and eccentric American woman named Joe MacLeod, follower of the Swami Vivekananda had asked Herbert – Nikos' old associate from UNESCO – to set up a meeting with Helen, who had already written a book of her own about Gandhi and had translated two of her husband's – and mentor's – books.

"I dislike rocks," she had made clear from the first moment of their meeting in Athens.

"I don't care for the Acropolis or for any of your ancient fare. I came here to meet people, to find out what kind of man Kazantzakis is, since you live with him. Let's go to Aegina right away; I want to meet him."

Tandin, as she was known by her pet name, may have been exceedingly wealthy but was certainly not wasteful. Once, during lunch, she had eaten only the white of her egg, offering Helen the complete yolk inside. Helen had declined, but Tandin had been quick to reply, "The yoke is unmarred and must not be thrown away." Helen had eaten it, to the sheer delight of their elderly guest.

"When I was a girl," Tandin had said, "I used to collect all the loose change I would find during house cleaning, above my door. I detest waste; to this day, I will pick up a stray match if I find it on the floor. Be frugal, Helen, don't permit yourselves any wastefulness. Not in yourselves, and not in others. But learn to be openhanded for important causes; there you can give freely, and God will reward you."

Tandin had observed the enormous manuscript on Nikos' desk, then, and how could she not? It was patently clear to anyone who stood in that office. She wanted to know more about it. "Is it the *Odyssey*, the one Jean spoke of?" she had asked, closing her eyes slightly. "Yes," Nikos had replied shyly. "This is our child, Tandin."

She had frozen momentarily.

"Well, what are you waiting for, then? If she's ready, why don't you publish? Tell me what is in it," she had commanded.

Nikos had begun to tell her about his Odysseus, who leaves Ithaca anew to traverse Egypt, then the whole of Africa, only to die in the Frozen South Sea, having organized plots and rebellions, known captivity, and founded a new city and a new God. Tandin had been enthralled with his narration. Though it was late, no one had stirred from their seat; he had continued, dauntless in his explanation of all he had written in thirteen years – in approximately fifteen thousand hours of work. Helen had asked if they needed the light on, when Tandin had turned to her bluntly.

"Go to my room and get my purse." When Helen had returned with the purse, Tandin had turned to Nikos.

"How much money do you need to publish?" Nikos had become flustered, not expecting such a question.

"I don't know... let's say fifteen hundred dollars?" he'd answered. She had pulled out her checkbook, then, and signed over a check to him.

That is how the *Odyssey* was published; it had circulated in a glorious edition with thirty copies, and he had dedicated it to Joe MacLeod. Nikos had kept the very first copy of that very first edition, and now, Helen reflected, that very first copy would accompany him in immortality.

Athens

Freddy walked with a different air each time one of his articles with his byline was published in the newspaper. His confidence flashed in his eyes, and poured out from his frame as he told his favorite kiosk vendor – who returned the sentiment, regardless of the profanities they'd occasionally exchange – to keep a copy of the paper for his grandfather, who would be by later to pick it up. And so it happened that Friday: he hadn't left home before telling his grandmother everything about his interview with Jane Mansfield, and the way his article was warmly received by Androulidakis and his other colleagues. He wanted her to feel proud of her grandson.

Peter Charis had told him to get to the newspaper as early as possible, because he wanted to give him information on Kazantzakis to read. When Freddy entered his office, he found a stack of old newspaper clippings waiting for him on his desk. He looked around for Peter, but he had stepped out on business. The coffee vendor had just delivered his coffee when he began to examine the newspaper clippings. The first one that drew his attention was an article dated March 31, 1955, with the headline "Man is a metaphysical, not a political animal: an interview by Robert Santulle."

"Largely unknown to a French audience when he published Zorba last year, the Greek novelist Nikos Kazantzakis has already emerged as one of the greatest authors of the post-war period. His new work, Christ Recrucified, translated by Pierre Amadou, has just been released by the publisher Plon, and justifies the reaction to the first novel of this great humanist, who today has withdrawn to the South of France."

Freddy focused on another paragraph.

"Romel, the local milkman had said to me, 'that man is a great man (i.e., Kazantzakis). He lives on an old road near the old town walls. He is easy to find. Everybody knows him.' At his home, the reception was quite friendly; Mrs. Kazantzakis prepared us some coffee, while her husband diligently filled his tobacco pipe."

The twenty-three year old reporter was fully absorbed by the text when he discovered something no one had written about yet. "'Do you plan to stay in France?'" the French journalist had asked Kazantzakis, to which the great thinker had replied, "'Yes, I plan to end my days here, in Antibes. I love this little town that reminds me so much of Greece. And I pray to have time to write a great deal more here.'"

Kazantzakis never intended to return to Greece. His self-imposed exile seemed easier to him than a return to Crete, to the land that had defined him as a person and as a thinker, Freddy wrote in his notebook.

What bitterness, what agony lay beneath his desire to be buried in the very earth upon which he took his first steps, yet made him determined to never step there again! How could his books be so infused with Crete and yet he not long to feel the Cretan air brush against his face?

Freddy could not comprehend it. What was the answer? What was the reason? Why had he chosen to leave? He decided he would have to discuss that with Peter, and continued to read the clippings.

A little under an hour had passed when the young reporter sensed a presence in the room. He looked up to see his chief-editor, smiling at him.

"Good evening, Freddy. What are you up to tonight?"

"I don't have anything planned, Mr. Androulidakis. Did you need something?"

"Yes. I want you to drop by the Grande Bretagne to see your girl."

"My girl?" Freddy asked, confused.

"Jane Mansfield! Don't tell me you forgot her already?" he asked in mock surprise.

"Yes, Mr. Androulidakis."

"Go around nine thirty tonight and come back and write a short article for tomorrow."

"Of course."

"What are you reading here?"

"Peter left a few clippings for me to read, of Kazantzakis' past interviews," he explained, enthused.

"However, there is something that is bothering me," he began carefully.

"Sure, I have some time. Tell me," his chief-editor prompted as he sat across from him.

"Kazantzakis loved Crete, he extolled Cretan culture, the overall Cretan stance on life, its traditions... Right?"

"Right!"

"Well then, why did he decide to leave and never return there but dead?" Freddy asked tersely.

"What's to wonder?" Androulidakis said with a smirk. "Haven't we told you enough about what they did to him?"

"But it's incomprehensible to me that he just backed down. That he let them win, that he surrendered," Freddy replied heatedly, as though his idol had betrayed him.

"How do you give in to a battle you haven't even waged? Kazantzakis left not because he was afraid, but so that he could create everything he had dreamed for himself, undisturbed. He didn't waste his energy fighting his detractors, he didn't permit himself to be lowered to their level, he didn't spend his strength on futile answers. He toiled, he wrote, he produced thoughts, ideas, he inspired. Unlike his moralistic abusers who sling mud at him, even today, unlike those pretentious Christians who curse him, those self-proclaimed patriots who rile up the gullible masses for their personal interests. So, don't get carried away, Freddy; Kazantzakis will go down in world history, not just Greek history, and his critics will be tossed aside into the trash bin of oblivion, forever enveloped by the stench of their foul misdeeds."

"I hope that's so," Freddy said softly, rather relieved by the assertion.

Androulidakis smiled.

"I'll tell you a story, Freddy, a recent one at that. About nine months ago, the cultural attaché at the American embassy, Mr. Emmerich, had invited a few journalists to inform them of the embassy's future cultural events. One of those events was a lecture on the *Odyssey* by an American professor. Our dear 'friend' Melas was also there, who, upon hearing about the particular lecture, practically exploded. He tried to convince the attaché and his colleagues that Kazantzakis was a 'Russian operative, doing their bidding', that the Americans ought to be more discerning of their friends and enemies, thundering that the lecture was unacceptable. Do you understand now, their wrath? Their fanaticism?

"And still, those 'ever willing servants to foreign agendas' hold strong public positions and try in every way possible to further along their own interests. Ultimately what matters is that you defend your own. That's true for each of us. If you get swept away, if you fall into their trap, then you're lost. And you don't just lose the game, the battle or the war; you lose your life."

"Sometimes I get the feeling you're describing Jesus. Didn't Kazantzakis have any flaws?"

"Of course he did. Of course..." Androulidakis pondered.

"Well, tell me one."

"I'll tell you what's been said about him by people who knew him well. He was very ambitious, so much so that he only cared about success, disregarding the problems of those around him. That's what Galatea says, anyway, and her circle seems to share that view."

"Well sure, but Galatea was his ex wife, so her credibility is to be taken with a grain of salt... But there's something else I want to know. From what I've read it's clear that Kazantzakis changed political camps over the years. In his youth, as a student in Athens, he was a follower of Venizelos. Soon after, he became a nationalist, a follower of Dragoumis. After that, he traveled to the Soviet Union, but after, called himself a meta-communist. Then he turned to socialism, even founded a party of his own, joined the Sofoulis government and then quit after two months."

"I've asked some of his friends about that, too. The explanation they offered is that he was always searching for the movement that will liberate people, until he realized that such a thing doesn't exist."

"And what about that interview with Mussolini?"

"He wanted to judge the measure of the man himself, to see the leader, his intentions, what to expect of him..."

"I see," Freddy replied.

"Kazantzakis wasn't a saint, he was a hermit, one who often couldn't bear to be with people. He liked to have his talent recognized, to be honored, but that was it. He often felt disgust with people. We're not dealing with a perfect man here, but with someone who wanted to change the world and just wanted to be credited for the effort. He certainly never harmed anyone. No one was forced to buy his books. And it doesn't matter if he was a brilliant novelist or a poet or a man of letters; what matters, in the end, is that he was persecuted every way possible by the official state and by the Church, and was forced to exile himself."

"Still, he didn't suffer the way other leftists and communists suffered," Freddy noted.

"Sure. He couldn't take it and simply left the country."

Freddy seemed calmer now. It wasn't that his outburst had settled him down, but that he now had an answer. That outburst would be one of a hundred during his lifetime, outbursts he would keep having until he figured out how to deal with each coming challenge, until he discovered the method he would follow to avoid being drawn into a battle that wasn't his own. *It doesn't matter if you win, only that you choose the battle that best represents who you are. Whether you win or lose, the stakes are what will define you,* he reflected.

Just then, Peter Charis stormed into Freddy's humble office which had fallen quiet. He was upset.

"Kazantzakis' remains are homeward bound from Freiburg. I don't know exactly when they will arrive in Athens."

"The body is being brought here first and then to Herakleion?" Androulidakis asked, thinking aloud.

"It's a little confusing on this point. I was told by a serious contact I trust, that Onassis offered an Olympic plane for the transport, but couldn't find Helen in time. So his remains are being brought back by hearse," Peter explained.

"Alright, gentlemen, we're in the final stretch," Androulidakis exclaimed with a serious tone befitting the historical moment. "Be on alert. Even the slightest detail can lead to something huge. And never forget: today's seemingly unimportant detail can lead to tomorrow's big story," the chief-editor said as he raised his right pointer finger for emphasis, and left the room.

"I may have heard that for the first time just now, but I'm fairly certain he's said that before," Peter Charis laughed.

"Isn't it obvious he's rehearsed that line?" Freddy asked humorously.

"Did you start reading over the clippings?" Peter queried.

"Yes, thank you very much. You saved me, they're invaluable," Freddy replied thoughtfully. "Did you know Kazantzakis didn't intend to return to Crete?" he asked, sharing the information he'd read.

"Why does that surprise you? When you are in center stage, internationally, and the whole of Europe is watching you, why return here to answer to Melas and everyone of his ilk?" his seasoned colleague replied quietly.

Freddy nodded. As he left his office, Peter suggested that Freddy call his Cretan friend in Herakleion, who was bound to have some information on the funeral of the great thinker. Freddy got up from his old weathered chair and looked out at Athens from the balcony. His face clouded over; he realized that, though he had impressed Androulidakis the day before with his approach to the Mansfield article, he had behaved earlier like a typical twenty-something, a frivolous boy prone to impulse, betrayed by his shallow, subjective judgment.

"That won't happen again," he said aloud, and his promise reverberated through his office, to be heard by the arms of the old weathered chair, the legs of the timeworn desk and the discreet drawer that opened and shut all those years, harboring so very many secrets.

It was still early in the afternoon when he placed the call to Herakleion, to the man he had never met, but imagined him as a short, dark, bearded man with large hands, flowing hair, and black pupils peering out of his bloodshot eyes. He didn't recall his name, though he looked for it in his old notepad. "The Cretan" was a good enough name at this juncture in the early, opportunistic phase of their relationship.

"Hello?" he heard his voice on the line and smiled.

"How are you doing, friend," Freddy said to him in an almost perfect Cretan accent. "It's Freddy Germanos, the reporter from *Eleftheria* newspaper."

"Freddy, good evening. I'm fine. How are you?" the Cretan answered with a familiarity unprecedented for an Athenian, though entirely expected from a Cretan.

"I'm looking for an update on the funeral....Have you heard anything down there?" Freddy asked in a lively manner, perhaps a bit swept away by his friend's colorful tone.

"A lot of meetings are taking place. Some say we should bury him in a cemetery, others at Martinengo, others still, that we should build a mausoleum."

"What's a Martinengo?" Freddy asked, having never been to Herakleion.

"It's the old bastion on the Venetian Walls. It's the highest point in the city, with a view of the mountains, overlooking the sea."

"And he's going to be buried there?" Freddy pressed.

"It seems like the Church might have to decide. I'm not entirely sure, though."

"You still don't know?" the reporter asked.

"Well, seeing as they think he's godless, they're not inclined to bury him in a cemetery," the Cretan explained in his frank, guileless manner.

"But do you think that's true?" Freddy insisted, having sensed a story there. Or was it blood in the water? Both were attractive to reporters. He pulled out his notebook from his desk and made note of everything he wanted to follow up on.

"I don't know for certain, but I'll call you if I hear anything."

Freddy was not satisfied with this answer, but couldn't really press further.

"Alright, friend. Thanks for the tip and for all your help."

"How 'bout you? Do you have anything to share?" the Cretan asked, emboldened by the exchange.

"I know your compatriot has left Freiburg in a hearse. It'll stop in Athens, first, and then will continue on to Herakleion," Freddy threw him the morsel, to make him feel important and trusted.

"I see. And when will you be down?" the Cretan asked. "I want to meet you."

"Oh we've been over that. We'll have a few drinks. I'll be down the day of the funeral."

"Alright. Goodbye, now," the Cretan said and hung up the phone before Freddy even had a chance to thank him. He ran to Peter Charis' office.

"Peter, they're going to bury him at Martinengo Bastion," Freddy yelled, reading from his notes.

"Martinengo? That's odd. There's nothing up there," the reporter said, perplexed.

"Maybe the Church doesn't want him buried in the cemetery," Freddy answered. "They're considering building a mausoleum," he added, flipping through his notes.

"That's the bad news...and the troubling news," Peter said, lowering his head. "But good job, Freddy! I'm going to go brief Androulidakis. If you hear anything else, let me know," his colleague said with an encouraging pat on the back in recognition of a job well done.

Freddy returned to his office. He started writing his column on overnight pharmacies for the next issue, but quickly gave it up and plunged headfirst back into the newspaper clippings on Kazantzakis, much the same way his chief-editor often was found headfirst in paperwork, which Freddy always found funny. Flipping through the clippings, he paused at an interview Albert Camus had given about Kazantzakis. It was from the Greek newspaper, *Vima*, with Leon Karapanagiotis, dated April 28, 1955:

"'Of course I know your poets,' he says. 'You have Sikelianos, Cavafy, but there is also a contemporary author whom I know well and admire, and that is Kazantzakis. I've read his tragedies, his Zorba, and recently his Christ Recrucified, which has been translated into French, and was very successful in Paris. To tell the truth, I prefer Zorba; it seems to me a work that is more Greek, more colorful...'"

Freddy read the article, sucking it all in, enjoying Camus' words as though they were the first coffee of the day.

"'My ambition is to one day direct his Melissa, a theatrical work that I admire and love very much. I gave it to Hébertot, the owner of the famous theater, who returned it to me, saying,

"Thank you for giving me this brilliant work, which I truly enjoyed, and which, if ever staged, would put me out several millions." His position of course was crushing, but I continue to hope, because, I know Hébertot.'"

Freddy removed his glasses and placed his thumb and forefinger over his tired eyes, pressing hard as though he were trying to squeeze out the defeat he felt. He rubbed his forehead several times. How entangled were the lives of great figures! A few days before Kazantzakis died, he had lost the Nobel Prize to Albert Camus, a worthy colleague. The summit is there to be conquered by great figures, who urge others to follow them: Camus, Kazantzakis, Sikelianos, all of them inspired by the same ideals, forged in the same quests, fulfilled in their travels, had all longed for ears to hear them, minds to understand them, kind hearts to accept them. *I hope I can stand next to great men like that when I am forty or fifty*, Freddy thought. *If they even exist by then...*

The clock struck half past nine, when Freddy suddenly jumped from his desk.

"Oh, no, Mansfield!" he cried out, and pulled his jacket on quickly as he ran down the stairs. Fortunately, the Grande Bretagne Hotel was nearby. He ran there in five minutes, and slowed down just before the entrance, straightened his jacket, ran his hand through his hair and crossed the threshold calmly. Assuming an air commensurate of the fine space, he inquired after the star, and was shown to a large ballroom, which he noticed was filled with the same reporters he'd seen the day before at Hellenikon airport. Freddy looked across the room to an empty red 'throne', which, he surmised, was awaiting its queen.

"Freddy, what can I say? Your article on her was quite sarcastic."

"Oh come on," Freddy said without seeing the man who was speaking behind him. When he turned, he realized he was standing face to face with the starlet's Greek manager.

"Where is she? When is she coming out?"

"In a little bit. Freddy, it was pretty sarcastic," the man repeated, trying to press his point. The young reporter was sure to let him know it.

"It was just a game with the actress, that's all. What did she do today?"

"She went swimming in Glyfada," the man answered.

"Where can I sit for a quick interview?" Freddy asked. "I'm in a hurry, I need to return to the office before this issue goes to print."

"Over there," the man pointed next to the 'throne'. "I'll signal her to start with you. This time, please ask her about her future plans."

Freddy moved to the seat indicated by the ruffled manager. From this spot he could view the entire room: businessmen, actors, Athenian socialites and journalists were all packed together, some to evaluate the Hollywood star, some to compare themselves to her, and some to have their photograph taken with her – proof of their status. Just then a vanilla scent wafted through the air to the other side of the room, where Freddy was watching everything unfold.

The crowd parted like the Red Sea, and the blonde enchantress entered, like a different Moses, swaying her attractive curves gracefully, knowing full well where all the men – and women – were staring. She was wearing silver heels and a tight-fitting red dress with a deep decolletage, and was just mere steps away from her 'throne' when the reporters started bombarding her with questions. She sat down, visibly vexed.

"What is it with everyone wanting to know about the bathtub? Is it so odd to bathe with champagne?" she complained, and the room fell silent.

"Not entirely odd," Freddy offered. "Only somewhat..." he said with innuendo, letting her know she had misfired with her question.

"Well that's because you haven't tried it. If you had..." Mansfield responded.

"So you bathed with champagne again today?" Freddy asked.

"Of course."

"Greek champagne?" he insisted.

"I think so."

"Were you satisfied?"

"Somewhat. I prefer pink champagne, you know."

"I see," Freddy said, beginning the interview where he had left off with the previous one.

"What did you think of the commotion at the airport yesterday?"

"Oh, it was *adorable*," she replied, smiling for the first time after their verbal sparring match.

"I beg your pardon?" Freddy asked, surprised.

"The crowd….It was just adorable. So lively, so spontaneous," she replied, maintaining her broad smile.

"Still, it seemed like you were frightened for a moment," Freddy noted.

"Me? Are you joking?" she asked, and her smile froze in place, betraying her annoyance. "Who do you take me for?"

"What do you think of Marilyn Monroe?" Freddy asked, going on the offensive.

"She's cute," was her immediate reaction. "Now if she could just act..." the barb followed seconds later.

"Can you?" Freddy asked with feigned innocence, annoying her to such a degree that she flashed him one of her most murderous glances, a look few had ever seen.

"I think so."

"They say you are more popular than Monroe," Freddy tried to compliment her to calm her down.

"You're very kind if you really think so," she shot back sarcastically.

"Truly Jane, to what do you credit your success?"

"To the kindness of the press," she said, clearly enraged.

"Is it true you went swimming at Glyfada today?" he asked as a formality.

"Of course. It was lovely. The blue sky, the blue sea, the golden sand."

"Are you a poet?" Freddy rejoined, dripping with sarcasm, while she sighed aloud like a first year acting student.

"I was...once."

"So...it was nice at Glyfada?" he circled back.

"Yes, it was a dream. Except for those little crabs..."

"What about those little crabs?" Freddy queried, trying hard to restrain his laughter.

"They pinched me," she pouted.

"You don't say!"

"Honest!"

"And what are your future plans?"

"Do you even care?"

"Very much."

Freddy recorded everything in his little notebook, then sped out of the ballroom. He exited the hotel and quickened his pace. *What a piece of work that Mansfield was*, he thought with a chuckle, knowing already how warmly his next article would be received by Androulidakis, his colleagues and his readers.

Antibes

Helen spent the rest of the day in Nikos' office, opening condolence letters on the loss of her husband, letters suffused with the scent of cinnamon and nutmeg which he always kept on his desk because he found the smell inspiring. When she wasn't bursting into tears, she was lost in remembrance. The view from the window was a palette of blues, from the deep blue of the Mediterranean to the light blue of the sky. Her gaze happened upon the trash bin which was filled with crumpled papers. She unfolded them and sat at the desk to read them.

"'I bid farewell to everything, and everything bids me farewell,'" it said.

He knew it, she thought, *but he wanted to keep his promise, to show me China and Japan.* Her tears flowed uncontrollably, a tribute to their selfless, embattled love.

She heard the gate rattle, and went to the window. A feminine silhouette was climbing the stairs, and soon knocked on her door. A young, dark haired girl, demure, stood at the threshold and motioned to her. Helen looked at her, silent.

"Good morning, Mrs. Helen," the girl began politely. "I'm Katerina Angelaki, daughter of John Angelakis. I just wanted to convey my deepest condol—"

"My dear girl, how you've grown!" Helen exclaimed and embraced her. She was their god-daughter; Nikos had baptized her and had been incredibly fond of her. It seemed the spiritual gifts of the godparent had had great effect on the young girl, though she was well influenced by her father as well. The first poem she had ever sent to her godfather had been published in a literary journal following his suggestion, and had made quite a stir.

"My parents told me I should come now, to help you," she continued.

Helen lowered her gaze.

"Come in, settle down," she urged, putting her suitcases aside. "You must be tired."

"Not at all. Don't worry about me. Tell me, how can I help?" the girl asked firmly.

"I'd like you to write to Goudelis. Let him know the funeral will be held on Tuesday, at Herakleion."

"Yes, I'll do that right away."

Helen went back up to his office, to his most private space, where she felt his presence the strongest. She sat once more, reading condolence letters, thinking to herself, how many letters she had read in her lifetime! How many letters of joy and sorrow! She tried to recall which letter had been the most joyous, which one sprang to mind most strongly. *Easy*, she mused a few moments later; *the one from April 13, 1947*. She remembered the date, remembered they had both sat on the bench, and Nikos had given her the letter informing him of the glowing review of his book, *Zorba*. She remembered how she'd celebrated with him, when he had smiled a bitter smile and said, "It's too late now."

That day marked the beginning of his rise to acclaim. A few years later, his *Zorbas* would be voted 'Best Foreign Book' in France and the whole of Europe – and soon after, the people would come to know the true life philosopher from Macedonia. Kazantzakis had been right. *It was late,* Helen thought. Such joyous recognition should come while one is still young and hungry, otherwise it is simply a vindication, which does not allow for celebration or joy, only anguish because it came late. He didn't even get to experience his vindication. Could one possibly not care? *Perhaps,* she thought, *if one had known relentless enemies and sorrows, perhaps one could.* Her mind turned to Aegina, to those first hours after the Liberation when the Germans had withdrawn, leaving the country to the British and to their cohorts, who just hours earlier had been German collaborators.

How could she possibly forget, that, at the moment she should have been overjoyed with the Liberation, two Greeks had come to their home with guns, threatening to kill them, and had carted them off to jail because, they had said, they were communists. It was incomprehensible to her. Only he had remained calm.

"Have you ever killed Nazis?" Nikos had asked.

"No," they'd replied.

"Well, have you ever killed anyone?" he'd asked again.

"No," they'd answered.

"And you're going to start with us!?"

They simply hadn't answered. The couple had been hauled to the basement of the local Gendarmerie. Perhaps it was then that Nikos decided he'd be more productive far away from his homeland, far from the maniacal pursuit the authorities had launched against him.

Helen began to read his mail, the letters he loved to read over and over again. She found the one from Albert Einstein: "We thank Nikos for sending us his German editions." Another, from Angelos Sikelianos, their best man, and Nikos' spiritual brother; then another, from Prevalakis, from Zorbas, from her. All of his life, his thoughts, his friends, his cares... Helen thrust her hand over it all, tumbling the letters to the floor, and broke down in tears.

"What made you give up?" she heard his voice through her sobbing, drawn out breaths. Her mind flooded with his words from their last trip to China, words that had affected her greatly. On one delightful occasion, when their Chinese friends from the Peace Committee had offered an impressive fete for their special guest, and though he seemed to enjoy the evening, he had suddenly sighed, "How I wish I could have a little water from my wellspring!" Helen tried not to make a big deal of it, for he would later tell her, "Don't worry. I'll die when I'm eighty-three, in the month of March."

Should she have ordered water from Crete? Would that have done him good? She faltered only to shake her mind clear moments later. *What am I saying? What am I saying?* she murmured, as she began to pick up the fallen letters and arrange his desk neatly. She laid in their bed, the one that had been so warm while he was still next to her, and which now was so detestably large that she was alone. She didn't cry that night; completely spent, she surrendered to sleep, hollow, her head aching.

SATURDAY, NOVEMBER 2, 1957

Antibes

Her two suitcases were ready, as ready as the sun that would accompany her to Paris. One by one, she had placed his things neatly in the suitcase: first, the *Odyssey*, then his pipe, and then his picture. The heavy items went in first; the lighter ones came last. She had grown accustomed to packing suitcases quickly, for she had learned the art long ago. Yet this was a trip no one wished to take, and knowing that she would have to endure the most devastating moment of her life on enemy ground frightened her. What would she find in Athens? How would she be received in Herakleion? What if the provocateurs tried to derail things? How can one bid their beloved farewell among enemies? *You hadn't prepared me for any of this,* she cried, despondent.

Her mind whirled to another memory, to the time he'd written an article on Greece for an American travel magazine. He had been asked to write about the beauties of the Greek islands. Privately, he'd always loved the aura of Mykonos, but for Crete, he had opted to write about a personal experience he'd had during one of his adolescent adventures.

He had loved nature since childhood, and so, when given the chance, he would put his satchel on his shoulders, grab a walking stick and hike up to the mountains. On one particular occasion, he had been hiking until late; night fell and caught him outdoors, so he looked for a little village, to find a place to sleep. An old woman, hearing her dogs barking, opened her door and invited him in, but he gently refused. "Just show me to the priest's house," he'd said.

The old woman had done so, but hadn't left, wanting to see what would happen next. The priest opened the door, asking, "Are you a stranger?" When Nikos nodded yes, the priest opened his home to him. Nikos could hear women's voices coming from inside the house, but hadn't paid attention, nor had he thought anything of the priest's red eyes or his pallid complexion; he had simply been enthralled with his flowing white hair and beard.

"My wife is a bit unwell. I will get you something to eat and make your bed," the priest had said kindly. The next morning the priest had prepared breakfast, and saw Nikos off, giving him his blessing. On the outskirts of the village Nikos ran into an old man who asked him where he'd stayed the night.

"At the priest's house," he'd answered.

"Ah, that poor man," the elder had replied. "Didn't you sense what was going on? His son, his only son died yesterday morning. Didn't you hear the women mourning?" Nikos had heard nothing, to which the old man replied, "They were probably mourning in quiet, so as not to upset you."

That is how Kazantzakis had chosen to speak of Cretan hospitality to his American readers in *Holiday* magazine.

She was certain he would walk in, at any moment, and march firmly toward her, caress her head lovingly, take her in his arms and say, "Hush now, we will make it." For that is how they had always walked, forever into the unknown. As for vindication, it had never been prompt on arrival; it was always a wretch, always late, save for the picture of them together with Melina Merkouri and Jules Dassin at Cannes, which adorned her nightstand – one of the rare exceptions.

She still recalled the first time she met Melina Merkouri, in 1955, when she and Dassin had come to ask for the film rights to the novel *Christ Recrucified*. She remembered Melina's large, green eyes and her imposing voice, and Dassin and Kazantzakis engrossed in conversation. That is, only after the ice broke, for the first moments of their meeting were decidedly awkward. "We won't make any headway like this," Kazantzakis had said, and proceeded to crush the ice.

He began telling stories and anecdotes from Crete, and in just a little while, he and Dassin seemed like two old friends who were catching up after a long time apart. Some months after that, Melina had confided in Helen that just before they'd entered their home on that first day they'd met, they had passed the doctor who had examined Nikos, at the gate. They happened to know the doctor, who had told them, "You're visiting a dead man. I've never seen anyone with such an advanced state of leukemia. He tells me he doesn't have time to die, he has a great deal of work to finish and he swears he won't leave this world without seeing China."

Helen had begun to feel better, stronger, filled with Kazantzakian confidence for the duty she had to fulfill. Katerina was in the kitchen, having gotten up earlier, and was tending to the home.

"Good morning, Katerina, dear. I'm going out on a few errands and then I'll be leaving."

"Alright, Mrs. Helen," the girl replied sweetly.

Helen walked down the hill to the post office. She had to announce her arrival in Athens. "I'm arriving tonight," she wrote in her laconic telegram to family friends. She felt ready for the final act; whatever might come, she was now able to deal with it.

Athens

Freddy's mother didn't need to look but once at her son to know his blissful state. After relaying to her how he'd handled Jane Mansfield and how his colleagues had shown their approval, he had moved on to the pressing matter of Kazantzakis' funeral, informing her that he was being dispatched to Herakleion to cover it.

He took his breakfast, then grabbed his coat and poured out into the street, the sun on his back as he crossed Skoufa Street on his way to the Deksameni coffee house. *A new day with fresh news*, he thought on the way, and it occurred to him, as he climbed up the hill, that Kazantzakis must have traveled the same path countless times on his way to his favorite haunt. He made sure to buy *Vima* and *Nea* newspapers to help him study the competition, to see what was being written elsewhere and to help him glean the information necessary for asking the right questions.

The sun shone brightly on Athens yet again, and all the little tables were out at Dexameni. Men tired from their trek up the hill sometimes stopped for a little rest and a seat, oftentimes forgetting their shopping bags there and returning home empty handed. Freddy spotted a table in the middle of the sidewalk and sat down comfortably. Children's voices sounded from below but did not bother him, but rather reminded him that it was a just another carefree Saturday for the coffee shop customers. He opened the first paper, *Vima,* only after his coffee arrived, turning to an article by Pavlos Tzermias that had drawn his attention.

"The entire intellectual world grieves for the death of Kazantzakis" was the title, and the article began with the global appeal of the author's works in the first sentences. Further on it referred to an article written about him in the *Frankfurter Allgemeine,* the German newspaper, entitled, "A spiritual Rebel," which highlighted the unconscionable behavior of the Greeks toward their compatriot. The German journalist asserted that while the Cretan thinker's thoughts on "true Christianity" might have been far afield the traditional view, even the harshest critics could not consider his books godless. Freddy's eyes darted along the page, to an article about Britain's intention to repeat its secret negotiations with Greece and Turkey over the Cyprus issue.

He then noticed that Monday was the premiere for the film *Boy on a Dolphin*, which had been filmed in Hydra and which starred Sophia Lauren, Alan Ladd and the Greek Alexis Minotis, of course. He wouldn't want to miss it, but was torn because he'd also read that another film he had waited to see, *Tea and Sympathy,* was also premiering on Monday. *Which one to go to?* he wondered. He wasn't about to give himself a headache over it; half an hour before the movies would begin – both of them at the same time, incidentally – he'd simply flip a coin.

He left the paper on the table and reached for his coffee. Everything he'd read so far he already knew. He looked around him, at pedestrians huffing as they came up the hill, at the children playing below. He cast his gaze at the horizon; before those trees had grown, the customers there could see all the way down to the Argo-Saronic gulf. He wondered what it would have been like, then, with Papadiamantis sitting at the table next to him, writing in silence, or with Kazantzakis seated behind him, laughing away with Markos Avgeris and their friends.

His thoughts were interrupted suddenly, immediately, as his eye was caught by a moving, beautiful trap. She couldn't have been more than twenty, and no taller than five foot four, Her impressive blue dress, with its delicate white polka dots was merely the bait – the call. The white belt, affixed to her waist, seemed to part her in half, and her elegant legs were in plain view, bare to her knees. The fabric fell somewhat tightly over her beautiful curves, accentuating her every step.

Freddy's eyes trailed upward. Above her lithe waist and taut abdomen, her proud, almost threatening bosom appeared, straining against the few buttons at the top of her dress, offering a hint at her cleavage to the indiscreet male – and jealous female – glances. Her tall neck with its lily-white complexion bathed her in an air of pride, and gave way to a beautifully symmetrical face, with dimples affixed to large, plush lips that made her seem like a girl and a woman all at once. Her chin and nose were delicate, and her eyes were slightly cat-like, with a dark, direct gaze. Her forehead was small, her hair black, coiffed with bangs and a short bob that fell just under her ear.

She looked down, then around, almost immediately sensing the young man with his newspapers and the coffee on his table, gazing at her intensely. She looked up slightly, and without turning her head, cast her gazed toward him, to get a better look. When their eyes met, she lowered her gaze, and Freddy felt electrified, for she was truly beautiful. He stared at her as she passed by, and kept looking at her until he felt he couldn't possibly turn his head any further. He went back to his coffee, and picked up the other newspaper.

"That right there is our neighborhood's pride and joy," a man's voice said behind him. Freddy turned to see the waiter in his white apron, smiling. He was no more than thirty, with dark, curly hair and an enormous fringe, and had a mole, high atop his right cheek, clearly his trademark sign.

"How could she not be?" Freddy said with a grin, and turned his chair so he didn't have to crane his neck to see the waiter.

"She makes our day whenever she comes by," the waiter added as he cleaned a table. "Too bad she's spoken for."

Freddy feigned his next smile; he didn't want to share his disappointment with a stranger. He picked up the newspaper again, though he didn't want to read it, he wanted to leave, even if he still had time before going to the office. He motioned the waiter over to pay.

"If you come back this time the day after tomorrow, you'll see her coming up the hill," the waiter informed him.

"Not hardly! She only had one chance and she lost it," Freddy said with a tight smile as he picked up his newspapers, though he was really talking about himself. He started down the hill, thinking he could ask the waiter to give the girl a rose from him. It would be a good test, to see if the girl would remember him. Or perhaps he could appear again, and ask her what club she was going to the following Saturday, without proposing they should go together. *No, that would be silly*, he thought, because even if she did tell him, she'd probably go with her beau. The flower was romantic gesture and framed Freddy's style perfectly, but not a rose, no, that would be entirely commonplace. A white tulip, perhaps, might better convey his good intentions; still, no battle was ever won just by thinking about it.

Was it even time for love? He wondered somewhat loudly, then realized that he often did that: he was talking to himself out loud. Perhaps the fact that he hadn't seen his friends for more than a week was to blame, but the events unfolding were so intense, that he really didn't have time for flirting, for love and revelry.

Antibes

Her suitcases were ready and the taxi was waiting. A sullen Helen opened the gate, and the creaking noise – a reminder of her loneliness – upset her terribly. Young Katerina had stayed behind, watching her from the stoop. Helen didn't turn, only faced forward. She gave her luggage to the driver and sat in the back seat. It was a short distance from her house to the train station; it seemed as though one moment she was in the taxi, and in the train car the next. Unrestrained by hardship, walking proudly, she began the journey for the final farewell to her husband.

She settled her things and reclined comfortably in her seat. She pulled *Zorba the Greek* from her purse. She wanted to familiarize herself with Crete, to read anew this adventure between the melancholy writer and the cynical laborer, between the man who remains true to ideals and the one who puts into action his every thought. In the book, the writer is trapped in his own moralistic civility, but admires the nonconformist laborer who chooses life. In the end, the writer could not break his chains, the laborer was unable to free him. Framing the story in Crete, Kazantzakis had written a novel of international magnitude, yet his primary goal was to illustrate his own personal struggle. He'd struggled his entire life to be a man true to his word.

He'd become an ascetic, turning away from every comfort, and that was perhaps, one of the reasons his marriage to Galatea did not last. He ate sparsely, and she wondered if he truly enjoyed living that way or if he was just a miser. It was certain that Nikos had loved Galatea, as equally certain that Galatea had loved him back; still, when they had lost their way together, Galatea saw to it that she burned every bridge they ever crossed. She'd left no room for reconciliation, not after the litany of complaints she levied against him. Was it the competition between two intellectuals? Was it a woman's envy?

Whatever it had been, her critique of Nikos to her friends and acquaintances, to her companions and admirers had been insulting, yet he endured it all stoically. He endured her affair with his best friend, Markos Avgeris, before they'd divorced, and even her libelous book against him, which she made certain he received, just a few months earlier, in which she practically made him out to be a monster. "Poor Galatea, she didn't deserve such an end," Nikos had murmured when he saw it, and refused to read it, allowing only Helen's review of it instead.

The monotone sound of the train kept rhythm with her thoughts, as though produced from her mind's inner workings. Like cogs in a chain, memories came and went before her; she recalled herself reading one of his letters that had moved her greatly. "As long as we are together, the world is tolerable, wonderful even. I would have died a thousand deaths if you were gone, because I've tired of people," he had written to her. The letters faded, the ink took over the paper, the monotone sound of the train, like the sound of her mind racing, finally subsided.

Athens

Androulidakis had asked him to stop by his office, expecting, at any moment, a new development in the Kazantzakis story. The doorman informed him that the publisher, Mr. Kokkas had arrived, together with his parliamentary friend, the "tall one" – Constantine Mitsotakis. Freddy headed straight to his office. He flipped through *Nea* newspaper, waiting to see what would happen. Was it truly a coincidence, that the publisher and Mitsotakis were both there on a Saturday afternoon? Perhaps what they were discussing had to do with him, also, since the last time he'd heard Mitsotakis' name was in relation to the funeral. He decided to work on his column for overnight pharmacies; he wanted to leave everything in order, in the event he had to leave suddenly for Crete.

He'd been working on his column for over an hour, when he heard footsteps in the hallway growing louder until a man's silhouette framed his door.

"Good evening, Freddy. Come to my office, I want you," Androulidakis said to him, and was gone in a flash. Freddy jumped up and was standing before his chief-editor in a matter of seconds, before he'd had a chance to bury his face in the stack of papers on his desk, as was his custom.

"Sit," Androulidakis said, indicating the usual seat. "You need to be at Hellenikon airport tomorrow at one p.m.," he informed him flatly, and the young reporter looked at him, surprised.

"What will I do there, Mr. Androulidakis?" he asked.

"You're flying to Herakleion. Onassis has offered an Olympic plane to transfer Kazantzakis' remains to Crete. You'll be on that flight. You're going to go there, cover the funeral, and fly back the next day. I've already made arrangements with Peter."

Try as he might, Freddy couldn't contain his smile.

"Pack a bag, a change of clothes. I'll need your report by ten p.m. You'll write it and phone it in, dictate it to the typist. I want you to be humble, to ask questions, and I want to hear good things about your article and about your presence there, understood?"

"Of course, Mr. Androulidakis," Freddy replied, filled with gratitude.

"I'm very worried, Freddy. I was just talking to Peter. I'm afraid there will be ugliness. Disturbances. Riots. I want you to be exceedingly careful."

"What happened?"

"Things in Crete are serious. Athenian priests are threatening their Cretan counterparts," his chief-editor informed him in his official tone.

"But how? In what way?" Freddy asked, astonished, though quickly regretted blurting out his question.

"Any priest officiating Kazantzakis' funeral is in danger of being cast out. Parareligious organizations are threatening the Metropolitan," he added, clearly shaken. "Can you grasp the scandal? Can you fathom the hatred of our highest spiritual leaders for a dead man?" he asked heatedly, and Freddy cast his gaze to the floor, as though he were somehow at fault.

"And, as would be expected, the Cretans are furious. They are such a proud and hot-tempered bunch where Kazantzakis is concerned – the man that glorified their homeland on a global scale. They understand the Church has wronged him. If they find out his burial has been condemned, I wonder who will be able to restrain them, or even how?" Androulidakis fumed in his clear summation of the facts.

"What if we posted it in tomorrow's issue? That way we could pressure the Church to reconsider. And the blame would shift from the Cretan clergy to the true authors of this strife," Freddy proposed, but Androulidakis shook his head.

"Then we might as well give the Cretans the go ahead to launch rampant protests against the Church. We will have suborned violence," the chief-editor explained. "We want to avoid all of that; we want to prevent a Cretan uprising against the Church, and we want to prevent the humiliating error of our clergy who are being so very shortsighted about things and can only focus on their thirst for revenge."

"Well, then, the only way out that I can see is through political intervention," Freddy surmised and waited quietly for Androulidakis' reaction, who was drumming his thumbs on his desk.

"This is one solution. It doesn't promise successful results, certainly, but on the other hand we are doomed to failure," Androulidakis commented, his voice no longer anxious. "That's what I said to Kokkas, who is also very concerned: 'We should mobilize Kazantzakis' friends. The Old Man was his dear friend. In 1945 Kazantzakis was minister without portfolio in the Sofoulis government. Papandreou and Sophocles Venizelos now both lead the opposition party. If they don't press now for this matter, when will they?'" the seasoned journalist asked as he laid out the facts.

"Do you think the government will have the strength to press? Or will the weight of it all fall to the opposition party?" Freddy asked. Androulidakis had stopped drumming his thumbs, and was now resting his head on his right hand.

"The funeral will be a public expense, by order of Karamanlis. I'm sure someone will be there to represent the government. Ordinarily, it should be Gerokostopoulos, the Minister of Education, who is also Minister of Religious Affairs. Everyone respects him, and I think if they use him, use his stature, the Church will be inclined to back down, especially if the Minister of Religious Affairs walks behind the coffin at the funeral procession," Androulidakis said thoughtfully. "Even if the hierarchy doesn't take back its threat, the Metropolitan of Herakleion won't be able to refuse officiating the funeral for the deceased when he is being honored by the titular minister himself."

"Who are you going to say all of this to?" Freddy asked, then quickly added, somewhat shyly, "If you don't mind my asking..." He sensed he'd overstepped somehow.

"I already spoke with our publisher, Mr. Kokkas, and he will put these ideas to the right audience," the chief-editor immediately replied, matter of fact. "I'm going to go discuss it with Peter."

"Yes, Mr. Androulidakis," Freddy said, and rose up from his seat.

He returned to his rickety desk, the ecstasy written all over his face, and dropped into his chair, finally relaxed. He felt ready. He *was* ready; he had prepared greatly for this. His mind unexpectedly turned to the girl in the blue polka dot dress from that morning; the image of her, stealing a glance at him came to mind. *Perhaps a red rose would do her more justice.* "What am thinking?" He muttered once more, aloud; he was talking to himself again. He couldn't help but grin. "I am ready," he yelled loudly this time. It was, after all, how he felt.

Paris

The train's whistle echoed in the half empty cabin car, where Helen, who had awoken just moments earlier, was fixing her hair and straightening her jacket. Her legs were numb and she'd gotten up to stretch just before the train pulled to a stop. She stood aside, letting the passengers who were in a frenzied hurry disembark first, as she usually did. Gradually, their commotion and voices faded as they left the platform. She felt a cool breeze, and hastened to open her suitcase, where she'd folded her light coat, having placed it in last for such a moment. It was pitch dark when she finally got a taxi for the airport in Orly.

The driver bombarded her with questions the entire drive. At first he thought she was Italian, due to her accent; when she told him she was Greek, he became enthused. He asked her many things, each time eyeing her in the rear-view mirror; Helen glanced at him when he wasn't looking, focusing mostly on the sight of autumnal Paris outside. Of the many questions posed to her by the driver with the thick black beard, thinning hair and enormous glasses, came one that caused Helen great discomfort.

"There's a Greek author, Kazantzakis, and he lives in France. I saw him on television, on some show where he was talking about Saint Sebastian. Do you know him?" he asked her.

"I've heard of him," she replied and turned her gaze to the window, having just experienced a scene she was bound to relive again and again in her near future. She only thought it right to leave a generous tip for the short driver who remembered her Nikos. Upon realizing his good fortune, the driver ejected himself from the car to unload her luggage from the trunk.

"Enjoy your time back home," he offered his unsuspecting wish. She returned his smile, then froze when she heard his words.

Once in the airport she walked straight to the desk of Olympic Airlines, which had passed into the hands of Aristotle Onassis just four months before. She took her ticket and headed to the airport bar, gazing at the huge corridor that stretched before her on the side of the building. It took about forty-five minutes to board the airplane, during which time they served a revitalizing warm tea. She would ask to stay at a hotel when she arrived in Athens, though she was certain that her childhood friend, Marika Papaioannou, would not hear of it, and instead, would take her to her home.

She calculated that the remains would arrive in Athens late in the afternoon, and was certain that Goudelis would have arranged for a public tribute at the Metropolis Church of Athens, for his friends and fans to pay their last respects. They would then take the ship *Angelica* to Herakleion, where another public wake would be held for one night. Next to her, she heard a couple speaking in Greek. She turned around, subconsciously, when she heard the woman tell her husband it was time to board the plane. Helen did the same, and followed after them; shortly before the runway door opened, the Greeks seemed to multiply. Ten minutes later she was in her seat, next to the window, with a young man in a dark suit, clearly a student, seated next to her. She was not afraid of airplanes, she was quite familiar with them. She remembered flying from Moscow to China on the world's fastest airplane, a technological miracle of the Soviets. She looked around as almost all the other passengers crossed themselves just before the plane began taxiing on the runway, so that it could attain its top speed and soar into the sky.

The passengers' anxiety lasted about five minutes, then dissipated at approximately six thousand feet. Helen glanced below, admiring the myriad bright spots on the ground, then turned to look at the student sitting next to her. *Just like Nikos, forty-five years ago*, she thought. Nikos had first obtained his degree at the Athens School of Law, then had continued to Paris for his master's degree, having studied under the great Bergson, whose views had influenced Nikos greatly. She remembered the photos he had shown her, how handsome he had been in his youth. Tall, proud, charming... She even recalled the story of his first love, which remained entwined with his life in all the days that followed. In his eighteenth year he had settled in Chania with an Irish lass who bore all of the traditional hallmarks of her people: red hair, green eyes, white skin. This twenty-five year-old became Nikos' English teacher, and the first woman he ever fell in love with.

It had been a secret love, until the young Kazantzakis was due to depart for Athens, to enroll at Law School. On his last weekend with her, he had suggested to his teacher that they hike to Mount Psiloritis, and she had accepted. They had been climbing the mountain for some time when night fell and a storm suddenly came upon them; they ran to a chapel for shelter and rest. There, they made their bed on the floor, drifting to sleep, exhausted, and when they woke in the morning, Nikos made love for the first time. If this was not a sign, then the word had no meaning, it was useless. Such was their passion and impulse that neither had any restraint or misgiving. Upon their return, Nikos had left immediately for Athens. Helen never did learn if this event was a figment – or not – of his imagination, which was constantly churning out beautiful stories.

On his first break back home in Herakleion, Nikos had gone to her house, seeking her out. The Irish lass, however, had left the island. Devastated and crushed by fever, he became bedridden for three days. He arose on the fourth, grabbed his pen and began to write unceasingly. This was perhaps the most decisive moment of his life.

"After a few days I was finished; I closed the manuscript, wrote the title upon it with red Byzantine letters, Serpent and Lily, and got up, went to the window, and took a deep breath. The Irish lass could haunt me no more; she had left me, I had committed her to paper, and she could no longer escape from there. I was free," he had explained to Helen.

Just imagine if the priests ever found out that Nikos had lost his virginity in a chapel! Helen thought and chuckled. She liked the thought, and not just the thought, but her reaction to it, since it was the same reaction Nikos had every time someone mentioned the Church to him.

She remembered those tragic events, shortly before *The Last Temptation of Christ* was published, which the Holy Synod had wanted to ban without actually having read it. Goudelis had come to their home in Antibes, and had explained that, after the book's publication he had received threats, that the reactions were fierce and that the Holy Synod had informed him that it would excommunicate him if he dared to release the novel in Greece.

"But that's not what bothers me – I didn't come here to talk about that," the publisher had said, "but about the fact that I don't think the novel will fare well."

"Is that the extent of your bravery?" Kazantzakis had asked him icily. "You're quitting?" Goudelis then tried to leave, but Kazantzakis had yelled after him, "There's the manuscript, take it if you dare."

That was it; everyone had waited with bated breath for the novel's release, and in the end, and after numerous attempts to find a printing press that would take it – for practically all the professional printers' feared the wrath of the Church – the publisher had managed to get it to print.

Helen recalled every word in the newspaper clipping she had been sent from Athens, with the total tally of the annual book sales for 1955. A total of one thousand six hundred fifty books had been released that year, more or less the same as the year before, and of those books, about three hundred fifty of them were original Greek works. The list was topped by the usual suspects with the highest sales: Karagatsis, Panagiotopoulos, Venezis, Myrivilis.

The quote came to her in full: "Undoubtedly, the greatest success this year, as with last year, belongs to Nikos Kazantzakis. His *Last Temptation of Christ* has broken every record in Greek book sales. On the first day of its release, it sold nine hundred thirty-seven copies in Athens alone, with hundreds more orders from around the country."

What a triumph, Helen reminisced. A strong shake that frightened the passengers jolted her out of her reverie and into the Greek clouds they were currently passing through. She looked out the window but couldn't discern anything other than a thick, dark haze. She stretched both legs as far as she could, stopping short of the seat in front of her, and asked the stewardess for some water. She could sense her time was drawing near, and it filled her with a sense of dread. If only she could meet with friends to mourn him, as she wanted; that would have been perfection. What would she do if the well-known bloodsuckers showed themselves - the ones that had been leeching off of his blood for years – in an effort to usurp his glory once more? What then?

It would certainly not be worthy of her husband's international reputation if she started an incident a few hours before his burial. Her only solution was to turn to the organizing committee for the funeral, and to their friends, to ensure that order would be maintained. The stewardess returned politely with the water she had requested. Helen drank it all desperately, feeling life flood back into her being. She was keenly aware of her own vicissitudes, but the last years had been anything but carefree. And there certainly was no clearer sign that she too, was aging and maturing, than her husband's death. Their frugal living may have strengthened her will and fortified her strength, but it was clear that she was exhausted. She was no longer the young girl who could throw herself into battle; still, she had faced so many hardships and setbacks in her life that she now had the experience to manage complicated situations.

The stewardesses announced the plane's descent to Hellenikon airport, and then took their seats. Next to her, the young man was sleeping; she looked at him furtively, and wondered how excited his mother and father must be, waiting for him at home. Perhaps her Nikos felt the same as he waited for her; she felt herself welling up at the thought, but restrained herself. She could see the hazy ground from the window, growing clearer and clearer as it rushed up to meet the airplane. She remained steadfast and composed, even as the wheels touched the Attic ground for the first time and the whole airplane shook with the impact.

For a brief moment she felt the young man clutch her hand in his – she saw it! - but when she turned to look at him, he was focused elsewhere. The wide-eyed passengers burst into applause and crossed themselves in gratitude for the relatively smooth landing; they seemed affably sympathetic in that short moment before they began to push and shove their way into the aisle in their efforts to disembark, signaling a return to the status quo for the uncivilized bourgeoisie. The student watched Helen from the corner of his eye, realizing that she too, had been studying him quietly.

"Shall I help you?" he offered, and picked up one of her suitcases.

"Bless you, my boy," she thanked him.

The airport lights could not hide the faces waiting in front of the building; about twenty-five people were standing there, holding up signs in their hands, shouting the names of passengers one hundred meters from the plane. She heard her own name being called, a sweet "Helen" that was too weak for her to ascertain from whence it came, though she was certain the sweet voice belonged to Marika. The chilly dampness permeated her coat, dress, even her skin, and she felt it, for just a moment, as she continued to search for that voice. The last *Helen* she heard was clearly coming from her right.

She turned to see her standing there: white coat, white gloves, noble features, large eyes. Her husband stood next to her. She started to walk faster toward them, forgetting the tired young man behind her who was carrying her luggage in addition to his own, and who had momentarily lost her in the crowd. There they stood in a tight embrace: the author and the pianist – the woman who had insisted she introduce her friend to Kazantzakis thirty years before, on May 18, 1924. Afterward, when Nikos had introduced Marika to his friend Emile Hourmousios, he seemed to be returning the favor, and since that moment their four lives had been bound together forever as they shared their cares and worries.

"My darling Helen," Marika's voice trembled as she sobbed.

"Oh Marika, hush darling," Helen said to her as she wiped away her tears.

"My condolences, Helen..." Emile said to her as he hugged her.

"Condolences to us all, Emile," Helen replied.

"A young man dropped off this suitcase and left. Is it yours, Helen?" Marika asked, surprised. Helen turned to look for the young man who had vanished.

"That's odd. He was sitting next to me on the flight and offered to help me with my luggage, and now he's gone," Helen explained.

"We should go, you must be so tired," Emile suggested, as he placed his right hand lovingly on her back. "Everything is under control. The remains should be here by tomorrow afternoon with Agnes, and I've spoken with Goudelis."

Emile chatted on in a swift but reassuring tone to calm Helen down. He succeeded.

"You can just drop me off at a hot—" Helen began, but was interrupted by Marika.

"There's nothing to discuss. We've already made arrangements for your room."

Helen smiled; she had been certain of this outcome. Emile took the two suitcases and moved ahead, leaving the two women to walk arm in arm.

"Are you alright, my little bird? Do you need anything?" Marika asked.

"I just want everything done quickly and quietly, Marika. Nothing else," Helen answered sadly.

"I'll tell you everything on the way."

The three of them entered the building, walking toward the exit where the taxis were parked.

"Are our enemies rejoicing?" Helen blurted out impatiently.

"There has been no rejoicing thus far, though I think it is important that Karamanlis announced it would be a state funeral and showed that there is no place for pettiness in such matters. But Emile said that Kantiotis is up in arms about it."

"That fanatic? And what does he want? Isn't it enough that Nikos is dead?"

"No. He's demanding that the clergy refuse the burial."

Marika's words seemed to daze Helen, who was utterly shocked by what she was hearing.

"Have they gone mad?" she asked, raising her voice. "What do they hope to win from a dead man?"

Marika tried to console her.

"Calm yourself, he's just a fanatic..." she said and linked her arm once more through Helen's as they continued their walk, trying not to lose sight of Hourmousios. They crossed the exit where he was waiting for them with a taxi.

"To Voukourestiou Street," he said to the bored driver.

The road was lightly lit like a film noir and added ever so slightly to Helen's agitation. As they entered the city, she remembered how much Nikos hated Athens. *The intellectuals at Deksameni had accused him even of that,* she thought to herself. Athens had changed a great deal since the last time she had visited. The bright signs had increased but could not disguise the poverty; on the contrary, they highlighted it if one looked closely enough. None of them spoke. Marika held Helen's hand tightly.

They didn't want the driver to overhear anything unusual, as the number of informants had dramatically increased since the Occupation and the Civil War, and Helen had suffered greatly at their hands. The taxi parked, Hourmousios paid and got the suitcases as the driver uttered a nondescript "goodnight" unworthy of reply. Soon, the three of them were sitting in the parlor of the apartment on 25 Voukourestiou Street.

"What we're going to do is ask for the remains to lay in state here in Athens for a day, and then go to Herakleion," Hourmousios said. "Agis Theros will speak on behalf of the Greek Literary Society. The city of Herakleion has set up an organizing committee for the funeral itself. It also looks like the Academy of Athens will not participate."

"Pathetic," Helen replied pensively.

"They've been hearing a great deal these last few days – especially Melas. The foremost Greek author of our time has died and the flag isn't even flying at half mast. Whatever. We didn't really expect anything better from him."

"No, not from Melas and his country 'Mellas', which has nothing to do with the real Hellas," Marika scoffed.

"They're going to inter him at Martinego Bastion, not in the cemetery," Emile hastened to say to Helen's surprise.

"And why is that?" she asked, disappointed.

"It is a form of tribute. Above him, the Cretan mountains and below him, the Cretan sea..." Hourmousios explained.

"I hope that's it and not something else," Helen countered anxiously.

"There is a rumor the Church won't allow him to be buried in a cemetery, but that has yet to be confirmed."

"Emile, what is Marika saying? That fanatic wants to make sure a priest can't bury Nikos?" Helen asked, visibly upset.

"Yes, but I don't think he'll get his way. I found out he even sent a letter to the Metropolitan, telling him not to dare offer the funerary rites. The same with all the Cretan clergy."

"And what if there are riots?" Helen persisted.

"Our man in Crete told us that they've received an order to lock down the military bases for three days, and there's even a directive to the officers not to attend the funeral."

"What does that mean, to lock down the military bases?" Helen asked.

"It means no uniformed soldier or officer will attend the funeral. They are trying to minimize the chance of any riots taking place," Emile explained.

"I see," Helen said emptily.

"Come, Helen, let's go to bed, you need to rest. Tomorrow will be a long day. Would you like to eat something first?" Marika asked.

"No, Marika, thank you. You are right, we should get some rest. Tomorrow will truly be a long day."

SUNDAY, NOVEMBER 3, 1957

Athens

The funeral drew an enormous crowd, but no one was mourning; everyone spoke in hushed, conspiratorial whispers. Even though they were all clad in black, none of them appeared sad, and the priests trudged through their words indifferently. She was inconsolable, and not a single friend of theirs could be found in the crowd. There were no floral arrangements, no one held flowers, and Helen was seated in the front row, surrounded by all those people who had fought him. When the priest stopped chanting, he told the pallbearers to wait before lifting the casket.

"Someone should speak," the priest commanded as the scene fell quiet.

"I will," a dark haired man in his sixties shot up, dressed in white – suit, shirt, tie, shoes, suspenders and all. Helen couldn't see his face, only the many papers he held in his hands. He passed behind the freshly dug grave slowly and stood silent.

"I had prepared," he began, "a nice speech. It took me several hours to write. But now that we are all gathered here, I think...why tire you all?" he asked, and tossed the papers into the hollowed grave. Helen tried to speak, enraged, but could not summon her voice.

"Alright now, do we all agree to tell her?" the dark haired man with the blurred face asked loudly, and the crowd below cried "Yes" and clapped and laughed all the while Helen struggled to scream "Shame on you!" but could not speak.

"Well, Helen Kazantzakis," the man in the white suit said to her, pointing at her with his left finger, "your tears are for naught, and your grief is in vain. Your husband is not in that casket. No, he didn't rise like Christ. He just tricked you. He isn't dead. He tricked you and abandoned you," he yelled and burst into laughter as everyone laughed with him. "Go look for him in Russia!"

She tried to yell "Shame on you!" She tried...Suddenly, she shot upright in her bed, drenched in sweat.

Marika rushed in, alarmed. "It was just a dream, my sweet Helen, just a dream," she said, holding her in her arms. Helen could still feel her heart racing, breaking. She slowly calmed down.

"Come now, its over," her friend cooed softly as she wiped her brow with a handkerchief she had pulled out of her robe's pocket. "I'll get you some water."

The sun's rays warmed Helen's face and sweat had begun to bead her forehead once more. Marika returned quickly holding a glass of water. Helen drank it in a single gulp.

"Are you better?" she asked.

"Yes, Marika, thank you."

"You were screaming 'Shame on you!'"

Helen told her about the dream.

"Now that I think of it...I could almost be at peace with him abandoning me... if only he were still alive," she confessed.

"What are you saying? He couldn't live without you. As if he would ever leave you! And even if he had, he'd still be dead, because he simply couldn't tolerate anyone else," she said with a laugh. It made Helen smile.

"Go and get ready, and I'll put on some tea," Marika said and left the room.

Helen pulled on her mourning clothes – that black uniform – once more. She was still upset from the nightmare, still reeling from all she'd learned from Marika and Emile. Her friend waited for her in the dining room with a freshly brewed pot of tea.

"Are you better?" she asked as she spooned the sugar into her cup.

"Yes, yes. Please don't worry, my dear Marika," Helen reassured her as she took the little serving spoon for the sugar.

"Emile should be back any minute. I'm sure he'll have news. Now tell me, how did it happen? You told me everything was going well," she asked earnestly.

"What can I say? He knew he was leaving. I saw it in his notes. 'I bid farewell to everything, and everything bids me farewell' he wrote in his notebook. He'd been writing similar things in *Report to Greco*, even before our trip to China. He could feel it."

"My sweet Nikos," Marika sighed and reached for Helen's hand. "You have us, you are not alone. I don't want you to worry."

"I just don't want them to dishonor his memory. They tried so hard while he was alive, and they didn't succeed. But back then, I could accept it; they thought he was dangerous, a communist, a corruptor, their enemy. But he was alive. Now that he is dead and unburied it is just immoral. Immoral, Marika!" she said, stifling a growing wail that sought release from the depths of her being, but was held back.

Helen glanced over and saw his book, *The Last Temptation of Christ* on the table. She reached out her hand, drawing it near, stroking the cover with her fingertips. She opened it gently to the first page and spotted an all too familiar sight – Nikos' letters in his handwritten dedication to the couple: "To Milios and Marika I gift this book, which I have so loved." Helen felt a hot tear slipping down to commit itself next to his signature, but she restrained herself once more at the last moment. Marika tried to lighten the situation, sensing how painful it was for her.

"I started reading it again, to remember it all. To go over it to see if it is really as unholy as they say – as unchristian as they say. To see whether it is communist in any way. To locate some passage that leads to corruption or scandal; I might have missed something or overlooked it because of our friendship. Yet I could not find a single thing – only his selfless love for humanity. And that, my dear Helen, that is what has them so riled up," Marika said tearfully. Helen let out a bitter, hollow laugh.

"Just think, he began thinking about it when we were in Aegina, during the Occupation in 1942. Do you recall the hunger, the hardships we faced? And while we all searched for someone to blame for our misery, he thought about writing a book that elevates humanity to bring it closer to God. He was going to call it *The Memoirs of Christ*." She sipped her tea and continued to stroke the cover gently.

"And when his German publisher had written to him, ecstatic, to let him know the Pope had included it in the Index of Forbidden Books, Nikos had shouted 'What hypocrisy, what rot!' The world could not accept a book written with such fire, such purity."

"What unfair reviews he received! What an unrelenting war he faced," Marika noted with disappointment.

"Just imagine what would have happened if Maria Bonaparte – the Princess George of Greece - had not intervened. Were it not for her speaking of Kazantzakis to her niece, Queen Frederica, the Greek Church might have simply excommunicated him on its own, without asking permission of anyone."

"What do you mean?"

"Didn't I tell you about this when it happened? You probably forgot," Emile's voice sounded as he entered the room, holding a cup of coffee. "Maria Bonaparte had read all of Kazantzakis' books. When she visited her niece, Queen Frederica, she spoke very highly of him. Then they met with Kazantzakis in Paris. A photograph of this meeting circulated in the Greek press, and the Church – which would never upset Frederica – seemed to soften its stance for a while."

"Wasn't Maria Bonaparte a student of Freud? Wasn't she the one who bargained with the Nazis to save her teacher's life?" Marika asked.

"Yes, that's her," Emile answered excitedly. "And to her, Nikos dedicated his *Last Temptation of Christ*."

"How did Nikos even find her?" Marika asked Helen.

"Oh he didn't find her; she found him. Maria Bonaparte is an author and a psychoanalyst. She lives in Paris, and, when she read Nikos' works, she sent him an invitation to Antibes so she could meet him. That first meeting, she came alone and brought all of her books for him to read and evaluate. The second time they met, she came with her daughter, the Princess Eugénie, and the third time, she came with her husband, Prince George," Helen explained.

"Oh oh!" Hourmousios exclaimed.

"Why, what happened?" Marika asked.

"I know why you say that, Emile, but let me tell Marika exactly how it happened. Prince George is considered the liberator of Crete, who was appointed High Commissioner of the island under the Great Powers in 1898. The day George set foot in Crete is a day etched in the memory of all living Cretans. Kazantzakis still remembers that day," Helen said, then corrected herself. "Kazantzakis always remembered that day... In 1905 the Cretans, under Venizelos as their leader, led the Therissos Revolt against George. He was forced to resign. Kazantzakis supported Venizelos, but even though Nikos wasn't in George's 'camp' so to speak, I'll have you know, Emile, that the two of them became instant friends."

"I believe it. Time has a way of quelling the past," the journalist mused. "That is why a person must live long; to right the wrongs brought forth from his vices."

"Well I don't think Nikos ever harmed anyone, not even unintentionally," Marika interjected. "I can only think of one instance – one to be exact – but even then he treated her better than most of her friends."

"You mean Galatea?" Emile asked.

"Of course."

"I hope I don't see her," Helen whispered pensively.

"I doubt she would make an appearance," Marika began to say.

"Still, though I do imagine her sister, Ellie, and their brother Lefteris would come," her husband added.

"Nikos was exceedingly kind to the entire Alexiou family, though I don't know how deserving they were. He loved them all. I cannot say the same for them; especially having read Galatea's last book, which is nothing more than idle gossip," Helen said, vexed.

"Come now, Helen, don't get upset. It isn't worth it," Marika caressed her shoulder tenderly.

"How about we go out just down the road to eat? It's almost midday..." Emile suggested, to everyone's agreement.

* * *

Freddy woke up alone. It was Sunday, and everyone was out and about, whether to Church, or the coffee shop, or on a stroll. He sat at the table to drink his Greek coffee. He still had plenty of time before going to the office. He thought about the girl he had seen yesterday at Deksameni; he could drop by today, to leave a flower for the waiter to give to her. Or perhaps he could give it to her in person. He wasn't certain of either move, much less who would be making the offer or even what kind of flower to give. He didn't want to give her something trite, like a rose for example.

Now there's a problem worth solving, he thought to himself. *She's so pure, so beautiful by nature...* "I've got it! A lily!" he exclaimed triumphantly as though he had solved a difficult puzzle. *She probably hasn't even made love yet*, Freddy continued to muse. *So very pure...*

He thought back to his first time, to the girl from cabaret Ritz who had been ten years older than him. Freddy had been fifteen at the time, a student still, and she had been twenty-seven, keeping company to the deep pocket sailors of the American Sixth Fleet. She had been with a client who had left around three in the morning; when he'd gone to sit beside her, she had turned to him, drunk and in tears. He had kissed her then, though he did not know how to kiss. Two hours later, they were entering his apartment, sneaking past his grandparents' bedroom hand in hand, and...

Freddy smiled in reverie as though lost in a scene from a movie. He had been very sad then; his beloved cat, his companion through the years of the Occupation and the Civil War had been laid to rest just the month before in his garden. Tears had welled in his eyes. "Are you crying?" she had asked him.

He had explained it to her, and she had listened. They fell in love, and years later, he could only remember two things: the silky skin of the girl, and the impossible image of his cat, still alive and wagging its tail as it watched them make love.

He laughed to himself as he sipped his coffee. He suddenly felt nostalgic for the Ritz and his romping days there. In just a month at the Ritz he had learned more than others learn in entire lifetimes. He hadn't simply learned the tricks men use to win over a woman, or witnessed feminine ingenuity and guile; he had truly learned how to read people there.

Life seemed quite like his grandfather's beloved sport, poker. Life is the dealer, tossing you a card, a passing event, and you are called to handle it, to integrate it into your life as you would into your hand, to be patient or aggressive, to combine your cards or cast them away, to recall what has been thrown down and to predict what will come next... In this way, if you connect the story of each person to two or three events, you can understand the measure of a person's hand.

Freddy had learned to read the hand of those around him quite easily. He learned to analyze their behaviors and their reactions, to figure out who was bluffing and who held the ace up their sleeve. His grandfather, who at some point in his life had squandered two factories, had spoken to him about that loss, saying simply, "I played the way I'd lived. I never did learn to separate the two." Freddy, however, was quite the opposite.

* * *

Back at the restaurant, Helen and her friends had barely stayed for an hour and a half before they quickly home, as they were all anxious about the developments. Sipping cocoa, they delved into the past once more, as is customary with funerals, keeping account of a turbulent life.

"What mistake do you wish you could take back?" Marika was the first to speak.

"Why talk about such things now?" Emile queried.

"But we're friends. We have talked about our problems so many times," his wife replied.

Helen thought a little, then spoke.

"I honestly don't know what would have happened if he had listened to me and had not resigned from UNESCO when we were in Paris. Do you remember, Emile?"

"Of course I remember!"

"Nikos was in charge of the office for the translation of classical works. I'll never forget the struggle we had to get him accepted into that position, since they'd requested reference letters from distinguished Greeks. The position had originally been offered to his friend, Jean Herbert, only he was working at the United Nations in New York at the time, and couldn't leave. So, he suggested Nikos in his stead. He knew however that the Greek state had 'issues', and was asked to supply three letters of reference for Nikos from prominent Greek politicians.

"Fortunately, George Papandreou, Sophocles Venizelos and Panagiotis Kanellopoulos all responded. Later, however, when the Ministry of Exterior found out Nikos had gotten the position, it 'chewed out' the Greek embassy in Paris because it had failed to avert his employment there. They could have cared less that a Greek had been chosen for the position," Helen concluded.

"But what is it exactly you regret in this story?" Marika insisted.

"The money was good. Nikos worked diligently, everyone was pleased. I had made my own plans: just one year more, and we could have bought two small apartments in Paris. We would have lived in the one and rented out the other; that way we wouldn't have had to struggle to make ends meet."

"A sound plan," Marika agreed.

"But he felt he had completed his work and wanted to resign. When I told him of my plans, he looked at me and said, quite angrily, 'How can you counsel me to take money without doing any work? My presence at UNESCO is now entirely unnecessary'. And a few moments later, he sighed and added, 'If I have to take the road to the office a single day longer I think I'll break down in tears'."

"Classic Nikos," Emile smiled wanly as he leaned back in his chair. The phone rang. The journalist sprang to answer as the two women watched on in suspense.

"Hello? Yes. What time? At 8 o'clock at Eleusis? Where exactly? At the entrance. Alright. Yes, she's here. One moment please," he said, then turned to Helen. "It's Goudelis. He'd like a word with you."

"Right away," Helen said as she took the phone. "Good evening, John... thank you so much... they won't give us the church? Call Prevelakis and Papandreou. And call me back to tell me what happened.

Helen hung up the phone upset, her eyes downcast.

"Helen tell us, what happened?"

"Goudelis told me they refuse to give us a church for the remains to lay in state for the public wake."

"That is unheard of!" Emile exploded. "How can they refuse that right to his thousands of his readers?"

"I told Goudelis to call Prevelakis and to mobilize Papandreou. He told me he is also looking for Archbishop Theoklitos."

"Don't worry, Helen, I'll make some calls of my own."

Helen hoped in his help; he was, after all, the editor-in-chief of *Kathimerini* newspaper. She sat back down, trying to shake the shock she felt. She could hear Emile on the phone in the background, informing, pleading, arguing. She knew she had to remain calm; she had to think of a way to rescue her beloved dead from this final humiliation.

* * *

A few kilometers away from Voukourestiou Street, at the offices of *Eleftheria* newspaper, Freddy had almost finished his column on overnight pharmacies when Androulidakis stormed into his office.

"The Archbishop forbade the public wake for Kazantzakis and his body will not lay in state. Stay on top of it. If you find out anything, come and tell me," he said and stormed out back to his office.

Freddy did not know whom to call; he had no source inside the Church. In fact, his only source was his Cretan contact from Herakleion who had shared some things, but mostly about the Kazantzakis family. Perhaps Peter Charis might know more, but surely he would have spoken with Androulidakis by now. Freddy thought it best to finish his column, and stay on hand for whatever his editor might ask of him, thinking he might even be sent to the Archdiocese for more information.

After thirty minutes, his column complete, Freddy walked to Androulidakis' office. "Come in, Freddy," the chief editor said calmly without looking up from his papers.

"Mr. Androulidakis, is there something I can do? Should I go to the Archdiocese?"

"No Freddy, I've already sent a reporter down there." Androulidakis glanced up briefly to bring Freddy up to date with the recent developments; he was, after all, the reporter who would be dispatched to Crete and had to be fully informed. "The Old Man, Papandreou, is on the phone with Archbishop Theoklitos, trying to change his mind. And I learned that Goudelis and Andreas Mothonios – the Old Man's right hand – are in constant communication, trying to find a solution."

"What do you think will happen?" Freddy asked.

Androulidakis hesitated.

"I imagine the Archbishop will succumb to the pressure," he said, "but I'm not entirely certain. In any event, you have to get ready to leave for Herakleion. Pack your bags tonight."

Just then, the phone rang.

"Yes, Mr. Kokkas," Androulidakis said as he motioned Freddy to leave.

Freddy went back to his desk, troubled. *How can they deny a public viewing of the body in a church? What could be more honorable than that?* He thought about all the stories he'd uncovered in the last few days and imagined them to be throwbacks to an age long gone. *Yet they aren't,* he thought. *Those outlandish people have power, so much power that they could influence an Archbishop.*

A moment later Androulidakis stepped into his office, visibly vexed.

"The idea was, that because the funeral would be a public expense, there would be no problem. The issue however is that the Archbishop is no longer answering the phone."

"So what happens now?" Freddy asked.

"They were told to take the remains to the funerary chamber at the First Cemetery in Athens. Freddy! You leave tomorrow on the Olympic flight Onassis has offered to transport the body to Herakleion."

"Onassis offered an airplane specifically for Kazantzakis' remains?" Freddy asked, astonished. "So as to avoid the obvious fiasco that is unfolding, I assume. And perhaps to advertise his new acquisition a little, too," he concluded somewhat cynically.

"Well, yes, that too. At any rate, it matters little," Androulidakis concurred. "You leave tomorrow afternoon around one, from Hellenikon airport. Stop by accounting and get some money for travel expenses, I've already issued the order."

"Yes, Mr. Androulidakis."

"Did you finish the column on overnight pharmacies?"

"Yes."

"Do the following day's column too. You might need to stay in Crete longer. Make sure you stop by my office before leaving so I can update you on any news."

"Of course."

"As you can see, Freddy, our civility is exhausted on the hollow titles we confer to those who make us proud. Beyond that, they are at the mercy of some who, given a chance, would cut them down if their viewpoints diverge. Even death gives them an opportunity to play politics and say, 'See what happens to those who oppose us?' Because that is the message they want to send."

"He became a target," Freddy said.

"If you think only one man has been targeted, think again. You don't need to simply persecute the person you are targeting, you can go after anyone who has ever been supportive of him, too. For example, Peter Charis had trouble with the law in 1947, because the magazine he headed at the time, *Nea Estia,* had published Kazantzakis' play, *Sodom and Gomorrah.* Andrew Karantonis lost his job on the radio because he dared to say that another of Kazantzakis' plays, *Constantine Paleologue,* was a tragedy of national proportions. Do you understand? Persecuting a person of letters is persecution of us all. Persecuting an innocent man is persecution of us all. Anyone can be the next target while they operate outside of the law with impunity, under the protection of the state, without having to answer to anyone..."

* * *

At the hotel, Emile told Helen and Marika it was time to get ready. The hour had come to go to Eleusis, to receive the remains. While the ladies got ready, Emile threw himself into one final round of desperate phone calls, though he knew there was no hope. Helen, too, had come to accept this defeat. Emile and Marika feared she would be devastated, but Helen seemed to care only for being punctual at the airport. Emile put the two women in a taxi for Eleusis and began to walk to his office at *Kathimerini* newspaper.

The evening was tender, and, under any other circumstance, the two friends would have had so much to say, yet they sat quietly in the taxi. Marika thought it would be better to leave Helen be, to give her the time to work through everything that was happening. Yet all Helen really thought of was how she would be with him again in just a little while. The next few hours would be her final hours with him, and she was determined to not let anyone desecrate those moments.

Helen looked out the window at the traffic, watching the tired passersby, the clunky trucks, the hungry city headed for rest. These were the hours when stories were born, and she hadn't just heard some of the best ones, but had starred in some of the stories that would regale the coming generations. She felt Marika's hand slip into hers.

"Are you alright, my sweet?"

"I'm fine, Marika. We're off to do our duty for our beloved," she said quietly, as they reached the entrance where a crowd was gathered. They told the driver to wait for them and got out. Alexis Minotis, Prevelakis, Tea Anemogianni, Nelly Evelpidi were all standing there, and once Helen came into view a sweetness transformed their somber faces.

Kazantzakis' widow fell into their safe embrace, into the arms of his friends. Tea told her that Goudelis was waiting for them at the First Cemetery.

"Helen, everyone tried to change the Archbishop's mind, but he was adamant."

"I know, dear Tea, and I thank you all."

She briefly had a chance to greet everyone when bright lights pulled to a stop before them. It was only when the driver turned off the lights that they realized they stood before the hearse they had been expecting. Agnes stepped out of the passenger side and ran into Helen's arms, not caring in the least for the arduous journey she had just endured.

"I heard what happened....this is a travesty!" she managed to say as Helen squeezed her hand.

"It's alright, Agnes. Let's just go to the cemetery."

The friends all disbanded to their cars and taxis, and a motorcade formed behind the black hearse. Hot tears slid down Helen's face, pounding her coat so loudly she feared they were audible in the deathly silence. Marika held her hand; Helen could not tear her gaze away from the casket ahead of them, illuminated in the headlights.

"*And at midnight there was a cry, Behold, the bridegroom cometh,*" Helen whispered to Marika, as her friend lost all control and broke down in silent tears. Helen did not notice, for she was on fire inside; she wanted to scream at the way such a wonderful, esteemed, just and honest man was being treated. There were so many traitors, so many black marketeers and informants whose crimes against the Greek people would never be punished like this, who would never suffer what her beloved – the man whose civility distinguished him to the ends of the earth – was forced to endure. She fell quiet, determined to do all things as he would want them, and nothing would sway her from it.

The hearse pulled to a stop at the gates of the First Cemetery. Agnes got out first, and Goudelis walked toward them. Behind him, Helen discerned a crowd. She opened the door, got out of the car, and walked toward him.

"My deepest condolences, Helen," he said.

"Thank you. Who are all these people?" she asked, somewhat frightened.

"Don't be alarmed. They are fans of Nikos, and they came here to honor him."

"And there really isn't anyone here from the Church?" she asked, a bit calmer.

"No, no one. We are alone," he answered, then turned to a group of about ten people and said, "come on, lads, let's get the casket."

The driver opened the back of the hearse and in a few moments Kazantzakis' casket was on the shoulders of six strangers, fans of the author. They placed it down in the funerary chamber. Helen pulled out a framed photograph and placed it atop the casket. Everyone bowed their heads. Goudelis approached Helen and Agnes, who stood next to her.

"And to think that at the border of Yugoslavia, when the customs and border patrol realized we were carrying Kazantzakis, they didn't even stop us out of respect for the dead. And here...." Goudelis lamented.

"I've been on the phone since this morning," he continued. "Since this morning! When they refused to let us have the Metropolitan Church, I asked for Saint Eleftherios Church. Then they told me about a church in Glyfada. But they couldn't find a priest there, they said. I begged them. Papandreou kept calling and his men were also on it. Theoklitos was resolute. Even the secretary of the Holy Synod, Sperantzas, called him, but in vain.

"'Put him in any church you like', we kept telling them. 'The body will soon be in Athens. We urge you, please reconsider!' And then the Archbishop replied, 'Take him to the morgue.' Just that. 'The morgue?' I asked. 'Kazantzakis??' 'Call back in ten minutes,' he said, but then we lost him, we could not get a hold of him after that.

"When we did finally reach him, he told us to place the casket in the funerary chambers of the First Cemetery. 'I cannot give you a church, though I personally appreciate Kazantzakis' works, because tomorrow the press will be all over me'," Goudelis went on.

"For shame!" Agnes cried.

"I told him, 'The press will attack you now, your Beatitude,', but he was unyielding."

"Beholden to the fanatics and the yellow press," Agnes commented.

Helen did not speak; she observed the anxious retelling of the events as though the story did not affect her personally, as though she had heard it all before and was now disinterested. She watched on stoically, devoid of all expression.

"Up until this very moment we have been trying to change his mind," Goudelis continued, exhausted. "We discussed all of it with Papandreou. He told me Onassis had contacted him, and has offered a private plane to transport the remains to Crete tomorrow afternoon, to minimize somewhat the almost certain fiasco that will follow, with all the foreign press coming to cover the funeral. Do you object, at all?" he asked.

"What a kind gesture in the midst of war," Helen said quietly.

"We'll fly out from Hellenikon at half past two in the afternoon. The Old Man will be with us, together with Minotis, Katrakis, Kakrides, and other notable friends."

"Thank you, John, for seeing to everything," Helen said.

"One more thing, Helen. The press is outside. Would you like to make a statement? Soon, if you can, before they have to go to print."

"Alright, John...in a little."

Goudelis left her and went to inform the somber group – which had been discussing the tragic turn of events in hushed whispers – about the schedule of the following day. Helen turned to the casket once more. It was enormous, black. She caressed it tenderly as though she were caressing her Nikos. She took her seat in the chair next to him; soon people would know who had risen to the occasion and who had circled the drain of indecency. Around her, everything was in constant motion; Marika was the first to come to her, asking if she needed anything, while Agnes tried to prevail upon her to make statements to the press. Goudelis awaited Agnes' signal that Helen was ready, and, when the signal came, Goudelis sped past them so fast to find the reporters he barely noticed as Helen stood up and made her way to the exit.

Helen emerged with her friend and attorney. The faint light barely illuminated their path and their faces. The three reporters gave their sympathies and then asked her to relate to them exactly what had happened after Kazantzakis' trip to China and Japan. Helen briefly recounted the events up until Kazantzakis' death, but when she was asked why the remains were not laying in state in a church somewhere for a public farewell, Goudelis stepped in to give the exact account.

Fifteen minutes later, the reporters had left; Kazantzakis' friends departed soon thereafter. They needed to rest, after all, for the flight to Herakleion the next day.

"What should we do, Helen? We should leave too, so you can also get some rest," Marika proposed.

Helen felt exhausted, but her duty to her husband demanded she remain at his side.

"I think I'll stay here until morning. Then I'll come to the house, take a shower and we can leave for the airport."

"I'll get Goudelis and we'll make arrangements."

Marika soon returned with the editor.

"John, I don't want to leave Nikos here alone," Helen said.

"This is unconscionable! There should be a priest here but he is nowhere to be found," Goudelis thundered.

Helen held his gaze with a knowing look.

"Don't expect anything from them, Giannis. Do you think you could come by tomorrow morning, so I can have a chance to shower and get ready for the flight to Herakleion?" she asked calmly.

"Of course," he replied. "I will be here at seven in the morning."

Agnes, Minotis and Giannis soon left, but Marika took up a chair next to Helen. "Dear Marika, you should go rest too."

"I'm not leaving you here alone. We'll leave together in the morning."

Helen reached for her hands, those hands that played Debussy better than anyone in Greece – perhaps in the whole of Europe – and squeezed them as she had when they were girls. What memories sprang forth as they reminisced the old days in the twilight; school games, traveling to Palestine – which had been Helen's maiden voyage with Nikos a month after his divorce had been finalized, and which had been attended by Marika and her sister, Katy, as the Papaioannou sisters had held a piano recital there.

"Do you recall, Marika, what Nikos had thought up? He was going on that trip for *Eleftheros Typos* newspaper, and he made me go to Vlachos, my editor at *Kathimerini*, to ask for press credentials. He suggested I tell him that I would send him travel pieces which he could publish if they were to his liking. Vlachos agreed, and you know, I still have that press pass. It's been thirty years, now."

"That trip was organized with incredible mastery," Marika said with a smile.

"It was my aunt Chariklea who had the idea; she thought it best to avoid the gossip of the orphan girl traveling alone with a man, and asked, 'Why don't you take a friend with you?' Well, I only had two good friends, you and Katy."

"Yes, and our mother consented on one condition: 'Bring me a piece of the Holy Cross'. And Katy and I arranged for a piano recital, too. And do you remember that Nikos had given each of us a Hebrew name?" Marika recalled with nostalgia.

"And do you remember, Marika, what a success that recital was? You got invited to Cyprus after that."

"We both know who made the recital possible in Cyprus; he did. He was going to Cyprus anyway for an interview, though I forget who he was interviewing with."

"With King Hussein of Hejaz, back when the Jews would freely visit Palestine which was under British jurisdiction at the time."

"How do you remember all that!" Marika asked, impressed.

"Yes, but I also remember the meetings we had with his –" Helen hesitated for a moment. "His exes, shall I say?" she finally blurted somewhat annoyed, making Marika smile again.

"You remember even that?"

"That is something not easily forgotten. When he was saying goodbye to Elsa Lange in Jerusalem, the gentleman was inconsolable!"

Listening to Helen made Marika burst into laughter.

"And as if Elsa was not enough, he then took us to Tel Aviv to say goodbye to Lea!" Helen scoffed.

They talked and smiled, fell silent and welled up with tears, gazed upon each other and reminisced. They hardly noticed how the hours passed and the fresh sunlight crept into the funerary chamber. It wasn't until a sleepy Goudelis appeared that they realized it was really morning.

MONDAY, NOVEMBER 4, 1957

Athens

"Freddy, Freddy...." he heard someone calling his name faintly. His mother had placed her right hand on his stomach, trying to wake him up. He opened his eyes and immediately sprang up from the bed. He had packed his things the night before: the blue suit, which his mother had bought for him as a gift for his second prize in the *Vradyni* Literary Contest, and which he'd only worn once, a black shirt, and some personal care items. He ate his breakfast amid his mother's admonitions and advice on his upcoming trip, then rose from the table and embraced his mother, grandmother, and grandfather and bade them farewell with a kiss.

Freddy was elated with his first reporting mission. He also found himself enthralled with his grandfather's farewell just moments before; the old man had thrust his hand into his right coat pocket during their embrace. Freddy expertly slid his bag over to his left hand and placed his right hand in his pocket where he found his grandfather's little 'treasure' - some spending money. It appeared to be roughly a quarter of his salary. "Oh grandpa!" he whispered, as though he stood before him and could give him thanks.

Freddy pushed past these sentimental thoughts to the excitement of his impending trip. He'd take a taxi, he thought, which he'd surely find on Asklepiou Street. He was right, as he spotted a large 1950 DeSoto Suburban sedan parked about thirty meters away from him. Freddy approached to find the driver fast asleep inside. He knocked on the window. The driver opened one sleepy eye, then another. He gave Freddy a look-over, then motioned him to enter the taxi. Freddy circled the back of the car, grasping the door handle and planting himself opposite the driver in the back seat.

"Good morning. Where's the lad off to?"

"Good morning. To Hellenikon."

Freddy felt somewhat riled with that 'lad' comment. He was wearing the coat, after all; *why not call me sir instead*, he wondered.

"And where are you off to exactly, lad, if I may ask...?"

"To the airport."

"You've got a flight or something?" the taxi driver pressed on sarcastically, to which Freddy curtly replied, "Exactly."

He felt pretty good to have astounded the driver; a small satisfaction for that 'lad' comment.

"Where to, if I may ask...?" the driver rejoined, fully cured of his sleepiness.

"To Herakleion. I'm a journalist," Freddy said with pride.

"I see."

The driver didn't seem too interested in Freddy's professional capacity, though he was certain the inevitable question of the trip's reason would soon come up. He decided not to speak until the driver succumbed to his curiosity – a common characteristic of taxi drivers everywhere.

"And what are you going there for?"

The question came a few moments later, to Freddy's utter delight.

"I'm covering Kazantzakis' funeral," he said casually, playing the driver's game.

"Was he a good one? Because I can't figure it out...why did the church folks excommunicate him? What did he do to them anyway?"

"They didn't excommunicate him. They tried, but were unsuccessful," Freddy said proudly.

"I see. But they read him everywhere, I hear. In France, in Germany, in America, in Australia... If they read him everywhere, he must've been good. That's how it goes, doesn't it?"

"I think so too, that is how it goes..." the reporter replied halfheartedly.

The driver seemed to realize he had tired his passenger and gave the questions a rest. Freddy looked outside at the bright blue sky. He felt tired; this silly game with the taxi driver seemed trivial since he knew he would win in the end. He opened his suitcase next to him and pulled out *Zorba the Greek*. He'd read it several times, but he wanted to get back into Kazantzakis' Cretan worldview. At any rate, reading prevented the driver from starting up again with his impertinent questions.

Letters came and went on the page, sometimes dancing, sometimes jumbled...he'd only slept a few hours the night before, as he wasn't accustomed to going to bed early. His body was now down to core functions, and keeping his eyes open wasn't one of them.

"Hey, laddie, we're here! Wake up!"

He squinted his eyes, then shut them again. He wanted to remain lost in the daydream of Kazantzakis seated at the family table in his kitchen, discussing his future with his grandfather, or his promising book, or his article on the arrival of Jane Mansfield which had so regaled fellow journalists and readers alike. And with every good word his beloved grandfather would say, Kazantzakis would utter the same monotone phrase, "Yes, but he must try harder."

There is no worse phrase for youth to hear. There is no phrase more graceless for an older man to utter. And yet, there is nothing truer to be said by a respected elder to a promising, up and coming talented young man. Talent is the most attractive trap set for the young by the devil. They do something remarkable with greater ease than others, and therefore never have to work hard to advance their skill, they can just get by on talent. And so the day comes, when what they do is no longer remarkable, and they stagnate, and whosoever stagnates, dies a daily death. Like Sisyphus, carrying nothing and remaining still. There were countless like Sisyphus, stagnant since the beginning of time, but none of them became legend. And they never will.

"Young man, I said we're here! You're going to miss your flight."

Freddy snapped completely awake this time; gone was the kitchen table, the chairs, his grandfather and Kazantzakis.

"Hey, young man..."

"I know, I know, 'wake up, we're here'," he said, echoing the taxi driver.

He paid the fare and got out without another word to the driver, that destroyer of dreams...

Athens – Hellenikon Airport

Helen and Marika arrived at the apartment and agreed to bathe and then sleep for four hours – the number of hours one's constitution needs to regain strength. They had already packed their clothes, so that, upon waking at around twelve thirty, they dressed and had breakfast.

Emile kept informed of the previous night's terrible events from his own reporters, and said the church was now mired in an enormous scandal. It didn't surprise him when a journalist called just then to inform him that Archbishop Theoklitos wished to make a statement; Goudelis had made certain to tell the press every sordid detail and now the Archbishop would try to stave the reactions. The scandal, naturally, would remain a scandal: the Church had shut its doors firmly to the dead Kazantzakis.

"Dear Helen, my sincere congratulations on your honorable stance. Nikos would be so proud of you," Emile said while they sipped their tea.

At around one o'clock the two women got up, checked their luggage one last time and went downstairs to find a taxi. That Monday was a sunny day, but no less tiring for the workers scurrying quickly on the sidewalks or driving their jalopies – some laden with ice, metal or wood, some laden with exhausted Athenians.

The steep downhill grade of Syggrou Avenue made Helen a bit anxious. She wasn't used to this.

"I'm going to bother you again," she whispered to Marika, who seemed to be overheating under her black knit sweater.

"I'm worried about what we'll find in Herakleion. Do you think those fanatics will have riled up the locals?"

"That's a step too far!" Marika fumed, more for the sweater than the question. "Just a second," she said, twisting her torso left and right, and, with Helen's help, who pulled the right sleeve, she was finally free of the oppressive heat.

"There is no way they'd do something like that there. And besides, we would have heard about it. Here in Athens everything happened covertly, which would be impossible to do in a town as small as Nikos' birthplace."

"You're right. I hope that's true," Helen said, a bit more evenly as she tried to quell her fear of the downhill drive.

With the seaview to her right, she felt instantly better. It was just another ordinary day in Athens, with very little traffic on the coastal avenue.

"Look, everything will be fine. You've been like this for eight days, stomach drawn tighter than a drum, constantly expecting the worst. That's just cruel. You'll get sick in the end!" Marika said, clearly concerned.

"I want Nikos to have the end he deserves. Only that. Then I can focus on me. But for as long as nothing is in my power and everything has been irrevocably decided, I need to have all my wits about me. There will be journalists everywhere. One slip, one heartfelt reaction could blow everything out of proportion," Helen replied.

It was a quarter to two when the car pulled up to the outgoing flight terminal at Hellenikon airport. They entered the first building and went straight to the information desk for instructions. It wasn't long before they discerned familiar faces, clad in black, coming toward them. First came George

Papandreou, who, realizing the widow of his dead friend had arrived, rushed to introduce himself and pay his respects.

"Dear lady, please accept my heartfelt condolences. I grieve first as a friend, and then as a Greek. The loss is enormous," he said to her mournfully. "Please allow me to introduce to you, the Vice President of the Liberal Party, Sophocles Venizelos."

"My deep condolences, Mrs. Kazantzakis. Our nation has lost a truly worthy son. The void he leaves behind can never be filled."

"Thank you," Helen replied in a taut but forceful tone.

Agnes approached next, and kissed her discreetly as they embraced. Pantelis Prevelakis, Nikos' alter ego, especially following the death of Sikelianos, kissed her cheek and offered his sympathies. Helen's confidence soared. All of their closest friends were there: Kakrides, with whom Nikos had translated Homer's *Iliad* and *Odyssey*, Alexis Minotis, Manos Katrakis, Hatzikyriakos-Gikas.

A young man with glasses and a dark blue suit awaited his turn to pay his respects. Freddy was struggling to find the proper way to present his condolences to the widow; he had never found himself in a similar situation before. He thought to say, 'my sincerest condolences', for they were indeed sincere and everyone else had used the word 'deepest'. When he finally approached he steadied himself, held her gaze and bent to squeeze her hand gently.

"Mrs. Kazantzakis, please accept my sincerest condolences for the death of your husband, a man who will shine as a beacon of inspiration for all the coming generations of Greeks and will be considered a pivotal point in our contemporary Greek literature. I am Freddy Germanos, from *Eleftheria* newspaper."

He kept his voice steady, devoid of dramatic pitch or contrivance. In truth, he hadn't intended on saying all of that; it had flowed rather effortlessly, and most importantly, sincerely.

"Thank you Mr. Germanos."

She seemed to him utterly so devastated, so fatigued. It was to be expected, of course; he had overheard Agnes say she had spent the entire night in the funerary chamber with Marika

Papaioannou. Still, her handshake was warm, just enough to remind others of whom stood before them.

They offered Helen a chair to sit down. Agnes stood next to her, holding her hand silently, looking ahead; Marika stood to her left. Helen could see Venizelos and Papandreou and recalled the days when Nikos had headed the newly formed Socialist Worker's Union. The Nazis had withdrawn from Greece leaving it divided and the ever romantic Kazantzakis tried to avert the seemingly unavoidable Civil War that ensued. Helen smiled as she recalled his plea in *Eleftheria* newspaper, especially that last paragraph:

"Let us overcome our differences, let us unite in our love of liberty, in a Democratic Coalition, let us fight while we still can for Democracy, for social and economic justice and for Socialism. Because at this very moment, these priceless human values are at risk. Working classes of the world, unite!"

How far ahead he could see into the future and yet what an incurable dreamer he was! He had managed to cobble together some of the left factions, but the main bulk of the union had come from the Communist Party of Greece. He was appointed to the Sofoulis government as minister without portfolio, only to emerge a month and a half later, disappointed, perhaps, in himself, that he had managed to do so little when the needs were so many.

She recalled his anxious letters from Athens – where he was temporarily living at his sister's home – in which he wrote that he would go to the ministry in the morning and return home at midnight. He had made arrangements with Sofoulis for a trip to the United States and to Mexico, to present the dire situation of Greece and to secure aid. He didn't even have the time to help Sikelianos with his requests for innocent citizens who were being slandered and hauled unjustly to the courts.

She recalled every measure of that farcical time. When the majority of the parliament was ready to vote on legislation that would have reinstated pro-Venizelos officers, it ran into opposition from General Scobie – the shadow leader of the nation

– and Nikos then made the decision to resign. Two months later, the ruling figures of the state made it perfectly clear to Nikos that they had not forgotten him. When the Royal Theater staged his play *Kapodistrias,* as part of the independence day festivities, the play was met with staunch protest and was withdrawn after just two shows.

Kazantzakis, that 'red communist', was a 'Bolshevik rabble-rouser' to the right, and an agent of British intelligence to the left. He would smile bitterly and say, "I have been a language purist and a nationalist, a champion of vernacular tongue and a scientist, a poet, a socialist, a religious fanatic, an atheist and an esthète and none of these things can deceive me."

Freddy ravenously recorded every gesture, every smile, every expression on the faces of those gathered at the airport. He noted the sadness in the Old Man's eyes, the distant Kakrides, the restless Prevelakis, the somber Venizelos, the dynamic Rousopoulou, the noble Minotis, the rugged Katrakis, the sweet Hatzikyriakos-Gikas – he noted them all, even the angular face of the unknown, composed gentleman who later turned out to be the Norwegian author, Max Tau.

Their discussions revolved around Kazantzakis and his works, which Venizelos noted, "would now finally be acceptable to all, as 'the dead are finally free from sin'".

The Old Man however was quick to correct him.

"To be 'free from sin' doesn't mean that the deceased is acquitted of his former sins, only that he can sin no longer."

Goudelis appeared at that moment, the fatigue visible in his eyes as he greeted the gathering, one by one, and informed each of them that the body had arrived and that in a few moments they would be boarding the plane. Freddy made certain to place himself next to this most interesting source.

"The Archbishop's decision is most unfortunate, gentlemen," he heard the editor say to the Old Man and Venizelos, speaking to them as though they were his representatives.

"We tried, Mr. Goudelis, to avert this terrible turn. It seems all of the parareligious organizations exert a far greater influence on the clergy than either of us," the Old Man replied testily.

"It is a blow to the Orthodox Church, not to Kazantzakis," Venizelos fumed.

"Theoklitos convened the press today. He told them that it is true that Kazantzakis' friends contacted him and requested a church for the body to lay in state, and that he was more than happy to oblige."

"What hypocrisy!" Papandreou reacted.

"Just listen to his statement! 'I asked to speak with the priest at the church where the body was to lay in state, to give him some final instructions, but the priest didn't show up until six in the afternoon, at which time I was informed that the body was being moved to Athens.'

"They asked him what happened next, and he said that he advised to move the body to the funerary chamber of the First Cemetery of Athens. And when pressed as to whether the Church had any reason to deny the dead Kazantzakis his funerary rites in a church, he answered, verbatim, 'Of course not. Kazantzakis was a wise man. If, in the past, he was somehow misunderstood, that is completely unknown to me and irrelevant.'"

"Spoken like a politician!" Venizelos exploded.

Freddy listened to the whole conversation rooted firmly in place, and did not move even when a police officer told them it was time to board the plane.

"To be clear, we must tell the whole truth because we will be asked by the press," the Old Man suggested to Goudelis. "We're not going to play this dangerous game."

Just before they exited the building, Venizelos bid farewell to Papandreou and Goudelis, as he would not be flying to Crete. Freddy walked past them casually, so as not to be obvious. Most of the passengers had already begun boarding the plane, and he followed up the stairs. He noticed two empty seats in the back of the plane and started to make his way when he noticed that Papandreou and Goudelis had sat away from him, near the door. He instantly regretted it, but it was too late.

Helen was engrossed in the gentle interplay of the clouds with the sun. High up in the sky, surrounded by friends, she felt at peace for the first time. She couldn't recall if she had ever felt such peace. Agnes was always at her side, her guardian angel, Marika sat behind her, Goudelis in front of her and Papandreou next to him, to his right; and below them all, lay the sea.

"How long has it been since you've been to Crete?" Agnes asked.

"I went last year, but I went alone, to the set of Dassin's film, *He Who Must Die*. Nikos didn't want to come."

"I never understood that. Why didn't he want to go home, especially when a film was being made there based on his book?"

Helen didn't answer. She didn't want to speak, she had already plunged deeply into the misty blue horizon of memory. The first time she had set foot in Crete, she had been a pretty girl; she had flirted with Kazantzakis, hoping to travel the world with him, and the last time he had visited her, her wish had come true. She had been proud that her husband's novel, *Christ Recrucified*, was being made into a film with international stars like Jules Dassin and Melina Merkouri. Helen would wake up early in the morning to watch the residents of Kritsas, that tiny village sprawled on the peaks of Mount Kastellos in Lasithi, give their best selves to the film each day, though they were not actors and though their lives depended little on the effort.

These memories played in her mind, like the clouds played with the sun, the way Dassin had played with his resident-actors – whom he would gather every evening in the local schoolyard and read to them the script for the following day, with Melina acting as their interpreter. And those resident-actors would listen, enthralled at their instructions for the next day, proud that they would utter words written by Nikos. She remembered how Melina had to split them up; how some of them were to play the residents of the rich village while the rest, the residents of the poor village. All of them wanted to be the 'good folk' of the poor village; it didn't matter how Melina shouted at them that the daily wage was bigger for the 'bad' village and that they would get to be on screen for longer in that part. They still wanted to be poor!

Kazantzakis' adamant refusal of Dassin's invitation to visit the set had truly mystified Helen. He had been equally dismissive when his friend, Demosthenes Danielides had written to him to inform him that the Peace Committee wanted to honor him with the Vienna Peace Prize. "That award should be given to someone who's suffered for peace," he had said. *Classic Nikos,* Helen gazed off, as though he stood before her. Danielides had pressed on, however, telling Kazantzakis that the decision had been unanimous, going so far as to remind him that this was the same prize given to Charlie Chaplin and Dmitry Shostakowich. This softened Nikos somewhat; that, and the knowledge that he would be honored together with the Chinese painter, Qi Baishi.

In Vienna, where the ceremony had been held, Helen had come to understand that the world viewed Nikos as a living literary legend. So many prominent figures attended the ceremony, yet the official Greek state was nowhere to be found. Not even the Greek ambassador made an appearance; under other circumstances, and, had any other Greek been the recipient of such an honor, the ambassador would have certainly been present. Helen had noticed that Kazantzakis seemed not to care. He no longer craved recognition, but rather delighted in being with friends, taking his strolls, getting lost in museums.

Goudelis, Maglis and Agis Theros had all traveled to Vienna especially for the ceremony, and yet, the most distinguishing hallmark of such Kazantzakian gatherings had been decidedly absent: his spirited laughter no longer filled the air. Helen would notice this behavior a year later as well, in Cannes. She started to put the pieces together, but was missing the most important one: him!

Herakleion

It wasn't the first time Freddy had flown in an airplane; an uncle of his had once gifted him a trip to Constantinople two years before. At the time of his visit, the relations between the two countries had been quite taut, and he had happened upon a gathering at Taksim Square where hundreds of thousands of Turks were listening to the main proponent of the anti-Greek bloc present his arguments. He had managed to make his way to the first rows near the podium, and when the speech had ended, he had approached a member of the security team, explaining in English that he was a journalist and wanted an interview with the speaker.

He had been told to wait, and in a few moments he was led before the Turkish politician, who had asked him for his name and where he was from. Freddy had replied that he was American, giving an assumed name and said that he worked for the *Chicago Tribune*, the newspaper Ernest Hemingway occasionally wrote for. Naturally his mannerism had been anything but American, and his English was even less convincing, seeing as he had picked most of it up in movie theaters, watching Hollywood films. When the interview was over, the Turkish politician had smiled and said, "My regards to Athens."

Now he had a second flight; *a second story I can tell into my old age.* Just a few rows ahead of him were some of the most prominent Greeks of the time, sitting in silence, transporting their fascinating compatriot to his final resting place. *If each one of them would tell me their favorite story of Kazantzakis, I'd write the most incredible biography*, he thought with youthful voracity.

The Herakleion airport was flooded with people, cars, dignitaries, honorary guards, and anguish. Grieving faces sought the comfort of their loved ones, and even the clouds seemed determined to shield them as they gathered around the sun, bringing about the most convenient dimness. The distant hum made faces tilt upward and bodies sit upright, straining to spot the sound in the sky.

"There it is!" an outstretched hand raised a pointed finger, and every head turned in unison to look. It was four o'clock in the afternoon. The back of the plane dipped, like a seagull hovering over the sea, prey in sight, ready to grasp it with its claws. At the same time below, the police gathered around the crowd, creating a barrier between the mourning multitude and the airplane. The buzzing noise became louder, frightful, but the crowd stayed rooted in place. The wheels touched down with a shrill sound on the first try, much like the sound made by the fish – if it had a voice – the moment the seagull plunges its talons into its flesh. The plane, perfectly straight now, taxied around the strip, approaching the crowd humbly before presenting it's treasured cargo. It soon was spent of power and noise, and the time of absolute silence was upon them.

Freddy looked around a bit flustered. He could see half of the passengers with their faces glued to the windows, and behind them, the remaining travelers from further inside the plane, straining to catch a glimpse outside. Freddy looked at Helen, trying to gauge her first reactions. She cast a discreet, enigmatic glance out the window. She could have been praying or thinking of nothing at all; no one could possibly know the thoughts of a widow.

The ladder was set in place, and everyone returned to their seats. Only the Old Man remained standing, making his way to the exit. He beckoned gently to Helen to stand up. He exited first and lingered on that first step for a moment, enough to see and to be seen by the crowd, and began his measured, composed descent from the plane. A hushed whisper grew louder and louder as people called out in recognition: "The Old Man!"

No doubt, the sight of Papandreou is a comfort to the people of Herakleion, whose spirits have been crushed by the Archbishop's disgraceful decision to deny a church for the public wake, Freddy reasoned.

It had also become widely known that Achilleas Gerokostopoulos would be attending the funeral, a political figure respected by friends and enemies alike, and so everyone was hopeful that the funeral would proceed in the manner befitting a man of Kazantzakis' stature.

Agnes straightened Helen's clothes one last time, and helped her wear her veil. Freddy watched as Helen closed her eyes for just a moment, then exited the plane. The Cretans did not know Helen, though they had seen her in photographs. She came out after Papandreou, clad in her veil and her mourning black clothes – and the tide immediately shifted from admiration and relief over Papandreou's presence to compassion and grief at the sight of Helen. Her steadfast air, as she descended the steps with her head held high, made it clear she was determined to thwart those who wanted to watch her fall apart.

Freddy looked out the window, taking it all in, jotting down his notes in swift, furious strokes in his notebook. His words looked more like an indecipherable doctor's script than the notes of a journalist. He watched on as the head of police saluted the Old Man and Helen who stood at the foot of the stairs. Alexis Minotis and Manos Katrakis followed next – their grief in plain view for all to see. One by one, Goudelis, Tau, Theros, Kakrides, Marika, all began their descent from the plane. Freddy exited last; he did not stand with the dignitaries, but moved towards the crowd for a better sense of the moment.

It took several minutes for the large, black coffin to emerge from the depths of the plane where it was loaded onto a waiting ambulance with great care. The pilots and crew had all disembarked by then, and were standing at attention, next to the esteemed passengers. Helen stood, knowing full well she carried on her shoulders the expectations not only of her dead husband, but of all wives. She struggled to remain composed, strong, dynamic. No one could comprehend what she was letting go of inside of that coffin. Who could possibly understand? Perhaps only his two sisters could; Anastasia and Helen were there to receive him, though the hadn't truly known him as an adult, for it had been so many years since they'd last seen him.

Freddy pulled out his notebook once more, jotting everything down, asking those next to him for information. The Prefect of Herakleion, the Mayor, the entire city council and numerous local authorities were all in attendance. Still, not a priest in sight. It wasn't just Freddy who noticed the glaring blunder on the part of the Church, which continued to stoke the fire. Was this a sign it would persist in its harsh stance?

"Where are the priests?" someone yelled from the crowd.

"Disgrace!" another voice rang out.

Everyone knew of the Archbishop's ignoble decision, who feared "riots from parareligious organizations," but only a few did not know how quick to anger the explosive Cretan temper was, and this unholy decision justified that anger.

"Freddy, Freddy!" he heard a voice call out amid the thronging multitude. The reporter tried but could not make out a face, though the deep voice grew louder and louder. A dark haired portly man of fifty, with medium height, a gruff gray beard, and a black suit with thin white pinstripes had been trying to reach him. Stepping on and getting stepped on, he finally prevailed through the crowd and stood before him.

"Are you Freddy?" he asked.

"Are you the Cretan?"

"I sure am!" he said and opened his arms wide to embrace him. "I was keeping an eye out for you."

"And find me you did. What is going on here? There are so many people, I honestly didn't expect it."

"I told you, all of Crete is in mourning. By the way, did you hear?" he asked, then, not waiting for an answer, pressed on, "Kantiotis sent a telegram to our Metropolitan, telling him he plans to come to Herakleion tomorrow to stop the funeral procession."

"Kantiotis?" Freddy asked to make certain.

"Yes, that monster," the Cretan replied. "And you know, he has a following here."

"Do a lot of people know here in Herakleion?"

"Well, everyone you see here, for sure," the Cretan answered and moved slightly so as to reveal to Freddy the crowd behind him, which had swelled to more than eight hundred people. Most of them were young men, bearded and dark haired; their blood was boiling, partly owing to the sun, and partly to their Cretan heritage.

"Come on, let's get going to Saint Minas Church to pay our respects," a young man in his twenties was heard saying to his friend.

"Let's see, will we find a priest there or will they have abandoned the church completely?"

"Yes, to Saint Minas," the crowd repeated, confirming the plan.

Freddy asked the Cretan if he had a car.

"No, but I have a taxi waiting."

"Alright, then wait here for a moment."

The reporter ran to Goudelis, to confirm that everyone would indeed be going to Saint Minas Church, and then went to pick up his luggage. He returned to the Cretan who had been waiting for him and it was clear from his dilated, teary eyes and his puffy, red cheeks that he had been crying.

"Shall we go?" Freddy asked, and the Cretan nodded.

Freddy tried to be discreet. One doesn't stare intently at a crying man, especially if he is a Cretan. He tried to lighten the air between them as they pushed through the crowd.

"Could we drive by the Martinengo Bastion? To see the tomb? I need to write about it," he asked the Cretan, careful to avoid his gaze, certain he'd say yes.

"Yes, let's go," the Cretan replied heavily, wiping his tears with a white handkerchief. "Follow."

He quickened his pace with his head hung low and his frame slack as he faintly seemed to stoop.

Freddy fell slightly behind, out of breath as he tried to keep sight of that hump in the crowd, for the people were many and they were all pushing in the same direction, where cars were parked and animals leashed to their carts were waiting. The dark haired man stopped at a parked car, opened the passenger door and climbed in. When he suddenly realized the young man from Athens wasn't with him in the taxi he hopped out and began to call out.

"Germanos!"

Everyone stopped to see who this 'German' was; Freddy sped up, rather embarrassed, and climbed into the taxi without a single word.

"So he's a German, is he?" the driver asked the Cretan suspiciously.

"No, friend, he's Greek. That's just his last name."

The driver turned the key in the ignition and looked past the back seat as he backed out. Freddy noticed that his eyes were also misty and his cheeks glistened with tears. Freddy lowered his gaze, trying not to intrude. He pulled out his notebook from his coat pocket and began to pour over his notes.

The driver took advantage of the slow pace and joined the motorcade of countless cars moving along reverently as they followed the giant coffin. Freddy did not look up from his notes; the driver and the Cretan were silent, like caravan drivers in the desert, following the long, drawn out funeral procession. They drove on, slowly leaving the airport behind them, passing by horse drawn carriages, shepherds with their flocks, sheep and guard dogs along the road.

There are some moments where one instinctively knows when to stay silent, when the moment is destined to be retold over the coming years. The three men may have wished to not see the day Kazantzakis would return to Crete in a casket, but since that wish could not come true, their next wish surely would be to experience every instant of that historic moment.

"I'd like to go to Martinengo where he'll be buried," the reporter said after he'd finished reading his notes.

"Alright," the driver replied crisply. "Who was that man with Katrakis?" he asked curiously.

"That was a celebrated actor, Alexis Minotis, perhaps the finest one we've ever had. He's played in films abroad, too, even in a Hitchcock film," Freddy informed him, then realized the driver had no idea who the director was and frankly didn't care.

"Ah, Minotakis' son. I know him! He's from Chania, isn't he? Yes, I know him. He's Paxinou's husband!" The driver exclaimed, pleased with himself for knowing this tidbit. Freddy and the Cretan smiled with him.

"Were there really eight hundred people out there?" Freddy asked.

"Maybe more," the Cretan replied, "but Freddy, you should be concerned with something else. I think we should first go to the church, to Saint Minas. We should see if everything is alright, if there will be any priests present, if they'll accept the casket. Then we can go to Martinengo."

He made a sound point.

"Fine, then, to Saint Minas," Freddy ordered.

Freddy turned several times to glance at the motorcade following the casket, impressed. It confirmed the more level headed view which held that the Church had made an enormous mistake on both, a public relations and a religious level.

Herakleion had commenced its grieving long before the coffin arrived in its winding streets. Freddy counted the women clad in black who stood by the side of the road to greet their fellow countryman. The muted silence was only pierced by the occasional funerary shout, "May his memory be eternal!" Old women with black kerchiefs on their heads knelt in tears and crossed themselves, damning Death.

Freddy was transfixed by all he saw: local shops with pictures of Kazantzakis in the storefront windows, terraces linked with ropes and little paper flags hanging from them, balconies adorned with Greek flags as though it were a national holiday.

Kazantzakis was being given the honor of a head of state. At some point, the cars could go no further, and the passengers disembarked and began to walk to Saint Minas on foot. The little side streets around the church teemed with people arrayed in black, waiting to pay their respects.

"Should we continue on foot?" the Cretan wondered.

"How far is it to Martinengo Bastion?" Freddy asked.

"Ten, fifteen minutes, tops. Can you take it, laddie?" the Cretan asked jokingly.

"It's you I'm worried about!" Freddy shot back with a laugh.

After making certain that the deceased had taken his rightful place inside the church, and that all was calm, Freddy and the Cretan began the ascent to Martinengo. They passed groups of old women gossiping about the arrival of Kazantzakis and what Helen and the other dignitaries were wearing, and shopkeepers who were discussing the day's events with their customers on the sidewalk. The shops were all shuttered, of course, to keep at bay the sorrow that had permeated the entire city, a sorrow both an orphan and a child of all.

"There it is!" the Cretan yelled as he pointed ahead to the spot that would become the author's final resting place.

Freddy had begun to sweat in the unbearable humidity. A couple of workers were leveling the path with their shovels; further down, another worker was patting a mound of dirt with his shovel as rapid strokes of soil came flying out from a hole in the ground. The smell of dirt commingled with the humid air.

"Good afternoon, friends. How are you doing?" the Cretan greeted them.

"Good afternoon to you, too," one of the workers replied.

The other worker kept tossing the dirt out of the pit, digging in silence. Perhaps he was greeting them in his own way.

Freddy hardly realized he had circled around himself as he soaked in the beauty of the landscape.

"Herakleion with the open sea below, and Mount Juktas and the Lasithi mountain range above. He would like the view," the chatty worker said to Freddy as he lit a cigarette.

"It's an incredible spot," Freddy agreed.

The Cretan swelled with pride, then turned to the workers once more.

"Are you done here, friends?"

"Well, we're done with the cleaning. We need to dig a little more and we'll be off."

"You need to go deeper."

"We'll be here tomorrow morning, too," the chatty local replied as the shoveling inside of the pit slowed to a stop.

Freddy took out his notebook. *Martinengo Bastion sits atop the highest point of the city*, he wrote. *It is a Venetian stronghold surrounded by trees. The vista here is panoramic – with views of Mount Juktas, the Lasithi mountains and the sea of Crete. The city of Herakleion lies at its feet below, with its shuttered windows, silent and mourning.*

He put his notebook away and turned to the Cretan and motioned it was time to go.

"Let's go down to Saint Minas. I want to speak with the people," he said.

It had grown dark by the time the two men walked down Giamboudi Street and passed by two old ladies standing at the stoop of a house where they were conversing in hushed whispers. One was in tears. A few meters away, a man no more than fifty stood outside of a basket shop, watching them. Freddy stopped suddenly.

"Good evening. I'm a reporter from Athens, from *Eleftheria* newspaper. I came here for Kazantzakis' funeral. Would you like to say a few words?"

"Do you see those old women there in tears?" the man asked him as he pointed. "That's what Crete was like when we heard Venizelos died," he said tersely, then stormed into his shop before breaking down. Freddy tried to follow him in but the Cretan restrained him by his shoulder.

"Come. We'll find more people further down the road," he said quietly but firmly.

Freddy jotted the man's comment in his notebook. Once at the church, they found many groups of people waiting outside and a long line leading to the casket inside. Several people left their group momentarily to greet the Cretan and went back to their line. Freddy found a good perch fit for a reporter, as he leaned against the church wall with the whole courtyard at his feet. He observed the people and tried to gauge their sentiments, beyond their obvious grief.

"I wrote a poem for Kazantzakis and I'm going to send it to the paper to be published," a young girl, no more than twelve, told him when he asked her if she knew the deceased.

"And what is the title?" Freddy asked.

"*Ode to Kazantzakis*," she replied boldly.

Freddy kept his notebook out; he spoke with a young waiter and an old man who could not stop crying, telling him how he had known the deceased since he was a child. The Cretan told him people were also paying their respects to the sisters at the Kazantzakis paternal home, but Freddy did not have time to go there. He needed to write the story and dictate it over the telephone. The time was eight-thirty; he thought it might be best to write the story on the spot, and the Cretan took him to a coffee shop a few meters away. He realized his hands were numb from carrying the suitcase he hadn't had a chance to set down.

"Greek coffee," he told the young waiter who looked at him curiously, trying to determine which of the famous figures that had arrived for the funeral Freddy could be.

"At this hour? But you've had nothing to eat," the Cretan said in fatherly protest.

"I write better on an empty stomach. I'll eat later, after it's done," Freddy answered, taking out his notebook.

"Alright. I'll walk around a bit, see how things are going and I'll be back in an hour," the Cretan agreed and left him alone.

Freddy settled comfortably in the wicker chair and started to organize his notes on the issues he felt were important and worth mentioning. He'd write about the teary crowd at the airport, the impressive motorcade, the enormous lines outside of the church; he liked the parallel drawn by the fifty-year old man on the death of Venizelos and Kazantzakis, and was certain he would include the riveting quote by the deceased himself, "I want to spend my last hours in Crete, to return to mother earth, the earth she lent to me."

The waiter, who was no more than nineteen years old, brought his coffee and placed it on the wooden table.

"Here you go, Mr. Writer."

"Oh, thank you," Freddy replied, realizing he had sounded like his grandfather just then. *I wonder how they are doing*, he thought, but had no time for a family phone call. He took one sip and dove straight back into his notes and ideas.

The text had a lovely flow, but he was stuck somewhere toward the end. The descriptions were short but concise, and the facts were presented in their true dimension, without exaggeration or pompous characterizations. But something was missing. He didn't despair; he drank another sip. And another. Around the third sip of coffee, he decided to walk back to Saint Minas Church. He motioned the waiter over to pay him.

"I'll be back in a bit," he informed him. "If a man comes in looking for me, tell him to sit and wait. And keep this suitcase safe," Freddy said with an air that had no effect on the young Cretan.

"Well if a customer comes in and sits down, I'm not making him get up. Are we clear?" the waiter asked, prompting Freddy to laugh.

"Clear," Freddy agreed, placing his notebook in his inner coat pocket.

He walked along, lost in thought, searching for the missing piece that would give his story it's impressive conclusion. He turned the corner to Saint Minas and saw the courtyard brimming with people. There were now three lines going into the church.

"Ah Freddy, you came," the Cretan said, who had spotted him some time ago in the crowd and appeared suddenly before him. "Come, let me tell you what I found out."

He drew him aside.

"So, the casket will remain closed. They won't open it at all."

"Well that makes sense," Freddy reasoned. "It's been so many days. It's been a week."

"Yes, and there's more. Over one hundred unions have pledged their participation in the public mourning," the Cretan continued with an air of grandiosity.

"Really? That's a huge number..." Freddy commented as he jotted down these last two points for his story.

"Yes, and the number is constantly growing."

"Alright then, I'm heading back to the coffee shop. I'll wait for you there."

Freddy weaved through the thronging multitude that had spontaneously left their homes to pay their respects, without any personal gain or purpose, like attending a election rally, or out of pleasure, like going to the fair. An old man leaning on his walking stick crossed his path. Freddy was struck by his almost biblical appearance, as though he had stepped out of an old post card.

"Grandpa, did you know Kazantzakis?" Freddy asked him.

"I knew him, my boy. I'm older than he is, of course I remember him."

"And what do you remember the most about him, grandpa?"

"I remember him saying, 'One day, I'll either be God or I'll be dead'." The old man laughed and started his slow pace toward the lines outside the church. Freddy chuckled, and wrote down the phrase in his notebook.

That old man had given Freddy the perfect ending to his story.

"Hey, grandpa...when did he say that?" he called out to the old man who hadn't gotten far.

"The year Venizelos took him into office," the old man answered without turning back. Freddy scratched his head, trying to recall when that was.

When he returned to the coffee shop, he found others sitting at his table. "Don't fret, I have a better one for you," the waiter said with a friendly pat on the back. It irked Freddy. "Here's your office," the waiter pointed to a wooden table set before a fragrant garden with beautiful colors. He swiftly wiped down the table.

"I'll be back with your raki."

Freddy sat down, took out his notebook, and added the new details to his text. He began to craft his epilogue, taking a deep breath, filling his lungs with the Cretan autumnal air. He wrote, erased, stopped, went back, wrote again, erased again. Perhaps he did more erasing than writing.

The raki came but he paid no attention. This was his moment. The piece he was submitting had to be worthy of the enormous trust placed in him by Androulidakis. Freddy's stern glance dissipated as he read over the article one last time. He took off his glasses and rubbed his forehead and downed the raki in a single gulp. He put his glasses back on and read over the last paragraph: "In 1912 Kazantzakis had predicted: 'I will either become God or I will die'. He kept his word as a fine, honest Cretan man. He became the God of Crete before death could claim him." That was it!

He raised the second raki to his health, and to the joy and sorrow he felt in equal measure. He drank it with his eyes closed, and when he opened them, he was already thinking about his next moves. He had to call the paper and dictate his article; for that, he had to get to the hotel where the newspaper had booked his lodging. It was probably the only place where he could place the call, anyhow. He decided to go there immediately, but first, he would stop by Saint Minas Church, to see how things were going and to thank the Cretan for all of his invaluable help.

The church was now swelling with people, most of them young. The elders were resting, for tomorrow would be yet another demanding day. Two were the names on everyone's lips: Theoklitos and Kantiotis. The provocative stance of the Church monopolized all conversation, and even now, mere hours before the funeral, no one knew whether the Metropolitan of Crete, Eugenios, would offer prayers and hymns to the deceased. Still, the fact that Kazantzakis' remains were in Crete at all within the walls of that church, was a victory for the Cretans, nonetheless, and a message of hope.

Heraklion, Saint Minas Church

Helen sat in chair, gazing tirelessly at Nikos' photograph atop the enormous casket. She could not get enough of it, being interrupted ever so often by people who came to give her their condolences. She saw the endless lines forming, growing larger as time went by. What a wonderful gift the people of Herakleion had in store for Nikos! How could she tell him now that he had been wrong not to visit Herakleion sooner? She finally felt she was on safe ground. She was not defenseless against the raging appetites of her husband's gutless enemies, of Melas and the rest who would live on in infamy for their evil pursuit, for censoring Nikos and slandering him.

Was all of this necessary? She wondered. *Of course it was.* She knew it now, though she never admitted it to him while he was alive. That had been the otherworldly charm of Nikos: to never falter while climbing his ascent. How it had bothered her, when he would simply smile when her courage wavered in the face of this relentless battle. The persecution, the exclusion that led to his self-imposed exile, the endless hunt across the farthest reaches of the world, were, to him, a badge of honor in the asymmetrical war waged by an entire system against a single man. Just then a commotion was heard outside, and heads turned in unison toward the church entrance.

"Antichrist! Rabble-rouser! May you rot, you communist!"

The disturbance lasted only a few moments, enough to evince the quality of Kazantzakis' enemies. Helen stroked the coffin calmly.

"More badges for your honor, my love," she whispered.

Agnes left her seat to see what was going on outside. She returned quickly, telling Helen that a few fanatics had started cursing outside but soon turned and ran when the men in the courtyard moved against them. Helen remained stoic, as those who knew her would have expected of her. She was used to this kind of harassment.

The mournful wake resumed. Helen looked at the long lines of grieving faces and thought of Nikos' struggle, not only for their friends but for all people who struggle, Greek and German, Austrian and Italian, Spanish and Chinese – especially the Chinese, who had gifted to Nikos the best godspeed anyone could wish for on his final journey.

She recalled a story Kazantzakis loved to tell: once, he had taken a walking stick from his satchel and had started to trek up the mountains. It was during the time the Germans were attacking Norway, but up in Psiloritis mountain, where he had been climbing, he had heard a voice call out to him amid the rocks.

"Hey friend, wait! Wait, let me ask you!' An old shepherd was climbing down swiftly, in danger of slipping. I stopped and waited for him. What could he want, I wondered? Why such a hurry? When he finally neared, he asked me, 'What's the news from Norway?' This old shepherd couldn't find Norway on a map, but he practically flung himself down the mountain in his hurry to ask me what was happening, if the Norwegian people were losing their freedom. 'Things are better, grandpa, don't you worry,' I answered him. He crossed himself and said, 'Praise be to God.' 'Would you like a cigarette?' I asked him. 'What would I do with a cigarette?' I don't want for anything, just for Norway to be well,' he said, and started climbing up the rocks to find his flock. Damn if he knew where Norway even was or how far it was from Crete."

The more time passed the less she could feel her legs. Still, she did not allow herself to abandon her post, for everyone who stopped by the casket wanted to impart a comforting word to the widow. Marika and Agnes told her she should move aside and rest a little, or perhaps leave entirely and return the following morning for the funeral, but Helen would not go. She could never forgive herself if she left him alone in his final hours.

"Agnes, did you remember to tell Goudelis his final wish? What it should say on the tombstone cross?"

"Don't worry, Helen. I've already spoken to him."

"*I hope for nothing, I fear for nothing, I am free.*"

"Yes, Helen. Everything will be done as he wanted."

This comforted Helen, but only momentarily.

"Agnes, did we put the *Odyssey* inside the coffin?"

"Yes, yesterday. Don't worry, rest easy. You will have to change clothes, though, and freshen up a bit. Eat something. When are we going to have the time to do all of that?" Agnes asked tenderly.

"When day breaks. Where is my luggage?"

"We dropped it off at your nephew Nikos' house."

Heraklion, Hotel Florida

Herakleion looked abandoned, a lifeless, empty city surrendered to the dark. Its ambiance had receded into the defeatism and self-pity imposed upon the defiant by the powerful. This is how the

Cretans thought of the game, anyhow, though they were losing and they knew it.

Freddy wasn't able to get in touch with the Cretan. He decided to go to his hotel, his mind already on the next day's events. The funeral was scheduled for eleven a.m. but he would have to be up by six. He walked downhill and found two young men, dressed in black, and asked them for directions to his hotel. They were headed to Saint Minas Church, no doubt.

Back at the newspaper, they had told him to take August 25th Street all the way down to Hotel Florida. The muscles in his legs felt the sting of a thousand tiny needles; he needed to rest, not to waste any more of his energy. He finally arrived at an imposing, stone cut building, and straightened his shoulders. *This must be it*, he mused as he entered and looked around at the distinctly Cretan décor on the walls. *Well it's no Grand Bretagne, but it's no hovel, either.*

"I'd like a room, please," Freddy approached the clerk at the reception.

"Certainly, sir. How many nights?" the clerk answered eagerly, trying hard to mask his heavy Cretan accent.

"Just one night and we'll see after that...."

The clerk scoured through half of the register with his pencil, in the strict manner customary of hotel clerks everywhere, then sounded a perfunctory, "hmmm" – to appropriately express his concern – before finally announcing he had found a room.

"Number 124. It's on the first floor, up the stairs, second door to the right. Breakfast is served between six a.m. and ten a.m. If I could have your identification, please."

Freddy pulled out his identification card from his pant's back pocket and handed it to the clerk.

"Enjoy your stay, sir. Let me get the key to your room."

"Actually, I'd like to place a call first, to *Eleftheria* newspaper," Freddy requested.

"Right this way," the receptionist said politely and pointed to the telephone on the counter.

It took Freddy ten minutes to dictate his piece to the typist at the paper. He could tell from the tone of her voice and her lively affirmatives as she urged him to continue that his article was interesting, which was good; he had seen and heard her in the past, exhaling loudly whenever she took a dictation over the phone that bored her.

He didn't know whether to feel guilty or not that he was thrilled with the notion his article was appealing. It seemed terrible that the messenger could be pleased with delivering sad news, but that was the way of the journalist.

So I must be doing it right, though perhaps I shouldn't say that out loud.

He took the key and his luggage and started up the stairs to his room. A single bed, a nightstand, a single closet, a bathroom door, a single chair – all a single color: dark brown. He threw his bag down on the bed and drew back the curtain to look out upon autumnal Herakleion. He was taking in the inky sea view when he heard a knock at the door.

"Coming," he said. The knocking stopped.

He paused for a moment, perplexed.

"Who is it?"

"Room service. I've brought some warm water."

Freddy opened the door to a young man, slightly younger than himself, holding a green basin.

"Thank you very much." He took the basin while the young man disappeared before the door could even close.

Freddy bathed and went promptly to bed. It was around a quarter past nine; though tired, as he was, he still could not fall asleep. He tossed and turned, thinking of nothing and thinking about everything in an effort to tire his mind, but hunger and tension could not be defeated by sleep.

How can you sleep up here without a care when History is in the making downstairs? he chided himself. He gave up staring at the ceiling and got dressed. In a matter of minutes he was back down in the hotel lobby.

"Any suggestions about where to go?" he asked the receptionist.

"Well, are you hungry? In the mood for dessert? Perhaps a drink?" the clerk tried to clarify.

"All of it," Freddy admitted.

"Well, the bride market is just up the street."

"I didn't say I wanted to get married, sir!" Freddy interrupted him.

"I didn't tell you to get married, sir. It's just what we informally call the local square where everyone meets. All roads lead to and end at the Lions' Square. Now this hotel," he said, "is on Illusion Street."

"What? I thought this was August 25ᵗʰ Street?" Freddy asked, confused.

"Oh it is, but we also call it Illusion Street. That's because the beautiful buildings on this street mesmerize the traveler, but there aren't any others in the city like it," the clerk replied with the certitude of a National Geographic report.

"Okay, so you are suggesting I go to the Lions' Square, then?"

"That's right. If you wish to eat or drink, just go to a raki parlor, either at Limnides' or Papatsaras'. That's where the high society goes. After that, you can also enjoy some lovely fresh pastries at Kirkor's."

"So, Limnides' or Papatsaras', and then Kirkor's. Got it. And where do I find it?"

"Just further up the road."

"Any suggestions on what to eat?"

"Just go on, now, and ask for some raki, and the good folks there will feed you, don't you worry," the clerk forgot himself and slipped in his natural Cretan accent, making Freddy laugh.

"Thanks a lot. So how do I get to the Lions' Square?"

"You just go out and up the hill, you'll see it on your right hand side in about four hundred meters," the clerk replied, somewhat embarrassed to have slipped into his native accent in his enthusiasm for the local delicacies.

Freddy walked out the main entrance and set course for the famous square. The light breeze made the uphill walk easier, and he could hear hushed conversations in the gardens of the houses he passed, though the people on the street seemed sullen and lost in thought.

"Excuse me, sir, I'd like to ask if you know where Papatsaras' tavern is?" he asked an older man with a white mustache and a black suit with thin white pinstripes, who was escorting a much younger woman in a light blue dress.

"About one hundred meters ahead, you'll see it," the man replied hurriedly.

Young and old, everyone was out on a stroll, talking quietly. Presently, he saw the famed water fountain adorned with lions. His hunger had become so unbearable, that he plopped himself at the first available table he found. The table was old and worn, much like his desk back at his office; he immediately felt a welcome familiarity. The emptiness he'd observed before had given way to throngs of pedestrians pouring into the town square; clearly, most of them had been at the church earlier, and he felt fortunate to have found this little table, set on the side of the building, propped against a mustard colored wall. A beautiful bougainvillea climbed up that wall next to his table, reaching atop the building. *It's the pink kind, definitely not the red.*

His mind trailed to the girl in the blue polka dot dress from Dexameni.

Perhaps I'll give her a pink rose, he thought, when the waiter interrupted him.

"What will it be, mister?" the young waiter asked. "Before you fix to tell me, have a raki, ease your troubles," he suggested, and left a small carafe of raki and a shot glass on the table.

Freddy offered a hasty "cheers" and drank the spirit in a single gulp.

"Now tell me, what is there to eat?" he asked as the waiter was setting the bread basket on the table.

"How about a salad, some chicory greens, and a fine lamb offal?"

Freddy smiled.

"Bring me that. Will it take long?"

"No, boss, don't you worry," the young waiter replied.

A man with a perfectly balanced mustache caught Freddy's eye; he seemed absolutely poised, holding a thick walking stick with its beautifully curved bronze handle. He was speaking to three other locals, and they seemed to be about sixty years old – or appeared old, at any rate, possibly from a lifetime of war and hardship.

"If the politicians can't bring the Church to its senses, they should let us know so we can do it."

"Is it certain, though?" asked one of the men, who wore wire-rimmed glasses. "The Athenians don't want our priests to give service to Kazantzakis?"

"That's what my priest said. Why would he lie? They say Kantiotis sent a threatening letter to our Metropolitan. 'Don't you bury him', it said."

"And what could they do to the priests if they do?" the man in glasses queried.

"That's what I asked. My priest said they'd be cast out of the clergy," the old man replied, grasping the small shot glass with his large fingers as he swallowed the raki in a single gulp.

"There's five hundred thousand Athenians, and they've produced not a single Kazantzakis between them. He brought honor to Crete, to his island, with its good and its bad. And now they're gonna tell us what to do from up there?" he asked incredulously.

Freddy absentmindedly drank two more shots, deeply engrossed in their conversation. A good reporter was always at the heart of events as they unfold. Even if Freddy was not yet a good reporter, he certainly was a lucky one.

"And why won't they bury him in the cemetery?" asked the other man who sat next to the one with the glasses, opposite the old man with the walking stick. He seemed shorter than the others, with white hair and mustache and pale skin.

"They said that Martinengo will be better. He can see his beloved Psiloritis mountain from there, and the sea."

"Didn't we say, the Church doesn't want to bury him in the cemetery?" old 'Glasses' chimed in again.

"Maybe so, but it worked out well for us. Martinengo is good," the old mustached man gulped down another shot.

Freddy naturally toyed with the idea of stopping by their table and asking a question or two of the old man but just then the young waiter brought his food to the table, and Freddy thrust himself into the battle with his dinner. He lifted his head occasionally as he chewed, observing a cute Cretan girl or two, then, thinking twice about where they come from, retreated his gaze back to his delicious meat.

He glanced at the bougainvillea once more, his thoughts turning back the girl in the blue polka dot dress. *How fun would it be if she were here with me?* He quickly panicked at the thought. No, he couldn't be in love at such a crucial time in his career; *but so what*, he comforted himself, *being in love doesn't make you useless.*

Even so, the girl in the polka dot dress should have been the furthest thing from his mind at that moment. The young waiter appeared out of nowhere, stopping by his table to replace the empty carafe. Freddy finished his dinner and poured himself a shot without a second thought. *It's pretty good after the third glass.*

He stood up suddenly and was momentarily dizzy; he composed himself and then walked over to the table he had been eavesdropping for some time.

"Good evening," he said as he drew near.

"Good evening, boy. What do you want?" the old man asked, stroking his proud, angular mustache with his right hand.

"I'm Freddy Germanos, a reporter from *Eleftheria* newspaper. I flew to Herakleion today to cover Kazantzakis' funeral."

"And you're a German, are you?"

"No, I'm a Greek journalist," Freddy answered patiently, "and I'm here to cover Kazantzakis' funeral."

"I see. Well, what do you want?" the old Cretan asked again, clearly suspicious.

"I accidentally heard part of your conversation about the funeral, the Athenian priests, and Martinengo. I was wondering if you could clear up some things for me."

"So you just happened to hear our conversation, and you're a reporter? And you expect us to believe you that you just accidentally overheard?" the old man asked with a booming laugh, eliciting others to laugh along with him.

"Well, don't just stand there, take a seat. Have a raki with us!"

Freddy pulled his chair from his own table and sat down.

"To our health....to Kazantzakis," the well groomed elder thundered as the small shot glasses clanged.

"So tell us, what do you want to know? It's just as you've heard it."

"What do you plan to do if your priests tell you they refuse to bury Kazantzakis?" Freddy asked. "And before you answer, let me tell you I'm not writing any of this down, I just want to be prepared. I just want to be able to express the local sentiment."

"Write it down, who cares?" the old man said boldly. "There will be trouble if they don't. Protests and demonstrations, that's what I think..."

"Are the priests here afraid of the Archdiocese in Athens?"

"I don't know about the priests. I know the people aren't spooked by that sort of thing. Kazantzakis was a worthy Greek, and they should bury him as he deserves. Not just as all Greeks deserve, but as an honored Greek does. Don't you agree?" the old man asked Freddy, and everyone nodded in agreement.

"Of course I agree. I'm a fan of this great man."

"Come, let us drink. To Germanos, friends," the old Cretan thundered and raised his glass to Freddy. "You see this square? This is where everyone is usually happy and relaxed because they come here for their evening stroll. How does everyone look to you now? Silent. Saddened. Defeated. All because those priests in Athens wouldn't allow his widow to place him in a church, wouldn't allow the people who loved him to attend his wake. It's a disgrace and they've brought disgrace upon us, too."

The more Freddy listened, the more he feared there would be trouble. It was clear that the decision to refuse the public wake wasn't made lightly, for even the Archbishop himself feared Kantiotis. *What was to stop them from continuing this hostility?* he wondered. He bid the old men goodnight, paid his bill, asked for directions to the Church and set out for Saint Minas on foot.

He kept a fast pace until he reached the church courtyard. There were plenty of people there, still, but at least now he could enter the church. On his way inside, he stopped by a group of men in their forties, just to get a sense of the crowd, although by now he was more or less certain of what he'd hear.

"Hello, I'm Freddy Germanos, a reporter for *Eleftheria* newspaper. I'm here to cover Kazantzakis' funeral," he said in an easy, hushed manner.

"A reporter from Athens?" asked a brown haired man, who was taller and more regal looking than the other three.

"Yes, exactly. Are you aware of what has happened? How the public wake wasn't allowed?" he asked, steering the conversation where he wished it to go.

"We know," the man who stood across from him replied. "We are saddened by it, and I heard that Kantiotis' men are coming around, trying to stop the funeral. Are these things godly?"

"Of course not," Freddy agreed, winning them over.

"Some people came around here earlier..." the third man in the group spoke up.

"What do you mean?" Freddy asked, surprised.

"Some of Kantiotis' men. They shouted a couple of times, saying, 'Antichrist!' and 'May you rot, you communist', but when they saw us coming at them, about fifteen people strong, they quickly left."

"Did you recognize them?"

"Two of them, yes – they are from here," the third man confirmed.

Freddy was silent for a moment, surprised by the turn of events which were clearly leading to disaster.

"And what will happen if they try that tomorrow? How will you react?" he asked them.

"That would not be good. Isn't that called defaming the dead?" answered the man across from Freddy, giving him the impression that people would take matters into their own hands if the fanatics weren't apprehended.

Freddy thanked them and walked a little further, pulling out his notepad. He suddenly felt a hand on his shoulder.

"So you came back, eh?"

Freddy turned to see his friend, the Cretan. He appeared quite upset.

"Yes, I sent in my article and now I'm here to see what's going on. I heard some of Kantiotis' men came by, hurling insults."

"It's true. I was here. We started toward them but they ran off."

"Who is inside now?" Freddy asked.

"Helen, the brother and sister of Galatea, Marika, Agnes, Prevelakis, Hatzikyriakos-Gikas, Kakrides, Kazantzakis' sisters and his nephews..."

"Do they know what happened?"

"It was hard to miss."

"Alright. I'm going in to take a look and then I'm off to the hotel for the night. I'll be back here at six tomorrow morning."

"Very well, Freddy. I'll be here early, too. Goodnight."

"Cretan.....thank you for all your help," Freddy called out but his source had already turned to leave. He didn't even answer.

Freddy entered the church, and locked eyes with Helen who was sitting in a chair next to the casket. The black and white framed photograph of Kazantzakis dominated the room. Agnes sat next to Helen, and Marika next to Agnes; the Alexiou siblings were whispering with Prevelakis, and Kazantzakis' sisters sat nearby. Freddy approached Helen with a resolute step.

"Are you alright?" he asked. "Do you need anything?"

"I'm fine, my boy, thank you," she replied softly.

"I'd like to speak with you. Not today, of course, nor tomorrow, but the day after tomorrow?"

Helen nodded.

"For the newspaper," he reminded her.

"Yes," was all she said.

The reporter started his trek home, satisfied with himself that, instead of enjoying a refreshing night's sleep, he was pursuing the story. And if Helen Kazantzakis did give him the interview it would be a success, and Androulidakis would certainly trust him with similar stories in the future. Freddy passed by the square, recalling the old men he had spoken to. It had been a turning point for him, for it hadn't only helped him appreciate Kazantzakis and his homeland more, but was the moment he'd felt the effects of the raki that lowers inhibitions and lets instinct and feelings flow. It seemed the great Cretan author was one of the few important figures to enjoy such wide acceptance, contrary to Jesus' statement that *"a prophet has no honor in his own land."*

Of course, it could just be that this was only true of prophets. But, wasn't Kazantzakis a prophet? Hadn't he had all the hallmarks of one? To look into the future, to rouse people? Why was he such an exception in the history of prophets? Perhaps because he never transformed into anything other than what he was meant to be. With a book in hand since childhood, he grew to be an intellectual; Jesus, on the other hand, was a lowly carpenter. What were the chances that his suspicious and jealous compatriots could believe he was the Son of God? None; but if you were to tell the people in Herakleion that Kazantzakis was still writing the stories of their ancestors – that, far from his homeland, he was searching every speck of dirt for something familiar, something Cretan, his compatriots would not be confused, for it would be expected. Perhaps they too would do the same if they found themselves away from their island.

Kazantzakis was one of them, flesh of their flesh, blood of their own Cretan blood, a spirit stirred out of the same Cretan pot. And, if again, you were to tell them that his books were read abroad, it would be all the more reason to treat you to a raki, to raise a glass with you, to bask in their pride for their compatriot. Not that there weren't envious souls in Crete, though, to be fair.

Heraklion, Saint Minas Church

Hundreds of people continued to pour through the gates of Saint Minas as the hour passed and the darkness of Herakleion filtered in through the church windows. Men, women, children, their heads bent low in silence came to pay their respects. People who might not have known him, might have never read a single line from any of his books were waiting patiently in the long cue to deliver their respectful farewell to their compatriot, to the man who'd had his memory defaced by fellow writers, journalists, and priests, to the man who had praised their Cretan heritage and had endorsed their land so proudly.

Helen wore a black scarf on her head, a woman of Herakleion, now, herself, she honored her husband in the Cretan way, the way he deserved and would have cherished. His friends all stood at her side. They had decided to spend his final night together, like so many nights they had spent being regaled by his spirited discussions and old tales. Of the many stories they told, the band of friends recalled the adventure Nikos had had with Cybele's daughter, Alice. Cybele was the ultimate film star in the decades preceding World War II, and, as is usually the case, had a staunch rival named Marika Kotopouli. Cybele's third husband was the 'Old Man', George Papandreou, who would later become Prime Minister and dear friend to Nikos. Her daughter, Alice, a star in her own right, had eloped with the theater owner Kostas Mousouris, with whom she'd stage performances.

Things did not go well for them, financially, however, and Alice had despaired. Nikos had told his friends that one night, a woman in a broad-rimmed straw hat came to knock at his door; it was August of 1937 in Aegina island. Helen was away abroad, and Nikos had been sitting on the roof terrace; when he looked down below, he had mistaken Alice for Helen's sister, Polly.

"I've come for your hospitality," she had said with a laugh.

"Who are you?" he had asked.

"You don't remember me? We had dinner one evening."

"Meaning?"

"I'm Alice."

He had ushered her inside, and, after some time on the sofa exchanging pleasantries, she had asked him, "Aren't you going to ask me why I've come?"

"The Ancient Greeks only asked that of their guests after three days. I too am an Ancient Greek."

"But I'm in a hurry! I've come because my theater is in shambles, we haven't any money, our bills are piling up and this evening I was supposed to be on stage and I walked out without telling anyone, not even my husband. I wanted to kill myself, but then I thought of you, and I ran immediately to you. Please, let me spend a few days here, by your side! It will invigorate me, help me to find a better path!"

Nikos had prepared the studio for her and the star had lived there quietly for the next few days, reading the books he gave her, wearing Helen's clothes from her closet. Two days after her arrival, she was the headline of every newspaper: "Cybele's Daughter Missing," or "Alice has Disappeared" or "Police Search for Missing Alice". Athens had fallen into pure pandemonium, with rumors raging as to the whereabouts of the missing star. The police had fully mobilized, and reporters wrote endless articles on her life and on her last days before her disappearance, speculating that suicide was most likely.

Nikos was due to tour the Peloponnese, however, for a series of articles he was writing for *Kathimerini* newspaper. He had told her she could stay until September first, at which time she decided to end her two-day "disappearance". She had contacted her husband, then, to let him know where she was. News immediately got out, and, in addition to the husband who came to get his wife, Nikos' house in Aegina was soon clambering with journalists and photographers as well.

The next day's newspapers featured photographs of Nikos' house in Aegina and were rife with headlines like "This is Alice's secret hideaway," or "This is where Alice had breakfast in the morning," or even "This is the hammock from which Alice gazed at the sea". And, naturally, many were those who had believed Nikos and Alice were having an affair.

The sensation around his name was enormous, as the matter remained in the news for more than three days. In fact, Nikos had received irate phone calls from the editors of *Kathimerini* newspaper, because he hadn't informed them that Alice was staying at his home, something that would have been quite the story for any newspaper.

"I am a lousy journalist but an honest man," he had replied. The newspaper editor however had been staggered by how famous the entire ordeal had made Kazantzakis. "Nothing you ever write, ever, will make you as famous as you are now," he had said. And so, when Nikos began his tour of the Peloponnese, when anyone mentioned his name, people were quick to ask, "Alice's Kazantzakis?" to which he'd readily reply, "Yes". He had related this story to his friends, laughing all the while, noting that, "I may have been a successful author, but my name would never become as famous as it was then."

He had laughed a small laugh, and his friends, whether commiserating or genuinely entertained, had laughed with him, since, in the end, he had indeed become a celebrated author who was no longer remembered for this incident with Alice which had occurred nearly twenty years before.

Someone recalled another story, of the time when Kazantzakis had gone on a stroll with his nephew into Herakleion, and had decided to buy a hat. Hats were the fashion for men at the time, and he didn't want to stand out for his lack of one. He had entered a shop and the owner had asked what hat size he wore. Kazantzakis had replied, "Give me one, any which one." The owner kept asking after the size, but Kazantzakis had assured him it did not matter. "How can that be?" the owner insisted. "It's simple," Kazantzakis retorted. "I won't be wearing it. I'll just hold it under my arm."

It was two in the morning and the church had begun to clear out. Helen needed to sleep, to have strength to face the funeral the next morning. The church windows were dark, bodies were sore, and every whisper in the chamber echoed up to the domed ceiling. Agnes approached Helen shortly before daybreak. She thought she was asleep.

"Helen, are you sleeping?"

"How could I?"

"Helen, perhaps now would be a good time for you to go to your nephew's house, to change clothes, to eat something," Agnes suggested tenderly.

"In a little bit," she answered, though it did not satisfy her friend.

"Helen, you've lost a lot of weight. The day will be difficult, I worry for you."

"Fine. Let the sun come up first, and then we'll go," she acquiesced.

"Do you know what I just remembered?"

"What?"

"How happy he'd been that time I had given him a jacket. We didn't have money then, and I had asked the tailor to alter my jacket into a men's jacket. He'd worn it on his name-day and felt so pleased."

Helen tried to smile a small smile but couldn't manage. Agnes hugged her as she tried to cry, but hadn't any tears left. She looked at his casket, surrounded by all the flowers the people had left during the wake, and her mind immediately turned to Nikos laying in a meadow in Gottesgabe. What an adventure that had been!

They had left Berlin with no particular destination in mind; at the train station, Nikos had purchased two tickets to Prague. Once on the train, however, Nikos had chatted with a coal miner who had urged them to change course.

"What do you need Prague for?" he had asked. "Get off with me at Joachimsthal. You can eat there, rest up, and then hike for three hours through the woods and you'll be at Gottesgabe."

It was as though she could see him now, his eyes twinkling as he pronounced the town's name: "Gottesgabe" – God's Gift. He had gently touched her shoulder, then, and he hadn't needed to say anything more, and she hadn't needed to ask anything else. After they'd slept at the inn, the had risen early the next morning in search of a house. They had traversed the main settlement at an altitude of 1,200 meters. If Nikos had been lucky at anything, it had been at finding a house to live in.

"I'm certain that somewhere nearby, at the edge of this street, a miracle awaits us! And if we don't find it there, then the fault is with our noses. Any dog would be able to sniff it out immediately."

And presently they had come upon Mr. and Mrs. Kraus, who had agreed to rent to them their wooden cabin with two bedrooms, large windows and plush beds with goose feathered covers. On the ground floor they had a spacious kitchen and dining area with a lit fireplace, and outside, a stable, two cows, a goat, a rooster and so very many chickens.

They knew an otherworldly peace in that home, on that mountain top. Ensconced in that peace, Nikos and Helen had lived two of the happiest years of their life together. It was here that Nikos had gotten the idea for Kapetan Ilia, forerunner of *Captain Michalis,* and it was here too that he had fleshed out his Letter to Greco, the forerunner to his *Report to Greco.* When it snowed, he'd lie awake in bed, refusing to get up. He'd wear his gloves and thrust himself into writing his *Odyssey* in freezing temperatures. In the summer, he'd write at the kitchen table, and on those summer evenings they'd lie in the verdant meadow, staring at the star-speckled nighttime sky.

When he had finished his book about his time in the Soviet Union, to which he had given the African name, *Toda Raba,* Helen had gone to discuss its publication with two German publishing houses. Despite the initial warm reception, the discussions had led nowhere. And how could she forget her meeting in Paris with the editor of the French publishing house, Montagne. She had shared with him, among other things, the letter from the German editor who had proclaimed Kazantzakis a literary genius. After a week however, the Frenchman had held an ugly surprise in store for her.

"Hahaha, a genius? Let me laugh! Who is this man who dares to write in the first person? Who does he think he is? Tell him, for my part, that no Frenchman will ever read his work!"

Were Helen were to remind Nikos of that incident now, she was certain he would smile softly and say to her, "You only remember the ugly moments, but I only recall the happy times we have shared."

The church windows took on a bluish hue and the sound of impatient roosters could be heard crowing in the distance. No one was weeping for Kazantzakis; everyone who had spent the night at the wake had been sharing stories about him and was now utterly spent. Agnes went to check on Nikos' sisters and quickly returned to Helen.

"Come Helen, get up. Let's go. The sun is rising. We need to be back here before the priests come," Agnes urged. Helen rose slowly. Her fingers caressed the casket tenderly as she gazed at his picture before taking her silent leave.

TUESDAY, NOVEMBER 5, 1957

Herakleion, Saint Minas Church, Martinengo

"Mister….Germanos! Mr. Germanos!"

Each call for his name came with three swift knocks on the door. The first signs of life came at around the fifth knock.

"Who is it?" he asked, still asleep.

"You requested a wake up call, sir. It's six a.m."

Freddy shot clear up from the bed when he heard the time.

"Thank you, I'm awake," he confirmed and began to dress hurriedly. Standing in front of the sink, shirt and pants still undone, he threw some water on his face, and, ten minutes later, he was out on the street.

Twenty minutes after that he had arrived at the empty church; peering inside, he discerned the exhausted family and friends of the deceased, but noticed that Helen and Agnes were not there. No matter; they might still be there, only he couldn't see them. The silence was unnerving, as vexing as the fact that it was six thirty in the morning and not a priest was in sight.

The sun began to warm up the benumbed city which was slow to rise, dreading its duty. The first townsfolk timidly appeared, cheerlessly heading to work. Timid was also the appearance of three middle-aged priests, who darted into the church from a side door, casting a suspicious look around. Soon after, three more priests joined them, entering in a similarly clandestine way.

"Good morning, friend," an old man greeted Freddy as he stood next to him, clothed in his traditional Cretan attire.

"Good morning," Freddy replied.

"Have you come to pay your respects?" the old man asked casually, lighting his cigarette.

"No, I'm a journalist. I came from Athens to write about the funeral. And you?"

"Athens, eh? Have you any good answer as to why the Church doesn't want Kazantzakis?"

"It has its own reasons, which I do not agree with."

"And what are those reasons?"

"It considers him an enemy of the Orthodox faith, of Greece, and a corrupting influence on the young."

"And if they're such good Christians, why don't they just forgive him? Isn't that what Christ teaches? Why do they leave him out of the churches? Wasn't he a baptized Christian?"

"I agree with you, on everything," Freddy said.

The old man blew his smoke somewhat calmer then, and studied the young reporter who was admiring the church's architecture.

"Saint Minas is the patron saint of the city. In every village of every city, children are baptized in the name of the patron saint. Have you heard of many people from Herakleion named 'Minas'?" the old man queried.

Freddy thought on it a little, or at least pretended to.

"No, come to think of it, no one I know from Herakleion is named 'Minas'."

"That's because in the old days, whoever had a child out of wedlock would leave it at the church steps. The priests looked after those children and would baptize them 'Minas'."

"So you're saying 'Minas' is a name for illegitimate children."

"There you go!" the old man said and inhaled his smoke deeply, pleased with himself for having imparted this morsel of information.

"Thank you for sharing that story with me," Freddy smiled.

"Look, they're coming!" the old man shouted, ignoring Freddy's thanks.

Freddy turned to see Helen, with her black veil in the lead, followed by Agnes, Marika and Nikos' sisters and nephews.

"I'm going inside for a bit," Freddy excused himself as the old man puffed on his cigarette, not seeming to care.

Helen had resumed her place next to the casket, which was now entirely covered in flowers. The people no longer came briefly and then left; rather, they took up their seats in the pews, to make sure a service would be performed. It was eight o'clock in the morning and the chamber was practically full. Freddy felt a sense of relief from the moment he had spotted the priests, and went back outside. The old smoker was no longer there, but others just like him stood in his place.

"Hey Freddy, where have you been?" he heard a voice behind him.

He turned to see his Cretan friend.

"How's it going? Good morning."

"It's crazy! Good morning."

"Crazy, why?"

"Because they've been threatening the priests. Our own Metropolitan, Eugenios, says he's being threatened not to bury him."

"Where'd you hear that?"

"From some relatives of mine. It's been going on since the day before yesterday, and now he's getting more and more messages to not allow the burial."

"But some priests are already inside."

"Yes, but nothing is certain yet. They say priests have come down from Athens, too. Shaved off their beards, ready for fight."

Just then the Metropolitan of Crete passed by, and the old Cretan elbowed the reporter. "There he is!"

Freddy turned to see the Metropolitan with five or so more robed figures in tow.

"I'll try to get near the office, see what's going on," the Cretan said.

"Alright. If you hear anything, come tell me. I'll either be out here or in there."

Freddy stayed outside for a little while. He had survived the Occupation and the Civil War, and yet still couldn't wrap his mind around what was happening. This persecutory mania against a gifted man was incomprehensible. The lines leading into the church were swelling once more, and the courtyard was filling up again, mainly with women this time. Freddy thought it prudent to speak with Goudelis; nothing was happening in the courtyard, after all.

He entered the church and sat near the entrance, scanning the crowd for the editor. Once spotted, he walked slowly toward him.

"What is happening, Mr. Goudelis? I hear there are threats against the Metropolitan Eugenios here and against any clergy who dare perform the funeral service."

"I heard so, too. But the Metropolitan *is* here."

"He's here, yes. But are you sure he will officiate?"

Goudelis did not reply, but simply looked at him and it was clear he was thinking the worst.

"Antichrist!"

"May you rot forever!"

"Where are you now, you Satan? Rot in hell…!"

The shouting distressed everyone. Helen bowed her head, as did practically everyone inside the church.

"Antichrist!" "Communist!" "Bulgarian!" "Burn at the stake!"

Freddy sped outside to see about ten people burning books, leering and shouting. The women who were waiting in line to enter the church were appalled at the sight of Kazantzakis' books being flung in the air.

"Shame on you! This is the house of God. Leave now. Now! Have you no shame? Have you no dignity? What you are doing is defamation of the dead and I will call the police!"

A young priest, tall and strong, with a direct, blue-eyed stare, had appeared out of nowhere and was shouting at the blaspheming fanatics.

"Boooo!"

"Get inside, priest. You don't know anything," the group howled, flailing the flaming books around.

"Get out of here now!" the brave priest insisted.

With the books charred beyond recognition, the group of fanatics turned their backs on the priest and casually sauntered away, pleased with their inhumanity.

"We could have had great trouble here if men had been waiting in this line," the priest turned to the young reporter.

"Certainly," Freddy replied. "Aren't you worried they'll be back? Or worse, cause more trouble later?"

"I'll be here to deal with them," the priest responded with the daring of his youth. "And I'll be sure to let the police know."

"May I ask you something? Will the Metropolitan officiate the service for the deceased?"

"Who are you, sir?"

"My name is Freddy Germanos, and I am a reporter for *Eleftheria* newspaper."

"I see. Well, as with every deceased person, he will have done for him all that the Church commands for those baptized in our Orthodox faith."

"I see," Freddy answered, as the priest withdrew.

The books, mere ashes now, were scattered in the wind; scattered too was the source of the havoc, yet the disturbance remained, with people coming out of the church to ask those who were outside what had happened. Freddy turned back to the church to see how the family and friends of the unwanted dead were holding up.

Helen had lowered her brow onto the coffin, surrounded by family and friends who stood by in shock, trying to swallow yet another unfathomable effrontery against their dead. Freddy approached Goudelis once more, but it was the editor who spoke first this time as he drew Freddy aside.

"Did you see what happened?" he whispered so that the others would not hear.

"Yes. There were about eight to ten people, obviously Kantiotis' men. They were burning his books and I think you heard what they were shouting," Freddy answered in a steady voice. "What will happen with Eugenios? Will he officiate the service?"

"I don't think even he knows. What can I say? I didn't expect this."

"Well, what is he saying?"

"That he is awaiting instructions. Don't ask anything else; I don't have an answer. That is all he said."

Freddy decided to go out once more, but was met with great difficulty, as the church was practically full and it was only half past nine in the morning. He spotted his Cretan friend smoking in the courtyard, conversing with two older men. Freddy swiftly took to the stairs.

"Did you see what happened here?"

"I was just hearing about it. Their nerve is beyond words."

"Exactly. What have you learned? I asked Goudelis, who said that even the Metropolitan himself doesn't know if he will be performing the funerary service. What's going on?"

"There is a sense of relief, because the call just came from Athens saying that Gerokostopoulos should be arriving any moment. He should be here before eleven. What can the Church do to Eugenios and the other priests when the Minister of Education and Religious Affairs is standing beside them?"

"Don't say that… We thought so in Athens, too, that there would be no problem, but it turned out that the priests are even better skilled than our politicians."

"I'll head back to the office where all the priests are gathered, and I'll come back when I have news."

"Alright, I'll be out here. I'm not going back in, there are too many people in there."

The Cretan left, leaving the young reporter to wonder what would happen with all these people if Eugenios refused to officiate the service. What would happen if those fanatics returned to provoke, now that so many men had arrived? Where was the police, anyhow? Shouldn't they have been there, since they knew there was a real danger of riots breaking out?

The sun shed its rays on the ominous questions Freddy raised, illuminating the disastrous possibilities. People were now fearing the worst, having heard of the blasphemous actions of Kantiotis' lackeys. Inside the church, things were largely the same. Helen was spent of tears and thoughts; her empty glance was locked on her husband's photograph. The uncertainty surrounding this funeral had the family and friends on edge, and the service hadn't even begun.

"Come with me. Come with me, I said."

Freddy heard the Cretan as he grabbed him by the arm and led him along the wall, down a corridor to a back office with the door slightly ajar, where the two could eavesdrop on everything that went on in the room.

"All the priests are in there. Eugenios, too," the Cretan whispered to Freddy.

"We should leave, this isn't right," Freddy whispered back.

"If you want to leave, then go. I'll come and tell you what I've found out."

Freddy left immediately. He certainly wanted to hear the conversation, but he also wanted to maintain his dignity. After all, a reporter couldn't possibly say he learned something by eavesdropping! But, if a "source" happened to inform him of the matter, then it would be different.

* * *

I feel you completely now, my Nikos, Helen whispered through clenched lips in her black veil, her eyes shut. She was vindicating him now, so many years later. His silence alone was enough to defeat the most profane blasphemer or the most fanatical enemy. He was on his ascent now, on the upward climb he had shown her; and how could he, from up there, possibly answer his detractors who were writhing in the mud below?

Agnes whispered to her that the priests were in the church. She didn't seem to care much. She had been so frightened the last few days, more than she ever had been in her entire life. She watched the people of Herakleion filling the chamber, waiting patiently in line, and it occurred to her that whatever trickery the Church or the State attempted, they had already lost. The faithful, the citizens had not been fooled, not this time. They weren't being called to stand opposed to a different religion or a different political party in order to slander it, to seek out its scandal, to search out an oversight to work themselves up over; instead they were called to oppose a man, a man who had loved and had honestly cared for his fellow human beings, a man who spoke their language, who lived their life, which is to say, an Invincible man.

If only he were here to speak to them, she thought, but instantly retracted. The truth was, though he could enchant with his spontaneity in a small setting, his voice would often crack in a public one, and he would need to read from something he'd written.

If only he were here for me, she wished; *to be back in Gottesgabe, surrounded by the snow.*

How she longed to see him writing in bed, in negative two degrees, to enter the room to bring him a cup of coffee, a corrected page, to ask him, "How goes the writing, my Nikos?" and for him to exclaim, "There she is!" in his sing-song voice before asking her, "Until when?" so that she could reply casually, fearlessly, "Until and including Death".

"Until Death," she whispered, and tears poured out from her withered heart.

* * *

Had he not been standing in front of a church, he would have had choice words for his Cretan source, who was looking for him frantically in the crowd. Freddy realized he probably had something important to tell him.

"I've been looking for you!"

"I told you I'd be right here. What have you heard?" he asked, almost imploringly.

"So….half of the priests were saying, 'we should perform the service', while the other half disagreed. Eugenios was hesitant. 'But we've been threatened outright', the first priests said. 'But we must do our duty before God,' the others answered."

"Alright….now tell me of Eugenios' Solomon-like solution. I'm ready for it," Freddy could foresee what would come next like an old seasoned reporter.

"The Metropolitan phoned the Ecumenical Patriarchate in Constantinople. He explained the situation in detail."

"And what did the Patriarch suggest?"

"They didn't speak long, but as soon as he hung up he turned to the others and said in a booming voice, 'Let's go' and—"

Just then, they were interrupted by the first words of the funerary service echoing from inside the church. Freddy hugged the Cretan excitedly as though they had just scored the decisive goal.

"Let's go inside!"

The church overflowed with people, making it impossible to move around. Freddy and the Cretan found themselves thrust against the main entrance, straining on the tips of their toes to see what was happening. They were able to observe six schoolgirls in traditional dress surround the coffin, when suddenly, the crowd began to push and shove. The reason was an 'official' one: Gerokostopoulos, Papandreou and Mitsotakis had just entered the church. Outside, the courtyard was brimming full with people pouring out on to the adjacent streets. The special platform that would carry the coffin had just parked in front of the church, flanked by young men in traditional Cretan dress, carrying Kazantzakis' books. The psalms emanated clearly from the open church windows, streaming through the entire town in sheer defeat of the muted sorrow that had kept the city quiet.

While the city descended into complete lamentation, the protagonists of this drama – the family and friends of the deceased – finally felt relief. The decision of the Metropolitan to officiate the funeral service was an enormous victory. Helen stood motionless, staring at his photograph with her empty eyes. She had experienced the miracle of their life together fully, and now, for the rest of her days, would only be able to reflect on it in her memories. *Perhaps it is better to feel the miracle at the end of one's life, to go happily while in the midst of the wonder.* What could possibly make her laugh now, what could concern her or even bring her sorrow now? What peak could possibly stand higher than the one she had achieved after that long ascent with her beloved?

Agnes nudged her gently.

"Helen, are you alright?" she asked, but received no answer. "Helen?"

Had she heard Agnes? She could feel her legs heavy, her arms burning, yet forgot all her pain when she looked up to see the church teeming with people. Cretans from Chania and Rethymnon stood motionless and proud, with the traditional black kerchiefs tied around their heads. It was a matter of honor for them to abide by their proud tradition, to give their fellow countryman the farewell he deserved. If she could, she would have thanked them one by one.

She turned her gaze to George Papandreou. He was so devastated he didn't have the strength to hide it. He had truly loved and respected Nikos; when the Nazis had withdrawn from Greece he had tried to arrange his entry into the Academy of Athens, where he rightfully belonged. That would have secured a life for him where he wouldn't have had to worry about making ends meet, leaving him all the time to devote himself to his writing. But the existing members of the Academy had reacted, insisting on a vote for any new members, and the uglier turn had come two months later, when Kazantzakis had officially applied and found that he had not been accepted into the Academy for just two votes! Where now was a single representative of the Academy on this day? *I'll take your Cretans a thousand times over, my Nikos*, she rallied.

The psalms ended without her taking notice. She suddenly saw Gerokostopoulos placing a wreath before the casket; the minister's deep voice seemed to slit the silence.

"I salute the dauntless Odysseus, who has finally returned home to rest," he began, and the people hung on his every word as he honored the greatness of their fellow countryman. Helen turned to Nikos once more; she felt vindicated, proud. The immortality Nikos had so desperately sought had come on her own, to find him in his homeland, Herakleion.

It was the Old Man's turn to speak. Everyone quieted, as he placed a wreath of his own before the casket.

"I will not speak," he said, with every gaze locked on to his teary eyes that shone brightly in the church. "I have come to the funeral of my friend," he said simply, and the Cretans and Helen were moved by his integrity and his intention not to exploit his friendship with the deceased – or the sorrow of the Cretan people – for his own political gain.

Constantine Mitsotakis went next, followed by Agis Theros of the Literary Society. Then came the Norwegian author and long-time friend of Kazantzakis, Max Tau.

"Nikos Kazantzakis sparked a flame in the contemporary person. No other poet felt so deeply the pain of his own time," he said, beginning his speech.

Freddy swiftly jotted down as many quotes as he possibly could. He counted forty more wreaths after Tau, submitted by various unions and organizations, including one from Prince George and his wife, Maria Bonaparte. The service would conclude at any moment, and Freddy and the Cretan needed to plan their next steps; they discussed it for a few moments and agreed they should walk at opposite ends of the procession, with Freddy in the front and the Cretan at the rear.

"I'm off to the back office where the priests are," his loyal, investigative friend said as Freddy patted him on the back.

Freddy ran to the sidewalk across the church and got in position, as throngs of people had begun to stream out of the building. The courtyard ran about seventy meters in length from the church entrance to the street, and the police had cordoned off a corridor in the center, approximately ten meters wide. Students in their traditional dress stood on either side of the empty space, and Freddy realized from the expectant gazes in the flooded courtyard and surrounding streets, but also from the rooftops and balconies, that the coffin would soon be brought out.

The students of the Herakleion Pedagogical Academy, who were holding Kazantzakis' books, swayed slowly, unable to move in the congested crowd. The police tried to maintain the open corridor from the church entrance down to the funerary platform which awaited the casket, unobstructed. The Cretans stood by, uncharacteristically stoic and silent under the sun as it rose higher in the sky until Helen, unable to conceal her devastation behind her black veil, began to descend the steps of Saint Minas, followed by friends and relatives and dignitaries.

Freddy spied the young priest who had chased away the fanatics earlier, take his place in front of the funeral procession, right behind the city's Philharmonic. It wasn't long before the coffin came out, carried by six chieftains from Chania; they set it down upon the platform, then took their places on either side of it. The moment grew awkward as people began to whisper, wondering where the priests were. Their hushed murmurs grew louder when the platform began to move, setting in motion the first steps of the funeral procession. The Philharmonic filled the deafening silence with the funerary anthem composed by Delivasilis, a dear friend of Kazantzakis', which had only been played once before at the funeral of another monumental Cretan, Eleftherios Venizelos.

Freddy could hear the people around him still wondering where the priests were. All of Herakleion was afoot. Helen lifted her gaze occasionally, knowing full well that after the coffin itself, all eyes were on her. Wherever she cast her glance she saw forlorn faces – on the streets, on the balconies, on the rooftops. She did not know her heart could hold so many people within it, and now found out in the most tragic moment of her life. Agnes, who had been trailing behind, sped up to whisper to Helen if she could see the priests. Helen did not answer; her Nikos, who had adored his walks more than anything, was out on his final stroll where he had taken his first steps, and all of Herakleion was walking with him.

Freddy moved along, keeping pace with Helen, when he suddenly felt someone press on his left shoulder. He turned around to see the Cretan.

"You aren't going to believe it. The priests aren't coming!"

"They aren't coming? How do you know?" Freddy asked, shocked.

"I know because I watched them go into the back office and lock the door behind them."

"What are you saying?" the reporter practically yelled.

"What you heard," the Cretan shot back, and slipped back to the end of the procession.

The brighter the sun shone in the sky, the more it illuminated the grief-stricken faces, the more pronounced was the shadow cast by the procession as it took the ascent. The asphalt road had come to an end; they were now walking on Cretan soil. Helen looked up to Martinengo and found people waiting at the peak, weeping. Her legs ached with pain, the veil irritated her as it brushed against the angles of her face where her cheeks had receded, but nothing bothered her any more.

This is our last ascent together. Her mind fleeted back to all the glorious summits they had conquered together, hand in hand.

"Enjoy it my darling," she murmured. 'I only think of the good times', his words echoed once more. *You leave me now?* she wondered, inconsolable, *now that we have reached the summit, after the war we waged, us against the world? Now, when you could enjoy the fruit of your labors, the nectar of your sweat and toil?*

How many good times were in store for them, still, though Helen was uncertain of the latter; they had reached many summits together, but had stayed at none of them. Nikos would survey the beauty from that height and then would be off to the next peak. His free spirit constantly soared higher and he continuously strove for greater heights, to "reach what he could not" and thus fulfill the blessing and command his "grandfather" had left him.

Helen walked on, downcast, peering past several pairs of feet that walked beside her when she spied a cat on the side of the road, frozen in fear. Their eyes met; she reminded her of Sminthitsa, Nikos' beloved cat from Aegina. Sminthitsa had rescued Nikos from certain death during the Occupation; he had been writing next to a heated cauldron filled with coal, when he noticed the cat sit upright, trying to walk. She had appeared dizzy as she walked toward the office door, a sign that she wanted to go out. Kazantzakis had sat up from his desk, opened the door, and lost consciousness out in the hallway, with the cat having passed out a few steps away, both having suffered carbon monoxide poisoning.

Had they not exited the closed room where the cauldron was burning, they would have died. Helen had been in Athens at the time; Nikos had described the ordeal in a letter. A few days later, she'd received another letter which said, "Sminthitsa is progressing nicely... If she stays with me a few months more, I'll either learn how to mew or she will learn to converse with me in Greek..."

Freddy walked on, recalling the path from his visit the day before.

This must be the last turn, he mused as he climbed up the hill and saw thousands of people walking in silence, as though following the devout procession of Holy Friday, but without the promise of the Resurrection. Therein was the root of their grave sorrow; there would be no Resurrection come morning, for the next day was simply Wednesday. He realized he had been keeping pace, unwittingly, with the Philharmonic bass drum, when he felt a hand pull on him once more.

It was the Cretan again, with his tried and true move in getting Freddy's attention. "Look down there," he pointed, out of breath. Freddy tried to follow the invisible line from his hand to the end of the line. "Can you see them burning books?"

"Yes, yes I do. Are they mad? What are they trying to prove?"

"I don't know. I'm going back down there," the Cretan turned, not waiting for a reply.

At the front, however, the procession continued its stalwart, lonely ascent to immortality. Children holding laurels and books, women with tears in their eyes, men trying hard to conceal their own welling tears all walked resolutely toward the unfinished pit that would soon receive its famous tenant.

The end of the journey came into sight, and Helen walked determined toward it. This pit would claim a body and the beautiful life of two people who left no battle unanswered. The platform stopped a few meters away. Suddenly there was unrest.

"Where are the priests?" voices murmured. Rage soon followed.

"Shame on them!"

"Where are the priests?"

"They were afraid and locked themselves away!"

Helen became upset.

"Who will perform the graveside service?" a voice queried, followed by other indignant voices.

"Let's go get the priests," some roared.

Freddy worked his way through the crowd, trying to reach the head of the line; the end of the procession was still quite far off, and he fully understood why the Cretans were now fuming. Just then a young priest seemed to appear out of nowhere.

"Here I am. Let us continue," he said in a powerful voice.

He was tall, lean, and handsome with green eyes, a young man of twenty-three. A hushed whisper fluttered through the crowd as everyone wondered who the young priest was. No one knew. The chieftains, who had been standing guard were preparing to lower the coffin from the platform when the undertakers appeared. Manousakas, the most imposing figure of them all held on to the coffin.

"Such men do not get buried by mere undertakers," he bellowed.

The other chieftains jumped in to help him lift it, forcing the undertakers back. Helen stood with her head bent down to the pit. The young priest began to pray without further delay. "May you rot, Kazan!"

"Antichrist!"

"Traitor!"

Shrill voices could be heard from afar while the priest raised his voice as loud as he could to drown them out. Reverence filled the hillside. Below, the city was empty. Everything seemed empty, even the people standing there seemed to fade, until all that remained was a coffin being held by the chieftains from Chania. Freddy did his best to endure the pushing crowd, trying not to miss a thing. He felt a friendly pat on his back; the Cretan was standing next to him once more.

"Could you hear their profanity up here?"

"Yes," Freddy replied sadly.

"They even got into a fistfight with some of the men at the end of the procession."

The reporter pulled out his notebook, but didn't write anything down on the religious zealots. He wanted to concentrate entirely on the extraordinary crowd made of people from all walks of life, who were deep in the throes of a herculean sorrow.

"Who's that holding the casket? The tall one with the big mustache? Do you know him?" he asked the Cretan.

"No, but we will find out." The Cretan turned to the man next to him, and so it went, down the line, until the answer came.

"That is Captain Manousakas from Chania. They also call him Hotblood."

"I guess he must be pretty fiery, then, eh?" Freddy asked.

"Well, yes. His real name is Manousos Manousogiannakis. So, Manousakas for short."

The priest concluded the prayer swiftly, and the chieftains descended into the pit, trying to lower the coffin. It was too long to fit, however, or perhaps the pit was too small to hold it. The young priest bent down, trying to assist; the right side of the coffin had become wedged, owing to its size and shape, and could go no further. With no other alternative, they broke off a piece from the corner of the coffin, allowing it to descend to the bottom of the pit.

Helen reeled a few steps back, and in that very moment thousands of tears fell to the Cretan earth. Captain Manousakas brought Helen before him for the traditional libation with wine, but she paused; she needed a moment.

"Rest well, my Nikos, rest in peace, my love. It is your time now."

She could feel the pain of her heart, and at once was fully aware of her size, her shape, no greater than the palm of her hand. Every heartbeat seemed to rattle her bones; she could feel her blood pounding in agony with every beat.

Manousakas wiped his tears with his broad hands and was the first to cast dirt upon the coffin, a handful of soil he'd carried with him from Chania. The other chieftains raised their hands in salute. People broke down in liberating sobs, unable to hold back any longer as they cast soil upon the coffin, one handful at a time. Helen watched as the coffin disappeared from view under the weight of the soil and flowers, and felt her agony unfurl, felt the sky closing down on her. *Our life was a miracle and now it is over.*

"We buried him but we will not forget him!" Manousakas exclaimed as the crowd succumbed to a collective lament. Freddy fought back his tears; the Cretan next to him made no such effort as he loomed over the grave that now held Kazantzakis, his hot tears flowing down to his sparse beard.

An entire city was redeemed by her finest son sacrificing himself on the altar of ultimate ideals; that had been his life's choice, his sacrifice. At this high peak, the crowd found release in one final cathartic lamentation, for the dead had now set them free. A few moments later, it was finished, and the people began to disperse, trickling back down to the city.

Friends squeezed her hand and hugged her, then left her alone to spend her final moments with him. Helen stood before him quiet, unyielding; the sun shone warmly upon her face, drying her tears. She bid him farewell with the sun shining upon her, as it had the first time they'd met on that beach, when he had stood over her to shade her from the sun, lest she leave and he lose her. She knew the moment she turned to walk away she would be leaving behind the life she'd chosen, buried in that tomb, and would have to begin a new existence, foisted upon her like a life sentence.

She had memorized the ending of his new book, the one he hadn't let her read. She trembled as she tried to recite it to him in a single breath:

"Did I win? Was I defeated? I only know this, that I am full of wounds and yet I am still standing. Full of wounds, all in the chest. I did what I could, Grandfather, as you commanded, and even more than I could, not to dishonor you. And now that my battle is done I come to lay down beside you, to become dust with you, to await the Second Coming at your side. I kiss your hand, I kiss your right shoulder and your left, Grandfather. I see you at last."

"Till I see you again, my love," she whispered, her eyes shut, before turning away to join the others. The absence of his physical being could never diminish his spiritual presence.

"His entire life he labored to transubstantiate matter into spirit, and he prevailed. I know he did, I feel it. You are here, my Nikos, with me," she murmured.

Six young Cretan boys stood steadfast around the wooden cross and the mound of wreaths and flowers. Freddy noted this detail in his notebook and closed it shut. He saw Helen leaving and tried to confirm their meeting.

"My condolences once more," he said to her, gently tilting his head in respect. She thanked him softly.

"I'd like to ask when you might be able to answer some questions," he continued, the timber of his voice growing softer.

She paused to consider.

"Tomorrow morning, around noon. I will be at the home of Mr. Saklambanis – Nikos' nephew," she replied formally.

"I see. Noon it is. Would you like to make a statement now, for tomorrow's edition?"

Agnes watched the interaction and leaned over to say something to Helen, which Freddy could not hear.

"Shall I get my notebook?"

"Yes. So much has been written about his death but it has been in pieces. I want to make it perfectly clear that no one expected

Nikos to die, and that was exactly what killed him. He was hospitalized in Freiburg for fifty-eight days and had recovered from the vaccine's side effects. When he was told that three other Greeks had died at the same hospital, he'd said, 'Poets hardly ever die'. But that 'hardly' was the point."

"I see. And his final words?"

"He asked for some water."

"Would you like to add anything?"

"Yes," Helen replied thoughtfully. "Now I know why Nikos loved Crete so much," she said after a long pause, referring to the incredible gathering of people who had given him such a heartbreaking farewell.

"Thank you, Mrs. Kazantzakis. I will see you at our appointment tomorrow at twelve. My condolences once more."

"Be well," she replied, and walked away with Marika, Agnes, and Nikos' sisters.

She would turn, every so often, to cast a furtive glance at the tomb which was guarded by the six Cretan youths. Her old life was entirely safe.

* * *

Freddy and the Cretan walked along in silence, trying to make sense of what they had experienced together.

"How many people do you think were at the funeral?"

"More than fifteen thousand."

They fell quiet again.

"Are you tired, Freddy?"

"Yes, and not just physically. And you?"

"Me too."

"I'm going to go write the article and go to sleep."

"It's still only midday."

"I know, but I don't feel up to anything else."

They parted ways. They would meet again tomorrow, when the Cretan would escort him to the airport. Herakleion seemed weary, with its eyes cried out, speechless, counting the moments before it could retire for the night. There was no curfew, yet had there been one, there would have been more people, out and about.

He found the only open coffee shop at the Lions' Square. He sat down in the sun and ordered a Greek coffee. He didn't want to write the article while he was still flush with emotion; he preferred for his thoughts – and the coffee – to cool down a little first. He had time. He wondered what he would answer if someone were to ask him to state, in a single sentence, what had stood out the most at Kazantzakis' funeral. Was it Helen's dignity, the despicable instruments of religious fanaticism, or the Cretan priests who had locked themselves inside Saint Minas Church? Was it the young priest who had managed to salvage the Church's integrity over the open grave, or the collective heartbreak, felt by all? That was it! Unlike the cold reception in Athens, and the Church's petty standoff with a dead man, Herakleion had spontaneously shown its love.

He had sipped his coffee halfway through when he pulled out his pencil and notebook and began to write:

"At approximately noon today, the land of Crete welcomed Nikos Kazantzakis into its loving embrace. The funeral was attended by a vast multitude of fifteen thousand people, who came from all parts of Crete to escort the deceased to his final resting place at Martinengo Bastion."

He began to outline in detail the events that unfolded from the moment Kazantzakis had arrived in Herakleion: he wrote of Papandreou and Helen, of Manousakas, of the true protagonists of the funeral, but not of the Metropolitan or the religious fanatics. He would make no mention of those who had tried to usurp the glory of Kazantzakis' name. He finished within the hour, paid his bill, and promptly took the road back to his hotel. Once there, he phoned in to the newspaper, dictated his article, and withdrew to his room.

WEDNESDAY, NOVEMBER 6, 1957

Herakleion, Hotel Florida

He opened his eyes, then shut them again. He turned to his side, then suddenly shot upright, as though he'd seen something terribly frightful. His eyes darted from the wall to the window, with the curtain unable to hold the sunlight at bay. He lay there for a moment, immobile, until he slowly realized where he was, why he was there and how. It was too bright to fall back asleep now; he reached for his watch on the bedside table - it was ten minutes to ten. He dressed hurriedly and went downstairs.

A gentleman in his fifties stood at the reception, dark-haired, with a mustache and direct, dark eyes: a typical Cretan specimen. Freddy had been dying to use the phrase his beloved stars used in the movies, and now he was finally ready to do so. He armed himself with the appropriately haughty look.

"Do I have any messages?"

"Good morning. For room 124?"

"Yes. Good morning."

The man looked down at the snippets of paper before him, and read the message out loud: "Mr. Androulidakis would like you to call him at his home."

"Anything else?"

"No, just that."

He asked the receptionist to put the call through and presently heard his chief-editor on the line.

"Hello."

"Good morning, Mr. Androulidakis. It's me, Freddy."

"Hello, Freddy. Bravo, you've done a great job. Will you be able to send in anything else? You're leaving today, we've made arrangements for your ticket. Write this down."

Freddy scribbled down the address of the travel agency.

"Mr. Androulidakis, you asked if I have anything else. I do; I'm meeting with Helen Kazantzakis in a bit for an interview."

"Bravo, Freddy! Bravo! Are you prepared for it?"

"Yes, of course. I will ask her about his last hours and what she recalls the most from his life."

"Well done, my boy. I'll let you go now. Call the office later and let me know how it went."

"Goodbye."

Freddy hung up the phone, euphoric with his editor's praise. He would have kissed anyone and everyone around him out of sheer joy, yet the events had triggered in him a vague melancholy too, most likely due to the futility of life. He turned to leave, but then remembered he should call home. His grandmother picked up.

"Yes, I'm quite fine. No, it's not cold, it's warm. I'll tell you everything when I get there. Don't worry, I'll be home tonight. Give my regards."

Freddy soon found himself at the Lions' Square. He felt he knew the city by now. The town had returned to its usual rhythm: traffic was intense, merchants were transporting goods, women were out shopping, deliveries took up parts of the sidewalk and pedestrians walked by, ogling the merchandise that overflowed on to the streets from the shops. The Cretan had told him to meet at Kirkor's pastry shop; in a few moments he'd be enjoying a fresh pastry with his Greek coffee.

He was soon feeling better than before with the pastry filling up his empty insides, sweet and warm. *A most amazing medicine*, he mused, as he gobbled it up. He asked for more, and was half way through his second pastry when he saw the Cretan approaching.

"Wasn't I right? Good morning."

"Good morning. You certainly were!"

"Did you hear the news?"

"More news? No."

The Cretan pulled out a wrinkled orange paper from his pocket, and unfolded it to the size of a newspaper. He handed it to Freddy as he ordered a Greek coffee.

"Read the part I've circled," he said.

Freddy however began at the top, where the title was. It was the *Spitha*, the publication circulated by Augustine Kantiotis. The article, entitled "The funeral of an Antichrist," was flanked by a sketch of the Antichrist on the left-hand side. The caricature was replete with horns and a tail on the body of a man who carried a book by Kazantzakis, peering over his shoulder at students following him, holding Kazantzakis' books, with politicians in their suits and top hats and even a metropolitan in tow.

Freddy became unsettled and went straight to the article.

"There can be no doubt, dear readers, that humanity has descended into the darkest periods of history," the article began, and went on to warn that the end of times was nigh!

Freddy read through the delirium which referenced, inexplicably, the last last hours of Jesus Christ before turning into a libelous assault on Kazantzakis and his works. Freddy skimmed through the drivel that had for years been written against Kazantzakis to focus on the part the Cretan had circled.

"[...] And lo, for this mocker, this reviler, this blasphemer of our Lord Jesus Christ, Greece – the only Orthodox Christian Kingdom in the Balkans – saw it fit to offer him a funeral with procession and ceremony and at public expense!"

The ranting went on to list those who had attended the funeral, and made an especial reference to the Metropolitan Eugenios.

"[He] did not wish to follow the example of His Beatitude, the Archbishop of Athens, Theoklitos, in refusing to accept the dead Kazantzakis even for one hour at any church in the capital, but rather caved to secular pressures and presided over his funeral. To offer psalms and prayers to whom? To an Antichrist! Praise ye, oh hallowed man of Crete!"

Freddy was taken aback by Kantiotis' vitriol, which continued unabated:

"On account of the presence of the Venerable Metropolitan of Crete at the funeral of this Antichrist, we had opportunity to hear a dedicated son of the Church exclaim, 'oh that I were the Venerable Metropolitan of Crete for a single day, the day of Kazantzakis' funeral, that I might shutter up every church and forbid the clergy from attending this funeral, and say to his defenders, take him to a mosque, to a synagogue, to a Masonic lodge, gentlemen, take him anywhere you like, but you will not set foot inside an Orthodox church'".

"This is vile! He calls him an 'Antichrist' yet admits he threatened Eugenios to not offer a church for the funeral."

"I was handed it this morning."

"It is immoral! Over the top! A low blow!"

"I agree," said the Cretan, sipping his Greek coffee.

Freddy no longer felt like eating the rest of the pastry he'd left on the plate. The Cretan observed his distress and tried to cheer him up.

"I told you, I cut out a lot of articles and ask people to give me what they can find."

"Yes, you've done an incredible job," Freddy praised him.

"Good. Then take this, too."

The Cretan pulled out another newspaper clipping. Freddy unfolded it and concluded that it was in French. It had a picture of Eleftherios Venizelos; the date was March 24, 1936 and the newspaper was *Le Petit Parisien*. Freddy looked at it, astonished, trying to figure out what it said.

"Hold on, let me get the translation, I'll read it to you," the Cretan said and pulled out another piece of paper with great formality, cleared his throat twice and, with the pomp of a country town clerk, began reading:

"'The body of the great Greek politician Eleftherios Venizelos has been transferred to Crete, without a stop at the capital of Athens, after information surfaced that the arrival would be met with public disturbances and riots. And so it happened. The Creator of contemporary Greece, who, with his political ingenuity glorified Greece anew to the ends of the earth, could not find temporary rest in a single church in the polity he edified, for the people to pay their respects before the soil of his homeland covers him forever.'"

"My word! That's amazing!" Freddy exclaimed, enthralled.

"I know," his friend agreed. They quickly fell silent until the chatty Cretan thought up something else. It didn't take long.

"Well, what time is your flight?"

"This afternoon. I have to go pick up my ticket from the travel agency. And I also have an interview with Helen."

"I'll take you. Give me the address. Come now, I'll take you to Saklambanis' house."

They stood up and Freddy motioned the waiter over.

"You're not fixing to do something foolish, now are you?"

"Of course I'm going to pay. I want it to be my treat."

"It can be your treat when I come to Athens."

"But no..." Freddy tried to protest, though the Cretan had settled the bill before he could finish.

"Imagine that, he wanted to pay!" Freddy heard the Cretan mumble indignantly as he started off.

They walked along slowly; they had become quite the team, mostly owing to the experience and discretion of the Cretan. Freddy simply added his talent to the venture.

"You know what we say in these parts...Whoever dies on the weekend is a good man."

"Really? I didn't know that. Let me check what day Hitler died..."

The Cretan laughed with Freddy's joke; it was the first time he had seen him relax. He was usually bringing him bad news, but, unlike people who would hate the messenger for the terrible tidings, Freddy owed a debt of gratitude to this selfless Cretan.

The sun was shining and the people had returned to the usual tenor of things: loud, intense, austere.

Such is life, Freddy sighed. *You strive to be on the side of the just man, the honest man, the fighter, and you keep at it until you are justified.*

It seemed a heavy mandate to follow, and he was always wide awake when the Furies appeared. Still, it made for peaceful sleep.

The Cretan stopped just a few steps from the home of Saklambanis.

"This is it," he said, pointing. "I'm going to go get your ticket and I'll be waiting for you at Kirkor's."

"I'll be there in two hours at the most."

The Cretan smiled at Freddy.

"You know, Freddy, my name is Manolios."

"And why do you say that?"

"Because, from the first moment we spoke you've never said my name," the Cretan replied.

"Oh no. To me you are 'the Cretan'. You are the person I'd like all Cretans to be. 'Manolios' is far too common a name. You are '*the* Cretan'. My truly special friend."

Manolios pulled out the French newspaper clipping from his pocket.

"I'd like for you to keep this," he said.

"No way."

"But you record History," he protested.

"And you, my dear Cretan, preserve it," Freddy replied with a wink.

Heraklion, Home of Nikos Saklambanis

"Please come in, Mr. Germanos. Mrs. Kazantzakis will be down shortly," a shy young girl greeted him. Freddy followed her nervous walk inside the house where she motioned to a heavy, brown couch.

"Sit here," she instructed, and disappeared into the house.

Freddy sat down and opened his notebook. He wanted an account of the author's last moments, and had some general questions on the life and preferences of Nikos Kazantzakis. He looked around the parlor at the heavy, baroque-style furniture and the large portrait of uncle Nikos hanging on the wall across from him above the ornate dining table. Nikos Saklambanis was the nephew of Nikos Kazantzakis, son of Anastasia Kazantzakis and Michalis Saklambanis, the Venizelos party parliamentarian and legal scholar.

Helen did not take long to appear. She glided softly – almost silently – in her large black dress, like a sprite. She seemed different today, even if she had not had the time to gain back some of her weight or to fill out her sunken cheeks.

"Good morning," Freddy said ashe rose from the couch.

"Welcome," she greeted him kindly with a wan smile.

They exchanged a formal handshake, but that smile, while fleeting, surprised him. He cast a few swift, understated glances her way, trying to ascertain what was different about the Helen that stood before him today from the one he had seen just the day before.

"I have tea ready. Or perhaps you would like coffee?" she offered.

"No, thank you."

"I will bring you some tea, then," she turned and left, only to return moments later holding a tray with a teapot, saucers and glasses of water.

"How are you feeling today?" Freddy asked in his habitually kind manner.

"Much better," she replied with a wan smile that was bitterly fraught around the edges. "Truly, you appear much better."

"Now I know I must not mourn. After what I witnessed yesterday at the funeral, that inconceivable multitude, I know I have no right to grieve," she said, the small smile returning to her lips. That smile could have dominated her face had her eyes not been so largely expressive, so tear-stricken. She sat across from him, perched on the edge of the armchair, perfectly alert and ready.

"Would you mind telling my about the last moments of Nikos Kazantzakis?"

"It all began in Copenhagen, where we returned from Tokyo via Alaska. There, in Copenhagen, our publisher had organized a celebration in Nikos' honor. Suddenly he fell ill, with a fever of 39 degrees Celsius. We attributed it to the pox vaccine he'd had. He stayed at the clinic there about twenty days. His friend, the famous hematologist Jean Bernard visited him and was quite optimistic.

"'You're much better than before,' he had said to him. We left for Freiburg. He had an amazing improvement there; he was given vitamin shots and the swelling in his hand gradually dissipated. The famed doctor Heilmayer told him, 'Kazantzakis, we saved your arm and your life.'

"Everything was going well. I was preparing to leave for Antibes; I was going to get money and clothes, but by Wednesday he had grown restless. 'My throat hurts', he said. He had a fever of 40.4 degrees Celsius. He had concealed it for a week, so as not to frighten me. The doctors weren't concerned, though. 'It isn't diphtheria,' they informed me, and so Thursday passed, and by Friday morning things seemed better. Albert Schweitzer came to visit him that morning, and told me, 'I have hopes he will get away this time, as well'. The doctors were so optimistic they wanted to stop giving him the injections altogether."

Helen's voice broke; she stopped speaking. She gazed at the curtain, at the small rays of light streaming in through the window.

"Would you like to stop for a bit?" Freddy asked, but she shook her head.

"Around midnight he woke up in a bad state. By Saturday morning, the doctors were worried. 'Mrs. Kazantzakis, we're concerned', they said. I sent a telegram to Crete, then. To complicate matters, his blood pressure had also dropped. He was given fluids intravenously then, and was able to eat a little yogurt. His forehead was so damp - his fever was 38.9 degrees Celsius. I leaned down then, and said to him, 'Nikos, dear, your blood is doing very well and your hand is no longer swollen, and you'll be able to write again in a day or two. But you have to fight this fever.' He smiled at me and said, 'I'll try.' 'You have to gather all your strength', I urged. 'I'll try', he repeated."

Helen lowered her head, unable to restrain her tears. Freddy remained composed and in one swift motion offered her a glass of water. Helen seemed surprised at the gesture from this stranger, this journalist. She touched the water to her lips, and pressed on, as though she was in confession.

"'Try', I told him. He did what he could. At about ten past ten that night he whispered, 'I thirst. I want water.' Ten minutes after that, Kazantzakis was no more."

Helen fell quiet, and Freddy did not try to fill the silence. He gave her time to collect herself, so that he could ask her a question that would lift her spirits.

"Tell me, Mrs. Kazantzakis, what are your strongest memories of your husband?"

"His civility and his pride. I swear to you, I never heard him utter an unkind word about anyone. He loved the common tongue – after Crete, of course – language was his great love. He could perish for a word. In poetry, he preferred Valéry; as a person, he preferred Schweitzer."

Freddy smiled, letting go of the stiff affect of a seasoned journalist to nestle into the couch comfortably.

"Which one of his own works did he prefer the most?"

"He always said *The Odyssey* was his greatest work. But he loved *The Last Temptation of Christ* for its language."

Helen seemed energized, livelier, no longer downcast, looking for a way to avoid or to escape. She held his gaze, and, no longer inhibited by her grief, she quickened the pace.

"There are some that complained because he published several of his books abroad first. But when he had published *God's Pauper* in *Eleftheria* newspaper, not one person sent him a kind word. Everyone was hesitant. Now that book is a staggering success in Paris."

Her forceful gaze impressed Freddy, who had realized what was different about her from the day before. He was certain: before him stood the woman that Kazantzakis had fallen in love with, not a newly minted widow. He decided to go beyond the bounds of the typical interview, and posed one final question.

"What did you think of the funeral?"

"Oh it was wonderful. Everything was wonderful; the people, the way everything was organized, the location of his grave...everything. I'm just sorry he wasn't there to see it," she said, biting her lip. "Though I do wonder..." her voice trailed off.

"Yes?" Freddy leaned in.

"Do you perhaps know who that young priest was, the one who appeared as a deus ex machina at the funeral? The one who managed to calm everyone down?"

"No," Freddy shook his head regretfully. "To be honest I thought you might have known him, that he was perhaps a part of the family. He certainly stood in open defiance of the Church and its political games."

Helen nodded softly, and Freddy knew he had the story. He felt he had understood her manner, the manner Kazantzakis had instilled in her. They sat there, their minds echoing the selfsame thought: *this is how I want my life to be from now on.* For her, to be speaking about the man who had defined her existence; for him, to be speaking with people who pushed beyond their limits.

He stood up to shake her hand, though what he really wanted to do was to hug her, to congratulate her for her poise, to tell her how proud her husband would have been. She shook his hand firmly, but Freddy could not get a word out; he swallowed hard, unable to move the lump in his throat.

"Thank you very much, Mrs. Kazantzakis," he said after a moment, his voice breaking slightly as he unexpectedly held her arms with his hands.

"May you live long to remember your husband, of whom I was an ardent fan."

Helen was taken slightly aback by the hoarseness in his steely voice and the outpouring of his emotion. She gave him a gentle smile and lowered her head demurely. This had been more than an interview – more even, than a confession, for through their conversation, the young man had helped Helen find the answers she had been searching for ever since her husband had fallen ill.

She was relieved of any residual toxic burden that persisted from the days before. Now she could feel her Nikos in every word she spoke of him, in every thought of hers that had him in it. She could feel him near her, intensely, completely, so much so that his physical absence was a mere technicality. She looked up directly into Freddy's eyes with her candid gaze.

"I thank you, Mr. Germanos," she replied, and gave him a mirthful smile, the first full smile of her new life.

"And let us see, now," she quipped, "how a dead man's heart can possibly beat, still."

About the Author

Yorgos Pratanos was born in Thessaloniki, Greece. He is happy because he is finally doing what he loves: writing exciting stories. He started working as a journalist in magazines and tv in his birthplace, and soon, his thirst for more impressive stories led him to the capital, Athens. Among others, he collaborated with *The Vice* (Greek edition) and he was Managing Editor of *People Magazine* (Greek edition). When he does not write, he erases words.

Note from the Author

Word-of-mouth is crucial for any author to succeed. If you enjoyed *The Unwanted Dead*, please leave a review online—anywhere you are able. Even if it's just a sentence or two. It would make all the difference and would be very much appreciated.

Thanks!
Yorgos Pratanos

Thank you so much for reading one of our
Historical Romance novels.
If you enjoyed our book, please check out our recommendation
for your next great read!

Fateful Decisions by Trevor D'Silva

"...Places you right in the action from page one."
–Luke Edison, Author Of *Valcarion: Sacrifices*

View other Black Rose Writing titles at
www.blackrosewriting.com/books and use promo code
PRINT to receive a **20% discount** when purchasing.

BLACK✿ROSE
writing™

CPSIA information can be obtained
at www.ICGtesting.com
Printed in the USA
BVHW030900290721
613050BV00001B/70

9 781684 337941